Harriet backed out of the office and opened the door to the basement.

"Wait here," she told Luke and started slowly down the stairs. She stopped to listen, and Luke bumped into her back. "I told you to wait up there," she whispered, glancing up at the landing.

Luke's eyes were wide, but he had a determined look on his face.

"If you're going down, I'm going down."

"Millie?" Harriet descended two more steps.

The muffled response was louder here. This time, it sounded like Millie saying . "Down here."

Harriet hurried down the last few steps, Luke on her heels. The scene they stumbled into was terrifying.

Millie sat in a chair facing the foot of the stairs, her hands and feet bound tightly, shiny gray duct tape wrapped several times around her head, covering her mouth. William lay motionless on the dirt floor a few feet to her right; blood seeped from a nasty indentation that started on his forehead and continued into his gray hair. More blood pooled around his head.

Harriet started toward William.

"Take another step, and it will be your last," an electronically altered voice said.

She froze.

"Now, turn around," the voice said. "Slowly."

Also By Arlene Sachitano

The Harriet Truman/Loose Threads Mysteries

The Harley Spring Mysteries

THE 12 QUILTS OF CHRISTMAS

A Harriet Truman/Loose Threads Mystery

ARLENE SACHITANO

ZUMAYA ENIGMA

2019

AUSTIN TX

THE 12 QUILTS OF CHRISTMAS

© 2019 by Arlene Sachitano

ISBN 978-1-61271-405-9

Cover art and design © April Martinez

"Zumaya Enigma" and the raven logo are trademarks of Zumaya Publications LLC, Austin TX, http://www.zumayapublications.com/ enigma.php

Library of Congress Cataloging-in-Publication Data

Names: Sachitano, Arlene, 1951- author.
Title: The 12 quilts of Christmas / Arlene Sachitano.
Other titles: Twelve quilts of Christmas
Description: Austin, TX : Zumaya Enigma, 2019. | Series: A Harriet Truman
    loose threads mystery
Identifiers: LCCN 2019008582| ISBN 9781612714059 (trade paperback : alk.
        paper) | ISBN 9781612714066 (Kindle) | ISBN 9781612714073 (epub)
Subjects: | GSAFD: Mystery fiction.
Classification: LCC PS3619.A277 A617 2019 | DDC 813/.6--dc23
LC record available at https://lccn.loc.gov/2019008582

Chapter 1

Harriet Truman shivered and cupped her hands around her mug of tea. "If it has to be this cold, I wish it would just go ahead and snow."

Her aunt, Beth Carlson, sat down beside her.

"You could wear a sweater instead of a sweatshirt. Wool is much warmer."

Marjorie Swain, the owner of Pins and Needles Quilt Shop, wheeled a portable radiator-shaped oil heater into the corner of the room and plugged it in.

"I'm sorry the meeting rooms are so chilly. The building's heat pump is on its last legs, and the back zone up and quit this morning. The guy from Ben's Heating came out a couple days ago to pronounce it nearing death and order a new unit." She sighed and fiddled with the dials. "It'll be another few days before it gets here from Seattle. I was hoping the old one would hang on until then."

"We'll be fine," Beth assured her.

Mavis Willis arrived and set a large project bag in the chair on Harriet's other side.

"I'm sewing the binding on my quilt today. If you sit by me, you can have part of my quilt over your lap."

Lauren Sawyer pulled her quilt from a new-looking canvas-and-leather bag.

"One of the perks of making a quilt for the outdoor store," she said when she noticed Harriet eyeing the bag. "And you're probably cold because you spent last week in Arizona."

Harriet laughed.

1

"You say that like we were at a resort. Working and living at the Indian reservation at Big Mountain for Thanksgiving week wasn't exactly luxurious. And the weather is about like it is here, minus the rain. Oh, did I mention we slept in a tent?"

Lauren put a teabag in her mug and added hot water from the carafe on the table.

"And why, exactly, were you doing this? I mean, the elders need help in the summer, too."

"James and I are trying to be good foster parents. We asked Luke what he wanted to do for Thanksgiving, and he said he wanted to do something that was a little less commercial. The first Thanksgiving after Steve died, I went with a group of people to help out at the reservation. I mentioned it as one possibility, and Luke jumped on it."

Mavis threaded her needle with green thread and began sewing her binding.

"You and James are doing a fine job with that boy. I almost didn't recognize him when I ran into him at the store last week. He's filled out so much in the three months since you've had him."

"He looks like he's grown an inch, too." Beth added.

Harriet smiled.

"We're trying. And with James in the house, he'll never go hungry."

"Did we miss anything?" Robin McLeod asked as she flipped her wool cape off her shoulders and set her purse and bag next to a chair. DeAnn Gault followed Robin in and shrugged out of her down jacket.

"Brrr.... It's cold out there."

Harriet picked up two mugs.

"Coffee or tea?"

They both chose coffee, and Harriet poured, adding sugar to DeAnn's and powdered stevia to Robin's before delivering them.

Carla Salter and Jenny Logan came in from the store, where they had been shopping for fabric.

"Sarah is buying binding fabric for whatever she's working on," Jenny said in a quiet voice. "I think she might be coming to our meeting."

"Good for her," Beth said. "It's time for her to get back in circulation."

Further discussion ended when Sarah Ness came into the meeting room.

"Is it okay if I join you?" she asked.

Connie Escorcia followed her carrying a plate of brownies.

"Of course you can," she said. "You're a part of this group whether you attend every meeting or not."

Sarah gave her a grateful smile and sat down.

2

Robin pulled a wool appliqué square from her tote bag and set it on the table in front of her.

"Before we get started, can we see the Christmas quilts?"

Several of the group had been asked by the Downtown Business Association to create Christmas-themed quilts for the shop windows. Another quilt group in town, The Small Stitches, was also making quilts for the display.

Harriet pulled a folded quilt top from her bag and opened it as she stood up. She had done an all-over pattern made up of various sizes of blocks using a variety of geometric shapes.

"As you can see, I still need to throw it on the machine and quilt it."

"I like the traditional block variations," Carla said.

Lauren sipped tea and set her mug on the table.

"Cutting it a little close, aren't you?"

Harriet smiled.

"I'm on the 'stress for success' plan. I've got time, though. Today's Tuesday, and they're due Saturday. And they don't need show-level quilting."

Lauren shook her head.

"If you say so." She pulled her own quilt from her new bag. It was a forest design with simple tree shapes in various shades of green. At the bottom of the quilt she'd appliquéd a scene depicting a clearing with a single decorated tree surrounded by woodland creatures.

"Oh, honey," Connie gasped. "That is *beautiful*. Is it your own design?"

"Why, yes, it is," Lauren said with a grin.

Robin sipped her coffee.

"You've outdone yourself."

Carla clutched her quilt to her chest. Her cheeks flamed.

"I don't want to show mine."

Mavis patted her arm.

"Your quilt is very nice. It's a perfect choice for the Sandwich Board window."

Lauren stuffed her quilt back in her bag.

"Let's see it, then."

Carla reluctantly stood and held her quilt up. Jenny stood up and took one corner, stepping to the side so the group could see the whole design. Carla had done traditional blocks using 1930s reproduction fabrics in Christmas colors.

"That is fabulous," Jenny said. "I agree with Mavis, it's a good choice for a sandwich shop."

Connie got up and, with Lauren's help, showed her quilt. Her design consisted of cupcake images decorated in red and green.

Mavis had just stood to show her quilt when Marjorie rapped on the door frame.

"Someone here to see you guys."

She stepped aside to let Glynnis Wilson enter. Glynnis came to the table and plopped down in the nearest vacant seat. Connie fixed a cup of tea and handed it to her.

Glynnis's normally tidy hairdo was flat on one side, with a strand hanging loose over her left eye, and her signature pink lipstick was missing.

"Honey, what's wrong?" Mavis asked.

Glynnis let out a big sigh and slumped. "Everything."

The Threads waited while she sipped her tea and visibly tried to pull herself together.

"Can we do something to help?" Beth prompted.

"The Small Stitches aren't going to have their quilts done," she finally announced.

"None of them?" Harriet blurted.

Aunt Beth glared at her.

"I mean, I'm sorry. How can we help?" she amended.

Robin folded her napkin and set her teacup on it.

"Is everyone okay?"

Mavis took a brownie from the plate and handed it to Glynnis on a napkin.

"Thank you," Glynnis said as she accepted it, then continued. "Everyone will be okay eventually, but right now, things are a bit of a mess. Frieda slipped and fell on the ice we had last week and broke her right leg and chipped a bone in her left elbow. I was going to do her quilt along with mine, but I just got word my daughter's toxemia has worsened, and they're going to have to induce the baby tonight, which will be six weeks early. I'm leaving for Seattle when I'm done here."

Harriet twirled her spoon in her fingers.

"We can finish two quilts, can't we?" she asked.

"I wish it were that simple," Glynnis said before anyone could answer. "Beryl got the shingles, and they go down her backside and thigh all the way to her ankle. She's spending her time in bed laying on her side. Mary has double pneumonia, so she's in the hospital. Betty called me this morning and said her studio caught on fire last night."

"Are she and her family okay?" Mavis interrupted.

"Her studio was in a separate building behind the house, and she and her husband were out to dinner when it happened. The firemen think her space heater caused it. Anyway, it's a total loss." Glynnis sighed and picked up her mug, taking a sip before continuing. "Kathy had knee-replacement

4

surgery a couple of weeks ago and is staying at her daughter's, and since Carol and LaRayne weren't signed up to make Christmas quilts, they went on a cruise and won't be home until a few days before Christmas."

Lauren drew in a breath.

"That *is* a mess."

Robin pulled her ever-present legal tablet and pen from her oversized purse.

"Okay, right now, Harriet, Lauren, Beth, Mavis, Connie, and Carla are making quilts for the Christmas in Foggy Point celebration." She wrote their names in a column on the left side of a page.

"And we lost Kathy, Betty, Mary, Beryl, Frieda, and myself," Glynnis said, and Robin wrote the names down on the right side of the page.

Harriet sipped her tea.

"That leaves Robin, DeAnn, Jenny…" She paused and looked across at Sarah, who nodded slowly.

"I could do a quilt if it's not too hard."

"Sarah," Harriet finished. "How many is that?" She counted on her fingers, "Four."

"We could ask Darcy," Mavis suggested.

"Beryl was making a quilt for my window," Marjorie said from the door. "She told me she has the pieces cut already. I could finish that one. I know everyone didn't want me to have to make one, since that's my business, but I don't mind."

A look of relief washed across Glynnis's face.

"That would be so wonderful. We Small Stitches want to do our share, but the sky just fell in on us."

Connie reached over and patted her hand.

"We don't mind helping at all. We quilters need to stick together."

Robin wrote her own name along with Darcy's, Marjorie's and the three available Loose Threads in a column in the center of her page. She drew a connecting line between Beryl's name and Marjorie's.

"Okay, we just need to pair up the rest of us." She looked at Glynnis. "Do you have any suggestions?"

"Betty's quilt is a total loss, so someone will need to start from scratch on that one. Kathy has the blocks done for hers. I think she thought she was going to be able to sit at her sewing machine after her knee surgery to sew them together and do the sashing and borders, but things aren't healing that fast."

Sarah raised her hand. Connie smiled at her.

"Yes, sweetie."

"Maybe I could finish that one."

Robin drew a line between Sarah and Kathy.

"Okay, two down," she said.

Jenny wiped her mouth on a napkin after taking a bite of brownie.

"I can do Betty's quilt. I'm done with my Christmas shopping, and I've finished all my holiday sewing projects. I might miss the deadline by a day or two, but no more than that."

"I'm sure everyone will understand," Marjorie said. "They're lucky they're getting quilts at all."

Glynnis leaned back in her chair, looking thoughtful.

"I'm pretty sure Frieda was mostly done with her top before she broke her leg. I think she wasn't happy with her border color and wanted to try something else, but otherwise the top is finished."

"That might be good for Darcy," Harriet suggested. "Since we're volunteering her when she's not here."

Lauren pulled out her smartphone and tapped out a text message.

"I'll ask her if she's in," she explained.

Her phone chimed before she could get it back in her pocket. She glanced down at the small screen. Robin drew a connecting line between Frieda's and Darcy's names.

"I think Mary only got hers cut out before she got sick," Glynnis continued.

"Mary lives in my neighborhood," DeAnn said. "Why don't I do hers? I should go check on her anyway."

Robin smiled at Glynnis.

"I guess that leaves you and me."

Glynnis smiled back at her."

"You're going to wish I'd done something else."

Robin raised her eyebrows.

"Explain?"

"I thought it would be fun to do a Christmas-themed crazy quilt."

Robin groaned.

"I swore I'd never do another crazy quilt after we had that workshop here."

The rest of the group made similar comments.

"I've got all the background squares done," Glynnis offered.

Beth tapped her spoon on the table. The group stopped talking.

"Since the six of us who are already making quilts are either done or mostly done, maybe we can each take a square or two and do the embellishments so Robin can concentrate on the final assembly."

Harriet looked at Lauren. "I can do one if you can."

Lauren grinned. "You're on sister."

"Do you have the blocks in your car?" Robin asked Glynnis.

"I do, and I have Kathy's blocks, also."

"I'll walk out with you when you're ready," Robin told her. "If you're leaving right away for Seattle, you should finish your tea and have another brownie first."

Chapter 2

Mavis turned her quilt ninety degrees and began sewing on the long edge.

"I'd make us a spreadsheet of all this, but my computer's in the shop having an upgrade. That boy Chris said when he's done sprucing everything up I should get another couple of years out of the old girl."

"Whatever," Lauren muttered. "I can make you a spreadsheet complete with deadlines, gating items and color-coded quilter names."

Mavis smiled.

"That would be very nice."

"As long as it doesn't keep you from getting your quilting done," Beth cautioned.

"Oh, please," Lauren shook her head. "I'll probably be done with it before you get home today."

Harriet folded her arms across her chest and thought for a moment, staring at the pile of quilt pieces Glynnis had brought in before she left.

"Do we know which stores these quilts are intended for?"

Conversation around the table stopped as the quilters looked at each other, hoping someone knew the answer.

"I'll take that as a no," Harriet said when no one spoke up.

Robin folded the page of her notebook to the back and wrote "Main Street Stores" at the top of the new one.

"Okay, starting at the far end of the street from here, name the shops."

The others called out names, and she wrote them down in order, adding the name of the quilter beside the businesses they were known to be stitching for and leaving blank the ones they didn't know yet.

Lauren pulled her phone from her pocket.

"I'll call the first three and see who they think is sewing for them."

Harriet looked at the list.

"I can do the last three, but there seems to be a problem. I see four more names."

"I can tell you about that," Marjorie called from across the hall, where she was filling a kettle in the small kitchen. "Serena Howard, who owns Kitchen Couture, wanted to make a bunch of quilted tablecloths in Christmas fabrics to sell this season. She wants to donate the profits to the Fallen Badge Foundation, so she asked the business association if she could put one of those in her window. Since it benefits the police and all, they decided it was okay."

"Her husband is on the Foggy Point police force, isn't he?" Mavis asked.

"I think Jorge said he recently transferred from the state police to our local force," Beth verified. "I've been working with her on the one for the window."

Lauren set her phone down.

"Okay. Jenny, you're making a quilt for Ruby's Jewelry Store. Sarah—Steen's Insurance."

Harriet tapped her phone off and slid it back into her pocket.

"Robin, your crazy quilt goes to the Print and Copy Shop, and, DeAnn, you'll finish Mary's quilt for The Melnyk Gallery. Darcy's is for B & B Clothing Boutique.

"That's it, then," Robin said. "As we already know, the sixth quilt was for Pins and Needles, and Marjorie is taking care of that."

Mavis folded her project and put it back into her bag. She stretched her hand across the table toward Robin.

"Let's have a look at the foundation squares for the crazy quilt."

Robin pulled a handful of twelve-inch squares from the pile of fabric and spread them out on the table. Glynnis had used the same irregular five-sided shape placed slightly to the right for the center block. She had then cut random shapes unique to each block from seven other fabrics to fill out the background. The centers were either pink or white satin, while the rest of the pieces ranged from wine-colored crushed velvet to pale-green cotton.

"She's certainly given us a lot to work with," Harriet said, and selected a block with a pink center. "Do we want to worry about using elements that are similar to tie things together?"

Connie chose a block and stood up.

"Marjorie has some beads that might work well on our blocks. Let me go get one or two colors, and we can all take some of them to use. That should be matchy enough, don't you think?"

9

The others agreed, and Connie left, returning a few minutes later with tubes of pink and green glass beads and a handful of small zipper bags provided by Marjorie.

Harriet scooped a dozen of each color into her bag and sealed it.

"I'll walk down to Blood Moon and see how Jade wants to hang my quilt, so I can decide whether to put a sleeve on it or something else."

Lauren collected her beads and tucked them into a pocket in her new bag.

"I'll walk with you if we can stop at the outdoor store on the way back."

Mavis, Beth, and Connie made a similar plan, and the group said their goodbyes, packed their quilts, and went out into the cold, damp afternoon.

✂ --- ✂ --- ✂

Bells chimed as Harriet opened the glass-paned door to Blood Moon Soap and Candles and she and Lauren entered the cozy shop. The scents of lavender and evergreen assaulted their noses. Neat rows of candles lined the dark wood shelves on one side of the shop, while bars of soap were arranged on top of a glass display case on the opposite side. Essential oils and diffusers were inside the case. A work counter stretched the width of the store at the back of the room. Scales, measuring spoons, and scoops littered the top, and Jade Meyers, proprietor, sat behind a row of plastic bottles filled with white lotion measuring drops of essential oil into each one.

"Hey," Harriet said.

Jade finished squirting two drops into the bottle in front of her and looked up.

"Oh, hi. I was concentrating so hard on my new blend I didn't even hear the bells."

Harriet walked to the back of the shop.

"No problem. It smells great. Is that pine and lavender?"

"Close, it's Douglas fir and lavender. I found a new supplier of fir-based essential oils. I thought they would be good for the Christmas season."

Harriet leaned toward the open bottles and inhaled.

"That one is a winner."

Jade capped each bottle, wiping it with a soft cloth before picking up the next one.

"How can I help you today?"

"I'm finishing the quilt for your front window this week and wanted to talk about how you want to hang it."

Jade came around the counter.

"Let's look in the window and see what our options are."

Lauren was in the window display area using a measuring tape from her messenger bag, stretching it from one side of the space to the other then repeating the process from the window platform to the ceiling above it.

"You might need to get a little creative," she said as Harriet and Jade joined her. She stretched out fifteen inches of tape and used it as a pointer, indicating the ceiling over the window's display shelf. "Notice how the ceiling is shaped, tapering on each end?"

Harriet looked and saw the problem.

"My quilt is wider than the tallest area of the display window ceiling," she explained to Jade. "Normally, we add a sleeve that runs the width of the quilt then put a dowel through it that's a few inches longer than the sleeve. We attach a wire or string to the dowel ends and run them up to the ceiling. If we do that here, though, the quilt will hang too low. Part of it will puddle on the floor."

"Can you turn it sideways?" Jade asked.

Lauren laughed.

"If you want the design to run sideways?"

Jade's face sagged, and tears filled her eyes. Harriet put a hand on her arm.

"Hey, don't worry, we have other options." Harriet glanced over Jade's head at Lauren. Jade's reaction was way out of proportion to the minor problem of hanging the quilt. "I can put triangle-shaped pockets on the corners, and we'll cut a dowel that's just long enough its ends tuck into the pockets. Most of the dowel will be exposed, so we just attach the hanging wires from the tallest part of the ceiling down to the dowel. It will be fine and is easier than doing a full-length sleeve."

Jade dabbed at her eyes with a crumpled tissue.

"I'm sorry, I've been under a lot of stress, and I'm not dealing with it very well."

The phone rang. Jade returned to the back counter and answered it. Harriet watched as Jade's eyes grew wide and the color drained from her face. She sank into her chair.

"That doesn't look good," Lauren whispered.

They strolled to the back of the store. The person on the other end of the line was still doing all the talking.

Finally, Jade said "I understand" in a quiet voice and hung up. She folded her arms on the counter and laid her head on them, her long dark hair covering her face. Her shoulders shook as she sobbed.

Harriet stepped around the counter and rubbed her on the back. Lauren went to a water dispenser in the back on the candle side of the store, drew a cup of water, and brought it back.

"Here, drink this," she said and held it out. When Jade looked up to take the cup, Harriet handed her a tissue from a box on the shelf behind the counter.

"I'm sorry," Jade blubbered. "It's just…"

"Take your time," Harriet said.

Jade snuffled and wiped her nose again.

"I'm sorry," she said again and stood up. "Do you need anything else from me?" She tried to smile; but her lip began to quiver, and tears slipped down her cheeks again. She sat down.

"Don't worry about the quilt," Harriet told her. "Is there anything we can do for you?"

Jade looked up at her.

"You want to buy a horse?"

Harriet raised her eyebrows.

"A horse?"

Jade sighed.

"If I don't have the best month my store has ever had, I'm going to lose the place. If I lose the place, I can't pay my stable fees; and if that happens, I can't keep my horse." She began crying again.

"Do you have family who can help you?"

"My parents are in South America with a vision team doing eye surgeries. They're in a remote area and can't be reached. They wouldn't bail out my store in any case, but they *would* pay for Becky if they knew."

"Have you told the stable?" Lauren asked.

Jade dabbed at her nose and shook her head.

"They have a waiting list. And they've raised prices three times since Becky moved there. New people pay the new prices, old people get the old rates. They'd love to kick her out so they can make more money."

"What sort of horse is Becky?" Harriet asked.

Lauren rolled her eyes.

"Don't tell me you're thinking about it."

Harriet glared at her and turned back to Jade.

"Tell me about Becky."

"She's really sweet. She's a Swedish Warmblood."

"Nice," Harriet said with a smile. "Do you ride dressage?"

"I'm learning. Becky's learning, too. Her original owner was going to use her as a broodmare because their daughter didn't ride, but they figured when she decided to start, she could use Becky to learn and, in the meantime, they could get a colt or two. They got into money trouble and gave me a good deal."

Harriet stared at the floor and paced a few steps away.

"Do you think you'll be able to have that good month you need here?" she asked without looking up.

Jade thought a moment.

"If we don't have any weird weather or anything else that keeps shoppers away, I'd give it a fifty-fifty chance."

"And how much is a month's-worth of stable rent?"

"We pay four hundred-fifty a month."

Harriet strode to the far side of the room and gestured for Lauren to join her.

"It's the Christmas season, right?" she said in a quiet tone.

Lauren shook her head.

"If we go halfsies, it would be two-twenty-five apiece, and we could be paid back in soap and candles," Harriet continued.

"I can't believe I'm even considering this," Lauren said. "But it *is* Christmas next month."

They went back to the counter where Jade sat watching.

"Lauren and I were thinking perhaps we could pay Becky's rent for a month, and you could pay us back in soap and candles after the new year."

Jade looked from one of them to the other and back again.

"You would do that?" she asked in a shocked tone.

Lauren shrugged.

"'Tis the season."

"I promise to pay you back every cent plus interest."

Jade went to her desk at the end of the counter and picked up a tablet and pen. She wrote on the pad, ripped the sheet off, crumpled it, and threw it in the wastebasket then started writing again. She crumpled this one, too.

"What's wrong?" Lauren asked.

Jade leaned back in her chair.

"Everything. If my parents are delayed getting back to the city, we're back where we started. And if I don't make enough money this month and have to shut down, Becky is all I have besides my inventory. If I lose her anyway to pay off my debts, it's all for nothing." Fresh tears began to fall.

Harriet though for a moment.

"How about this. Sell me Becky."

Jade stopped crying.

"How would that help anything. I mean, I know you'd take good care of her and I'd be able to pay my debts, but my horse would still be gone."

Harriet smiled.

"I don't want to take your horse away from you. But hear me out. Sell her to me for a modest price, and I'll pay her stable rent this month. That

13

separates your horse from your business. I'm assuming your business isn't a corporation, or you wouldn't be worried about losing your horse in the first place. At the end of the month, after your business situation is sorted, I'll sell her back to you or your parents, depending on which way things go."

"You would do that?" Jade asked, incredulous.

"She's a pushover," Lauren said.

"I spent a Christmas in Sweden one year, and the only comfort I had was the horse that was assigned to me that year. So, yes, I'm a sucker for a horse story."

The door bells jingled, and a woman with a small child holding her hand came into the shop. Jade swiped at her eyes, swept her hair off her face, and put on an Oscar-worthy smile.

"Hi, Jenna, I have your soap all ready." She turned and went through a doorway into the back room. She returned holding a square package wrapped in silver paper and tied with a blue ribbon.

Harriet stepped toward the counter and leaned close so only Jade would hear.

"Let me run this past our attorney friend, and if you still want to do it, I can have her write up a contract."

"Thank you," Jade said and turned to ring up her customer's order.

Lauren shook her head and the pair went out the door and into the cold.

Chapter 3

"Have you lost your mind?" Lauren asked as soon as the shop door had closed behind them. "I get it that you want to help Jade keep her horse, and I'm fine with donating funds that we may or may not get back in future soap and candles, but to buy her horse? That's a whole other story."

"Hear me out."

"This better be good."

They started down the block.

"Jade said Becky is a Swedish Warmblood."

"Whatever that means."

"A Swedish Warmblood is not just any old horse. If that's truly what Becky is, and even if she's completely untrained, she's still worth somewhere in the neighborhood of fifteen thousand dollars. I'm guessing the fact Jade's parents have been willing to pay for the mare but not for the soap-and-candles business means the horse is worth that or more. I'd hate to see her fall into the hands of Jade's creditors, whoever they are. Unless they know horses, they could end up selling her for pennies just to get what they're owed."

"Why doesn't Jade just sell her? She obviously knows how much she's worth."

"Given her parent's absence, I suspect the horse is her family. Jade would probably live on the streets if that meant she could keep Becky."

Lauren stopped and turned to face Harriet.

"On a related topic, I'm surprised Jade isn't doing better financially. I mean, there are always customers in her shop when I go there. And she's been teaching classes in all kinds of stuff—soapmaking, candlemaking, some-

15

thing to do with essential oils. Aroma therapy, maybe. I know she opened an online store, too."

"Now that you mention it, I am, too. Even if she's paying all the expenses for her horse. I know she used to donate money to pay for holiday meals for the people in the homeless camp."

Lauren started walking again.

"Like I said, I don't mind donating money to pay the stable rent for a month, but you're nuts getting any more involved than that. Especially without knowing more."

Harriet blew out a breath.

"I'll talk it over with James and see what he thinks."

"And Robin?"

"Yeah, her, too."

Chapter 4

I s your quilt ready to hang?" Harriet asked when they reached the Outdoor Store, two doors down in the next block.

"That will depend on what they have in mind. I put a sleeve on it, but I guess we'll see." Lauren pulled the door open and entered the shop.

A fit-looking man with thinning dark brown hair met them in the center of the room.

"Hey, Lauren. Are you ready to hang our quilt?"

"That's the plan. You know my friend Harriet, right?"

"Sure, she's a regular customer these days." He turned to Harriet. "How did your young man do with his new boots?"

"They're great, Vern. He really enjoyed working on the reservation, and I think his clothes all worked fine."

Vern rubbed his hands together, and Harriet noticed the shop was a bit chilly.

"I'm not sure how you want to hang it," Vern said, "but I suspended a shower-curtain rod from the ceiling using climbing rope."

He led the way around a display table sparsely filled with aluminum water bottles of various sizes to the front window.

"If the rod isn't too thick, it should work fine." Lauren set her tote bag on the floor and pulled the quilt out. She located the side with the sleeve and held it up while Vern lowered the shower rod using a pulley system he'd rigged up.

Harriet browsed while they worked on threading the rod into the sleeve. She'd expected to see new inventory since she'd last been in before Thanksgiving, but that wasn't the case. It was surprising, given that Christmas was only a few weeks away, but maybe Vern had a big order coming that hadn't arrived.

Lauren stood at one end of the quilt holding a piece of climbing rope, while Vern held the rope on the other side.

"Harriet, can you go outside and let us know when the quilt is as high as it can go and still be visible from the sidewalk?" she called.

"Sure." Harriet went outside, directing them with hand signals until the quilt was in place. "It looks great," she said when she came in.

Lauren and Vern went outside to check for themselves, returning quickly.

"It's perfect," Vern said. "It's so nice of you ladies to do this for the business community. I wish there was something we could do for you-all."

"It's our pleasure," Harriet said. She was interrupted by her cell phone playing her aunt's ringtone. "Excuse me," she said and stepped away to answer. Vern was explaining the pros and cons of frameless backpacks to Lauren when she rejoined them.

"I'll leave you two ladies to your business. If you need anything, holler. And, Lauren, thanks again for the beautiful quilt."

He returned to the back of the store, where he began rearranging water shoes, spreading the remaining pairs over the shelf space.

"That was Aunt Beth," Harriet said. "She wanted to know if we could meet for coffee at the Steaming Cup. I told her I could, and you probably could."

Lauren shivered.

"Sounds good to me. I'm freezing."

✂ --- ✂ --- ✂

Beth, Mavis, and Robin were seated around the large table in the middle of the coffee shop when Lauren and Harriet arrived. Harriet carried her mug of hot cocoa to the table and slid out of her jacket.

"Just who we wanted to see," she said to Robin.

Robin smiled at her. "That sounds a bit ominous."

Aunt Beth held her tea mug in both hands and peered over the edge as she took a sip.

"Are you in legal trouble?"

Lauren slid into the chair next to Harriet, piling her tote bag, messenger bag, and coat onto the chair on her other side.

"Oh, it's much worse than that."

Mavis raised her left eyebrow but said nothing.

Harriet shivered and took a sip of her cocoa.

18

"Well, don't keep us in suspense," Robin prompted.

Harriet explained their encounter at Blood Moon. The table was silent when she stopped speaking.

Robin leaned back in her chair and blew out a breath. "I understand your desire to help, especially this being the holiday season and all, but…"

Lauren looked at Harriet and laughed.

"There's always a *but…*"

Beth scowled at her.

"Let Robin finish."

"Before you get too involved," Robin continued, "I think you need to check out her story. Make sure there really are parents off in South America who could reasonably be expected to return and take over financial responsibility for the horse."

Harriet opened her mouth, but Robin held a hand up.

"While you're investigating her story, if you and Lauren don't mind losing whatever amount you're willing to give her, there's no harm paying a month's stable rent, especially with this being Christmas and all."

Beth set her mug down.

"But you don't think she should get involved so far as to buy the horse?"

"I don't. If Jade's parents really are financially solvent, they should be the ones to step in and buy the horse. And with such a valuable personal asset, she should have her business set up as a corporation so no one could come after it."

Harriet twirled her spoon in her cocoa.

"As long as Becky doesn't end up being sold for dog food, I'm good."

The group was quiet while a barista brought Lauren her gingerbread latte. She took a sip and set the cup down.

"Harriet and I were just saying how fast Blood Moon seems to have gone from a thriving business that was donating funds to every charity project in town to barely hanging on by its toenails, teetering on the brink of financial disaster."

Harriet wiped her mouth with her napkin.

"You know, speaking of teetering on the brink, the Outdoor Store doesn't seem to be doing all that well, either. We were barely able to find what we needed for our Thanksgiving trip, and when we were just there hanging Lauren's quilt, I noticed they haven't brought in anything new since then."

"I'm surprised," Beth said. "Vern's always been an astute businessman. And he's been successful for something like twenty-five years. Now that you mention it, though, he *hasn't* been making donations to the various charities like he used to. He used to be a named sponsor for the community

Thanksgiving dinner. This year he served meals, but I don't believe he donated any food."

"You never know," Mavis commented. "Things change. Maybe he developed a gambling problem."

Beth looked incredulous. "Vern Jenkins? I don't believe it."

"What don't you believe?" Connie asked as she came to the table with a cup of tea and an oatmeal raisin cookie.

Beth and Mavis quickly brought her up to speed as she sat down opposite Harriet and Lauren.

"I stopped by Sunshine Bakery to check out the window, and I have to say, Sunny and her crew had baked goods on every level surface and in all stages of completion." She paused a moment, thinking. "But you know, there was a weird frenetic energy to it all. I can't quite put my finger on it, but it wasn't the normal, cozy atmosphere it usually has."

"Honey, get me one of those raisin cookies, would you please?" Beth asked Harriet.

Harriet stood up.

"Anyone else?"

Mavis raised her hand and started to dig her coin purse out of her bag, but Harriet waved her off. She returned a few minutes later and handed out the cookies, including one each for herself and Lauren.

Beth nibbled hers.

"Everything seemed normal at Kitchen Kouture," she said. "Their shelves are bursting with merchandise, they had plenty of shoppers, and Serena's taking back orders on her holiday tablecloths."

Robin finished her drink and set her empty mug on the table in front of her.

"I better go. I need to stop by Print and Copy and see their space and then take Glynnis's crazy quilt pieces home and see what I can do with them. Do you want me to write up a loan agreement for you for the stable rent?"

Harriet chuckled.

"No, there's no need. She's either going to pay it back or not. If she doesn't, I'm not going to try to squeeze blood from a turnip."

"Still," Robin cautioned. "If something were to happen to her, it would be good to have something on paper to show her estate."

"There's a happy holiday thought," Lauren said dryly.

"Hey, it's the business I'm in. And you never can be too careful." She looked from Harriet to Lauren and back again. "I'll write something up tonight and email it to both of you. Print it out and have her sign it before you hand over the cash."

Lauren saluted as Robin stood up.

"Yes, ma'am."

Robin was barely gone when DeAnn arrived, bringing a blast of cold air with her. She ordered her coffee and joined the group at the big table.

"I'm ready for this cold snap to end," she said and sat down.

"How did it go at the art gallery?" Mavis asked when she was settled.

"A client came in wanting to buy a print, so I have to go back in thirty minutes."

Lauren set the remains of her cookie down on a napkin.

"Has Valery told you which window you'll be hanging your quilt in?"

"He hasn't said, but I'm expecting it to be to the right of the entrance. He's been working on a display in the bigger window, and I don't think he'd be doing that if the quilt was going to go there."

Beth shook her head.

"That's too bad. Your quilt is going to attract attention wherever it is, but the bigger window would show it off better. If I were him, I would have made it the centerpiece of a display of all his Russian ornaments."

"That's sort of what I was thinking when I used the nesting doll images on my quilt blocks," DeAnn agreed. "People come from as far as Seattle to buy those Russian ornaments. It seems like he does pretty well with them, but I did overhear him telling someone on the phone that the ornaments didn't have a very high profit margin."

"So, what's he putting in the big window?" Harriet asked. "I heard he has a collection of icons that are pretty pricey."

Lauren scoffed.

"It's hard to imagine there'd be much of a market for Russian icons in Foggy Point, Washington."

"Like DeAnn was saying, people come from Seattle for the ornaments, so they probably would come for icons, too."

"I guess," Harriet said and picked up her cup again.

Connie ate the last bite of her cookie and rubbed her hands together, brushing off the crumbs.

"Is everyone going to the opening event next Friday night?"

"I've seen the poster talking about the tree lighting on Friday, but is there more to it than that?" Harriet asked.

"The high school choir is going to sing Christmas carols, and Sunny told me we were supposed to each be in the shop where our quilt is hanging. They're doing up some sort of passport people will take to each shop,

21

and when they answer a question about the quilt, they get a stamp. When they get all the stamps, their passport is put in a drawing for a prize basket."

"Sounds fun," Beth said.

"I wonder when anyone was going to tell *us*?" Lauren commented.

"I think each business was supposed to tell their quilter," Connie said.

Harriet crumpled her napkin and put it in her empty mug.

"Do you need any help?" she asked DeAnn.

"I'm just looking at the space at this point," DeAnn said. "But I'd be happy to have the company."

Chapter 5

A h, DeAnn, thank you for waiting," Valery Melnyk said in slightly accent-
ed English when she, Harriet, and Lauren came into the art gallery. He
wore an immaculate white dress shirt open halfway to the waist no matter how
cold it was outside. Harriet imagined a closet in his house with nothing but
carefully pressed white shirts.

"These are my friends Harriet Truman and Lauren Sawyer," DeAnn
told him. "They're here to help me figure out what I'm doing with the quilt
I'm finishing for Mary."

"Very good, very good," he said, joining his hands together behind his
back. "Glynnis told me Mary has pneumonia. I hope she will be okay."

"I think she has to spend a few days in the hospital, but Glynnis said
that was more of a precaution because of her other health issues."

Melnyk pulled his phone from a pocket and made a note.

"I must send her flowers to thank her for the work she's done."

He was a stout man with a round head and dark hair and eyes. Strictly speaking, he looked more Ukrainian than Russian to Harriet, but the
two ethnic groups had probably been intermarrying for many generations
before the dissolution of the Soviet Union.

As expected, Valery directed them to the smaller of the two display windows. He looked embarrassed.

"I'm sure you were hoping to be hanging your quilt in the larger window, but things are a little tight this holiday season, and I need to put as
many pieces as I am able in the big space to bring more customers in."

"We understand," DeAnn said and set her tote on the floor in front of
her. "It's not a problem."

Harriet reached into the bag and pulled out a handful of blocks, handing several to Lauren and looking at the others herself.

"As long as you're displaying the quilt however the business association wants, it should be fine."

DeAnn took a carpenter's tape measure from her purse and handed one end of it to Harriet, stretching it the width of the window opening and making a note on a card she'd also pulled from her bag. Valery brought a small stepladder over and steadied it while DeAnn climbed up and stretched the end of the tape to the top of the display area. Harriet pressed it to the bottom edge of the window.

"Looks like it's exactly six feet," she said.

DeAnn stepped off the ladder and noted the measurement.

"Given the size of the window, I may leave off one of the borders Mary had planned."

The door chime rang, and a slender woman in an ankle-length wool coat came into the gallery. Valery turned toward her with a smile.

"Mrs. Whittier, have you made a decision?" He glanced back at DeAnn. "Let me know if you need anything else," he said and led his customer to the back of the store.

Harriet watched until he was out of earshot. She held up one of the quilt blocks, barely suppressing a grin.

"Has anyone else noticed the striking resemblance between the faces on the blocks and Mr. Melnyk?"

Lauren laughed as she looked at the blocks in her hand.

"Now that you mention it."

"Mary, Mary, Mary, what were you playing at."

"Maybe they're friends," DeAnn suggested.

Harriet handed the blocks to her.

"Let's hope so. Or at least hope he has a good sense of humor."

DeAnn took Lauren's blocks and stuffed them into her tote bag.

"In any case, I don't have time to redo them."

Harriet shook her head.

"Maybe he won't think it looks like him. People often don't see themselves the way others do."

"Thanks for your help," DeAnn said. She held up the tote. "I'd better get home and start working on this."

"See you at the next Threads meeting, if not before," Harriet said as she went out the door and headed for her car.

24

Harriet and Luke were sitting at the kitchen table when James came in from the garage, a baguette sticking out of a paper bag under his arm. He set the bread on the table and went to the slow cooker on the counter, lifting the lid and inhaling the aroma it emitted.

"Ahhh," he finally said. "Smells just right."

"I hope so," Luke said with a grin. "It's been killing us."

"Sorry. We've got people coming in for Christmas tea already. I had to stay and help prep for tomorrow. I don't want my people to burn out this early in the season."

Harriet had bowls sitting next to the cooker, and James began ladling out beef barley stew. Luke carried them to the table. Neither spoke until they'd eaten their first bowlful.

"Help yourself to more," James told Luke.

Harriet waited until Luke was back at the table with his seconds.

"Okay, guys, since this is going to be our first Christmas together as a family, we need to decide how we want to celebrate."

Luke put his spoon down.

"I got to choose what we did for Thanksgiving, so someone else should have a turn. What do you guys usually do?"

Harriet's face flushed, and she looked away. Luke's smile vanished.

"Did I say something wrong?"

James reached across the table and took Harriet's hand.

"No, you're fine. We haven't been together for a Christmas yet, so we don't have a tradition."

Luke relaxed.

"I keep forgetting. You guys seem like you've been together forever."

Harriet gave him a rueful smile.

"It does seem like that sometimes, doesn't it?"

James let her hand go and took a piece of bread.

"Back to the question. What *do* we want to do?"

"Luke," Harriet said, "I know your experience at the foster home wasn't ideal, but did they do anything for the holidays you'd like to keep going?"

He laughed out loud, then put his hand over his mouth.

"I'm sorry. They tried, in their own way. Linda had this ratty artificial tree she'd gotten at Goodwill…and Paul liked that stringy foil stuff."

"Tinsel?" James guessed.

"Yeah, that. Lots and lots of it. It was…" Luke grappled for a word.

"Hideous?" Harriet suggested.

"Hideous," Luke confirmed.

Harriet fetched a notepad and pencil from the kitchen island.

"Real tree," she said as she wrote the words on the pad. "Okay, that's a start."

James broke off another piece of bread from the baguette and popped it into his mouth, chewing thoughtfully.

"Well, we need one of those 'first Christmas' ornaments."

Luke and Harriet both turned to stare at him.

"Come on," he said. "I know we can't do 'baby's first Christmas' but we could do 'Luke's first Christmas' and the date, or 'family's first Christmas'."

"Or maybe 'Our first Christmas Together'," Harriet suggested. "And the date, of course." She added *First Christmas ornament* to the list.

"I do have a collection of ornaments," she said. "I got one in each of the countries I spent Christmas in when I was growing up."

Luke finished his second bowl of stew.

"That sounds cool."

"Back to the tree," Harriet said. "Tree lot, U-cut, or wild capture."

"What's wild capture?" Luke asked.

"You get a permit from the forest service, and they give you a map of where they need trees thinned." James explained.

"And then you hike all over and find the perfect imperfect tree," Harriet finished.

Luke smiled.

"You two really are like an old married couple—finishing each other's sentences and everything."

"When my uncle was still alive, I got to come here one year, and we went up into the woods to get a tree," Harriet said.

"My family always got wild trees until my sister and I were in college," James added. "But given the quilting Harriet has to do for the business association as well as the extra events they're having, maybe we should save the wild hunt for next year."

Harriet picked up the pencil again and wrote *U-cut*.

"Good enough compromise?" she asked.

Luke and James both nodded. James leaned back in his chair.

"My parents will probably expect us to come to their house on Christmas Eve. They like to go to my sister's and spend time with the grandkids on Christmas day."

"My aunt and I usually have breakfast and open presents, and then she does a dinner and invites people over on Christmas day."

"Sounds like that'll work, then."

Harriet made a note of the two expected invites.

"All right, our plan is coming together. Anything else?"

Harriet tried not to smile as Luke leaned back in his chair in unconscious imitation of James. He picked at his lip then, when he realized what he was doing, put his hand on his thigh.

"Is there something else, Luke?"

He struggled for a moment before speaking.

"Do you think I could get presents for my half-sister and brother. The ones I know, anyway?"

"Do you know where they are?" Harriet asked.

"Not really. I think they're somewhere in the county. My brother went to live with his bio-mom, but I'm not sure if he's still there. That was four years ago."

"Children's Services should know where they are," James said. "I can check with your social worker."

"Do you want to see them?" Harriet asked carefully.

Luke sighed.

"I don't know. I mean, I'd like to see that they're okay, but I'm not sure I want to talk to them or anything. We never got anything for Christmas, and if they still don't get anything, I thought it might be nice to give them something. It's probably a dumb idea."

"Sweetie, it's a nice idea. And very thoughtful of you. We don't have to figure it out tonight. Let's find them and see what their circumstances are, and then go from there."

James stood up.

"Who wants ice cream?"

"I'll take the dogs out while you dish," Luke said.

James carried the three empty dishes to the sink.

✂ --- ✂ --- ✂

"I have one more thing to add to the Christmas activities list," James said when Luke was back inside and they were back at the table, dishes of ice cream in front of them.

"What's that?" Harriet asked and reached for the list.

"We need a picture with Santa. I mean, we need a picture of Luke with Santa, but if we need to have it be a family Santa picture, I guess that's okay."

"Seriously?" Harriet said.

"Don't tell me you don't have a picture with Santa from your child-hood," he said.

"I do. But I was in middle school, and my friends and I were at the Christmas market in Annaberg-Bucholz, Germany."

"But still, a Santa picture. And even though you weren't a baby, I'm betting you still have your Santa picture."

"What do you think, Luke?" she asked.

He shook his head.

"To tell you the truth, I don't know what to think."

The smile left Harriet's face.

"Are we being too pushy?"

"No, not at all. I just have no idea what's normal."

James patted him on the back.

"How about let's not worry about what's normal and just think about what feels right to you. If you want a family picture of all of us with Santa, we'll do it. But if you don't we'll skip it."

"While you guys are pondering that, let me tell you about the horse I almost bought today." Harriet said.

"What?" James said.

"For real?" Luke said at the same time.

She laughed.

"Let me explain," she said and proceeded to tell them about her visit to Blood Moon.

Chapter 6

Annie's Coffee Shop was strategically located through a short alley and around the corner from Pins and Needles, and was a favorite hangout of the Loose Threads.

James parked in a prime spot across from the door.

"Perfect." Harriet said and reached into the back seat to get her tote bag. "Lauren's meeting me at the quilt store, and then we're going to run up to Blood Moon and hang this up. You guys can get us a good spot in the plaza to watch the ceremony. When the tree is lit and the choir has sung a few carols, people will walk down Main Street and store by store, the lights in the windows will be illuminated, revealing the quilt displayed therein."

James gave her an affectionate squeeze.

"Sounds like a plan."

She got out of the car and slid the tote bag over her shoulder. James and Luke joined her on the sidewalk. She gave James a quick kiss and squeezed Luke's arm.

"Keep an eye on him. It appears he follows an 'I spy, I buy' philosophy at Christmas time. If he shops his way to the plaza, you'll never get there."

Luke grinned. "I'm on it."

Harriet headed down the block and ducked into the alley, entering the quilt shop through the back door. Lauren was in the small classroom, a cup in front of her. She looked up when Harriet came in.

"I'm ready," she said and stood. "Let me get my coat." She carried her cup to the kitchen then slid into her down jacket and followed Harriet through the quilt store and out the front door.

"Your display quilt looks great," Harriet called to Marjorie as they exited.

"Thanks," Marjorie called back.

"Geez, slow down," Lauren said and slowed her own pace. She glanced at her phone. "We've got thirty minutes."

Harriet acceded to the request.

"So, have you heard anything more about the whole horse thing?" Lauren asked.

"To be honest, I haven't had time to think about it. I took Jade a check made out to the stable the morning after we talked to her."

"Good thinking, making it out to the stable."

"Since then, I've been chained to my machine, stitching quilts. It's a miracle we got them all done in time for tonight."

"Hopefully, Jade will have that big month she needs."

They arrived at Blood Moon and entered.

"Wow, Jade, it looks great in here." Harriet surveyed the display shelves. There appeared to be a modest increase in soap and candle inventory, but the big change was that Jade had filled every blank space on her display shelves with fir boughs and holly and puffs of baby's breath, with blood-red fabric bows tucked everywhere.

"Nicely done," Lauren agreed.

Jade came out from behind the counter.

"Thanks, I made as much inventory as I could, but it still looked a little empty."

"It looks great now," Harriet assured her. "Did you get that dowel hung?"

"I did." Jade led them to the window where she had placed a step stool, ready for someone to hang the quilt.

"Hold this," Harriet said, and handed one corner of the quilt to Lauren. She set the stool onto the wide window deck and used it so she could reach to unhook the dowel from the wires. She stepped down, and Lauren slipped one end of the dowel into the triangular pocket on the back upper corner of the quilt while Harriet put the other end into the pocket on the opposite upper corner. She climbed back up onto the window deck and carefully climbed on the stool, lifting the quilt by the dowel and reattaching the wires.

"See how it looks from the outside," Harriet suggested.

"Thanks again for paying Becky's rent," Jade said when she and Lauren were back inside, having proclaimed the quilt-hanging a success. She went to her work counter at the back of the store and returned carrying two boxes wrapped in gold foil paper with a big red bow on top of each one. "These are for you two for helping me so much. And it's not part of your payback. It's a thank-you."

"Well, thank _you_," Harriet said. "You didn't have to do this."

"I appreciate your help so much. With Becky safe, I was able to concentrate on making the shop the best it can be. Hopefully, it will be enough to turn everything around."

"We better go," Lauren held her box up. "Thanks for this."

Harriet collected her empty tote bag and slid her box inside.

"I'll be back for the window lighting."

When she and Lauren were outside, she paused, looking at the fir-branch, ribbon, and candle arrangement along the bottom of the window. "I probably should have used a bluer red." she said.

"It looks great. Besides, she could have told you she was going to do the blood-red ribbon thing."

"I suppose."

✂ --- ✂ --- ✂

Harriet and Lauren bought steaming cups of apple cider from a kiosk at the edge of the plaza and continued on to the front-row spot James and Luke had secured.

"Wow, good job getting the best spot," Harriet said as she slipped between them.

James grinned.

"It's sort of embarrassing—everyone made a place for us, and I'm pretty sure they did it in hopes of getting a better table at the restaurant the next time they come."

"You didn't ask them to do that, so it's their problem," Lauren said after a sip from her cup

James blew out a breath.

"It's a little more delicate than that. I don't want to lose customers if they can't get a window seat."

A group of teenagers pushed through the crowd and wedged themselves into the front row. Two girls were giggling and trying to catch Luke's attention.

"Do you know those girls?" Harriet asked him.

He turned slightly so his back was to them.

"They go to my school."

"If you want to go hang out with your friends, you can. We won't be offended."

Luke's face darkened, and his jaw tensed.

31

"They aren't my friends, and I don't want to hang out with them. I'm going to go get some cider. Do you want any, James?"

"Sure, that would be nice."

Harriet watched the young man skirt the crowd, avoiding the girls, before continuing on to the cider station.

"I wonder what that was about?"

"He clearly doesn't like that pair, at least" Lauren said.

Harriet sipped her cider.

"I wonder why? I've asked him if he wanted to have any friends over to the house, but he sort-of brushes me off. He doesn't really talk about school at all. I don't know if that's a boy thing or if he's having issues."

"Are we allowed to ask the school counselors how he's doing socially?" James asked.

"I wouldn't," Lauren said before Harriet could answer. "My brother Les had some problems in high school, and believe me, the counselors made it all worse. And if Luke found out he might feel very betrayed."

James rocked back on his heels.

"Okay, scratch that."

"Maybe we can volunteer at the school. That would give us a reason to be there, and maybe see how he interacts," Harriet said.

Lauren tilted her head back, hoping for a last drop from her cup, but it was empty.

"We should talk to Connie about it."

Harriet smiled.

"We?"

"Yes, we. I'm practically his aunt. That should count for something."

"Of course it does," James assured her. "It takes a village, right?"

✂ --- ✂ --- ✂

Thankfully, the mayor's speech was short and stuck to holiday greetings and announcements of upcoming events. The junior high choir sang several Christmas carols, accompanied by the high school band.

"Whoa!" Harriet exclaimed when the tree was finally lit. "They've outdone themselves."

"I'm glad they used colored lights," Lauren commented. "I'm getting tired of everyone using those little white ones everywhere."

Jorge and Beth joined them, and Beth slid her arm around Luke's waist, giving him a squeeze.

"I swear you've grown another inch," she said with a smile.

Luke blushed. "It's hard not to with all the good food James makes."

Jorge clapped James on the back.

"Hey, my man, have you picked up your Christmas tickets yet?"

"Not yet," James replied. "I thought I'd ask Daniel when we get to his shop. He's one of our stops on the window quilt trail."

"What are Christmas tickets?" Luke asked Harriet.

Harriet tossed her empty cider cup into the recycling bin behind him.

"Each participating business in town will have a ticket with some sort of discount or free gift or something. When you shop in a store, they'll give you a ticket to be used at any other participating business, and when you use *that* ticket, you'll get another one. The idea is to encourage people to shop local."

"That's cool," Luke said.

James took Harriet's hand.

"The crowd's moving. Shall we follow?"

Members of the Foggy Point Business Association led the procession up the street. The lights had been dimmed in the shop windows so that each quilt could be dramatically illuminated as the crowd arrived.

Connie was in front of The Cupcake Shop, and Harriet, James, and Luke crossed the street and joined her.

"Your quilt looks fantastic," Harriet told her.

She pressed her lips together.

"I wasn't sure about the crystals. I think people are starting to overdo them."

Harriet moved closer to window and examined the cupcake images on the quilt.

"I think they're the perfect accent on the frosting. Was Sunny thrilled?"

Connie considered for a moment.

"I'm not sure 'thrilled' is the right word. I'm sure she likes it all right, but she's been overwhelmed with Christmas business. I know bakers keep long hours, but her lights are on here past midnight and she starts in the wee hours of the morning."

"Seems sort of early in the season to be that busy," Harriet said.

James twined his fingers in hers.

"Lots of groups do their Christmas parties early."

"If she's got that much business, why doesn't she hire help?" Harriet countered.

"I asked her," Connie said. "But she just changed the subject."

James put his free arm around Connie's shoulders.

"Well, whether Sunny appreciates it or not, I think your quilt is beautiful."

Connie smiled and looked from him to Harriet.

"This one's a keeper," she said.

"Who's next," James asked, his face turning red.

"Mavis and the yarn store," Harriet answered.

✂ --- ✂ --- ✂

Harriet's quilt in the Blood Moon window was the last display on their side of the street. She stepped close to the window and stared at it.

"I should have realized that, with a name like Blood Moon, she'd decorate with a bluer red."

Aunt Beth patted her arm.

"You had no way of knowing. Besides, I think your traditional shade of red, and the green and gold work better with the quilt blocks you've chosen."

Harriet shook her head.

"That's kind of you to say, but I still think a more blood-red would have worked better."

"It's done now, so no point in fretting about it," Beth told her. "Let's go across the street to the print shop. I haven't seen Robin's crazy quilt since she put all our blocks together."

✂ --- ✂ --- ✂

"Wow, you've outdone yourself," Harriet said as the group gathered around Robin on the sidewalk in front of the print shop. Aunt Beth stepped closer to the window and peered at the quilt.

"How did you have time to embroider all the seams?"

"I had a lot of help. DeAnn did a lot, plus I taught my daughter how to do the herringbone stitch," Robin pointed to the lower left corner of the quilt. "She did this whole section.

Harriet leaned in for a better look.

"Wow, she did a great job."

James put his hand on her arm.

"I'm going to go inside and see if Daniel has my tickets ready." He headed inside along with Jorge and Luke.

Harriet shivered and rubbed her arms.

"I'm going inside to warm up."

Robin pulled her cape more tightly around her shoulders.

"You *all* should go inside. Daniel has a coffee and hot cider set-up for the public. I'm going to wait out here for my family."

Daniel Muhler was by his computer screen behind the shop counter. He was a tall, slender man with thinning hair and deep laugh lines etched into his tanned face. He looked up as they came in.

"If you're looking for your Christmas tickets, I've got the Tico's Tacos ones ready, but, James, yours won't be ready until tomorrow morning. If you wait until noon or so to pick them up, I'll have your holiday menus ready, too."

"That'll work," James said. "Can I go ahead and pay for them now?"

A look of relief came over Daniel's face.

"That would be great. I mean, I can invoice you if that's more convenient."

James smiled. "I'll take care of it now. I know things can get tight around Christmas."

"That was nice of you," Harriet said when they were back outside.

He put his arm around her shoulders.

"I heard from some of the business owners that this Christmas ticket thing puts Daniel in a real bind. He has to front the cost of printing all the tickets plus all the holiday cards and advertising flyers and things like my menus that people do this time of year. Under normal conditions, businesses pay sixty days after the work is received."

"That sucks," Luke said.

"It's how business works," James explained. "A lot of people start businesses without realizing how much money they have to have up front to cover that time period. They need more money to cover the people who take more than sixty days or don't ever pay."

"As busy as the print shop seems to be, I'm surprised Daniel isn't more solvent," Harriet said.

James blew out a breath.

"You just never know. Maybe his expenses are high. He could be making payments on all those printers and copiers."

Harriet stared through the window into the shop.

"I suppose."

Beth and Jorge came out of the print shop and paused for another look at Robin's quilt.

"That has to be one of the nicest quilts in the group," Beth said. "No one would ever know how quickly it was put together." Her gaze shifted to the shop directly across the street. "I wonder why Keystroke Computers doesn't have a quilt?"

Jorge shifted his package of tickets to his left arm, freeing up his right to encircle Beth's shoulders.

"It's a voluntary activity. Chris declined. The committee pressed pretty hard, since he's the only one who didn't want one. They tried to get him to put *some* sort of display in his window, if not a quilt, but he wasn't having it."

"I guess that's his right," Harriet said. "Is he anti-religion?"

Jorge shook his head.

"I don't think that was it. He just didn't want to be bothered. He's not doing Christmas tickets, either."

"Well, bah, humbug," Luke said, and everyone laughed.

Chapter 7

Beth, Mavis and Connie were sitting at the big table at The Steaming Cup, Foggy Point's other, larger coffee shop, on Monday when Harriet arrived. She unwrapped the knitted scarf from her neck and slid out of her jacket.

"I thought it was supposed to get warmer this week."

"Go get a hot drink, and you'll be fine," Aunt Beth told her.

"I can't stay too long. Lauren is meeting me here, and after we go to the quilt store to find some fabric for her brother's quilt, I've got to pick up James's printing. I've got time for a quick hot chocolate, though," she added and headed for the counter.

"I know we can't expect everyone to be as enthusiastic about our quilts as we are," Connie said when Harriet returned. "But did anyone else think the shop owners were a little subdued?"

Mavis sipped her tea then set her mug down on the table.

"I wasn't going to say anything, but I thought Mildred would be a little more appreciative. I mean, they get a free quilt out of the deal. She didn't seem to care what I made for the yarn store or how I hung it, for that matter."

Harriet stirred the whipped cream into her cocoa.

"Jade is having financial problems at Blood Moon, so I wasn't surprised when my quilt wasn't the first thing on her mind, but she did thank me."

"There are a couple of dominate members on the Business Association committee," Beth said. "Maybe this whole month of Christmas activities is too much for the smaller businesses, but they were afraid to go against the bigger players. Now, the expense of the extra activities is threat-

37

ening their survival." She leaned back in her chair. "Serena's doing a land-office business at the kitchen store. She's selling all the quilted tablecloths she and her friends can make, and her shelves are well stocked with kitchen tools, dishes, and cookbooks, and every other possible item that could be associated with a kitchen."

Connie pulled a plastic zipper bag filled with small prepared hexagons from her purse.

"Jenny and I were talking last night, and she said the jewelry store was so busy she had to stand outside on the sidewalk for the first half-hour before she could go in."

Mavis looked into her empty cup.

"Busy doesn't necessarily mean profitable."

"At the prices Tony charges, he has to be making money," Harriet observed. "And he has two apprentices now."

Mavis stood up.

"I'm getting a refill. Anyone want anything?"

"Could you get me a mini-bagel?" Connie asked. "With plain cream cheese."

Lauren came in and joined Mavis at the counter.

"I'll take mine to go," they heard her tell the barista.

Harriet draped her scarf around her neck and put her jacket on.

"Will I see everyone at Pins and Needles tomorrow?"

"I'll be there," Beth said.

Connie and Mavis said they would also be attending the Loose Threads meeting the following day. Lauren came to the table, latte in hand.

"Are you ready?"

Harriet smiled.

"If fabric is involved, I was born ready."

✂ --- ✂ --- ✂

Harriet and Lauren left Pins and Needles and headed up the street toward the print shop, a block and a half away.

"Make sure you wash that flannel twice before you use it," Harriet recommended.

"I read on the internet that you don't need to wash it since, once it's quilted in, the stitching will keep it from going anywhere."

"That hasn't been my experience. The stitching on functional quilts isn't dense enough to come into play. Besides, dark-colored flannels can bleed."

"I don't have time for a do-over if I don't get it right the first time, so I will definitely heed your advice. Marjorie suggested I buy a quarter-yard more than I needed for that reason."

38

"It wouldn't hurt to throw a color-catching sheet or two in when you wash the finished quilt, too."

Lauren shifted her shopping bag from her right hand to her left.

"I can do that."

Harriet looked across the street to the Outdoor Store.

"Your quilt design is perfect for the store it's in."

Lauren grinned.

"I do have my moments."

The print shop was on the corner of Main Street and Fourth Avenue. Harriet could hear Christmas music playing before she opened the door.

"Daniel must really have his stereo cranked up," she said as she stepped inside.

Fir garland festooned with large red bows outlined all the interior doors, and a Noble fir sat next to the counter, decorated with samples of personalized ornaments, with *your* name here in various sizes and scripts, that could be ordered and delivered before the holiday. Large wrapped boxes with oversized bows were stacked at the opposite end of the counter, and a display of photo Christmas cards on the top surfaces had with a discreet sign promising a three-day turnaround time.

"Wow," Lauren said and surveyed the retail area of the shop. "Looks like he caught the Christmas spirit after the quilt unveiling."

"Daniel," Harriet called out. "Are you here?"

Lauren crossed the room, reached over the counter to the boom box responsible for the music, and pushed the off button. In the silence that followed, Harriet heard the rhythmic *thunking* of a large printer.

"Daniel!" she tried again. "Anyone home?"

"He must not be able to hear over the machines," Lauren said and lifted a hinged section of the counter. "After you," she said, and waved Harriet through.

Harriet started through the swinging door that led to the production area and stopped abruptly, running into Lauren as she backed up. She felt the blood leave her face, making her dizzy. She staggered to Daniel's desk chair and collapsed.

"Call nine-one-one,"

Lauren pulled her phone from her pocket.

"What?" she asked as she dialed.

Harriet took a deep breath.

"Daniel is…" She took another breath and started again. "Daniel is hanging from the rafters in there."

"We need the police," Lauren said into her phone. "We're at the Print Shop, Four-oh-five Main Street, and there's been an accident."

"I don't think it was an accident," Harriet said when Lauren had finished the call.

"Are you sure it's Daniel?"

"Whoever it is, is tall, skinny, and wearing an apron with the shop logo on the front."

"Sounds like Daniel."

They heard sirens almost immediately, and within minutes two paramedics followed by Officer Hue Nguyen came into the shop.

Harriet pointed.

"He's in there."

The paramedics rushed into the back room while Officer Nguyen stopped beside Harriet's chair. He looked at the two women and shook his head.

"What happened?"

"I came to pick up James's printing," Harriet said in a rush.

Nguyen looked from her to Lauren.

"What she said. We came to pick up tickets and menus. We couldn't find Daniel, but we heard the printers running. We started to go into the back, but as soon as Harriet opened the door, she saw Daniel hanging from the rafters, so we backed up and called you."

Nguyen tapped his pen on his notebook.

"And you didn't go back in for a look?" He asked Lauren.

"No, I did not. This may come as a surprise, but some of us do not enjoy looking at dead people and, in fact, avoid it at all costs."

"And Detective Morse has lectured us on how not to contaminate a crime scene," Harriet added.

Nguyen closed his notebook.

"It's not a crime scene yet," he said. "If he's really hanging, as you say, it's likely a suicide."

If *he's really hanging?* Harriet thought. *Seriously?* Did Nguyen think a person could make a mistake about something like that?

Lauren glared at the man.

"Do people often mistake a man hanging from the rafters for something else, in your experience?"

"If you only glanced, as you say, maybe it wasn't a *man* hanging from the rafters."

"Oh, for crying out loud," Harriet said, her voice rising. "Don't you think the paramedics would be back out here if it was just a dummy or an I-don't-know-what hanging from his rafters?"

"Calm down. I'm just trying to wrap my head around the fact that, once again, we have a dead person in Foggy Point, and once again, you are the one to find him."

"Maybe you can wrap your head around the fact that in every single one of those cases, we—myself, Lauren, my aunt and all of the Loose Threads—had nothing to do with the murders that took place. I moved to Foggy Point thinking it was a nice, safe small town."

Nguyen gave her a grim smile.

"And strangely, it was just that until you moved back."

Lauren stiffened.

"Oh, so, now *Harriet* is responsible for all the crime in Foggy Point?"

Nguyen's face turned red, but he was kept from further comment by one of the paramedics' coming through the door from the press room. She was a short, blonde woman Harriet had encountered before.

"I think we're going to need the medical examiner for this one. I'm sure it will turn out to be just what it looks like—a suicide…"

"But?" Nguyen prompted her.

The woman chewed her lip before answering.

"There are a couple of small things that may be nothing, but I'd like someone who knows more than I do about this sort of situation to take a look."

"Do I need to call the detectives?"

"They can't come into the scene until the medical examiner releases it, but it might not hurt to give them a heads-up. I called the ME already, but it will take her a little while to get here."

"Thanks," he said then turned back to Harriet and Lauren. "You two stay right here."

With that warning, he went outside to his car to make his calls.

Chapter 8

Harriet and Lauren stayed rooted to their spots until ten minutes had passed and it became obvious Officer Nguyen wasn't coming back anytime soon. Harriet stood up and leaned to her left so she could see around the quilt in the front window.

"Looks like Detective Morse's is headed this way."

Lauren came to the counter beside her. Detective Jane Morse was a quilter and the only woman in the Foggy Point Police Department detective squad. They watched as she parked her car and approached the shop.

"Good, maybe she can let us out of here. I've got a video conference later, and I'd like to do a little prep for it."

"I wonder if James will be able to get his menus."

Lauren looked at a work table beside Daniel's desk.

"Is that them?"

Several bundles of printing were stacked neatly on the table, each with a slip of paper on top. Harriet went to look and checked out the bundle that was the right size to be menus. James's name was on the job ticket.

"I could slide them into my bag," Lauren said. "No one would be the wiser."

Harriet shook her head.

"If this does turn out to be a crime scene, we'd both be in big trouble."

"It was just a thought."

"And what thought was that?" Detective Morse asked. She had come in while their backs were to the door. Both jumped at the sound of her voice.

"Nothing," Lauren said a little too quickly.

Morse crossed to the counter.

"What have you two gotten yourselves into now?"

Harriet sat back down in Daniel's chair.

"Like I told Officer Nguyen, we were just trying to pick up James's printing order. Daniel wasn't out here, but we heard the printing machine. I know it's probably not legal for us to go into the workroom, but I was just going to stick my head in the door and call out to Daniel to see if he was there."

"And Harriet saw him hanging from the rafters, so we shut the door and called you guys," Lauren finished for her.

"Wait here while I see why they need a detective at an apparent suicide," Morse told them.

"If it's a suicide, why do we have to wait here?" Lauren said to her back as she disappeared through the connecting door.

Harriet pulled her phone from her pocket and tapped out a quick text to James, apprising him of her current situation. She knew he wouldn't see it until things slowed down after the lunch rush at the restaurant but wanted him to hear it from her. He knew she'd planned on picking up his printing, and she didn't want him to hear about the trouble from one of his customers.

Lauren checked her messages then paced the width of the office area a few times. Harriet looked idly around the desk in front of her.

"I wonder if he left a suicide note."

Lauren stopped pacing.

"It can't hurt to look. You check the desk; I'll take the computer."

Harriet pulled open the flat drawer in the middle, using her shirt sleeve to cover her hand as she did so. It contained pens, pencils, paper clips—the usual small office supplies. The top drawer on the right held pads of pre-printed invoices, receipts for cash purchases, and business cards.

"This is interesting," she said as she pulled open the second drawer on the right.

Lauren turned away from the computer screen.

"What?"

"We've got a regular pharmacy in drawer number two." She took a tissue from a box on the desk and used it to pick up one of the amber bottles. "This one's Triumeq." She set it down and picked up another. "Descovy," she read before dropping it and picking up another. "Retrovir."

"Whoa, that last one is an HIV drug. The rest of them probably are, too. Are they in Daniel's name?"

"They are," Harriet replied. "There's no reason we should have known that, but it does add to the possibilities, I guess."

Lauren returned to the computer.

43

"Why would someone commit suicide if they were being successfully treated?" she wondered aloud.

Harriet went back to searching the desk.

"Maybe no one wanted to be in a relationship with him because of it."

"I find that hard to believe in this day and age." Lauren frowned and slid off the stool she'd been sitting on in front of Daniel's computer monitor and bent down below the counter. "Well, this is interesting," she said in a muffled tone.

"What?"

Lauren slid the side panel off the computers tower.

"I think Morse is going to want to see this. Someone has removed the hard drive from the computer."

✂ --- ✂ --- ✂

It was another thirty minutes before Detective Morse reappeared.

"They took Daniel out through the back delivery doors. If you ladies don't have anything else to tell me, you're free to go." She headed for the door but stopped when neither Harriet or Lauren moved. "Is there something else?"

Lauren cleared her throat, stalling while she figured out the best way to tell Morse she'd been touching the computer.

"Umm…well, I thought you might want to know if Daniel left a suicide note on his computer, so I just tapped the enter key to see what might come up."

Morse closed her eyes and put her hand on the side of her face.

"It's probably useless at this point to tell you two to stay out of police business. But, okay, what did you find?"

"Nothing." Lauren answered.

Morse's eyes opened wide.

"All right, so you touched one key and found nothing. What aren't you telling me?"

Lauren squirmed on the stool.

"Well, when I hit the enter key, I got no response at all, so I thought I'd check the tower and see if it had been turned off."

"Had it?" Morse interrupted.

"Yes, but that's not the significant part. I slid the side panel off just to have a peek, and someone has removed the hard drive."

"That *is* interesting." She thought for a minute. "Please tell me you didn't touch it with your bare hands."

"I used a tissue."

"Make no mistake, I would prefer it if you wouldn't meddle in police business, but thank you for not leaving prints on what may turn out to be evidence."

Harriet leaned forward in the chair.

"Have you confirmed Daniel committed suicide?"

"You know I can't talk about an ongoing investigation. I guess, having said that, you might conclude there is an investigation to not talk about. That remains to be seen at this point. The ME is going to do an autopsy before declaring the cause and manner of death."

"Well, that's interesting," Harriet said.

Lauren stood up.

"Shall we go?"

"I don't suppose there's any chance I can take James's print order," Harriet said to Morse.

"Not until we process the scene. *If* we process it."

"Great. I guess I'd better break the news to James."

"Shall we go in person?" Lauren asked. "I mean, we did miss lunch and all."

"Sounds good to me."

Chapter 9

The lunch crowd had thinned by the time Harriet and Lauren arrived at the restaurant. They had barely gotten their coats off and settled in at their table when James appeared carrying a plate of tea sandwiches and another laden with small cakes and cookies.

"You guys want to evaluate our new high-tea offerings?"

Lauren reached for the sandwich plate.

"Yes, we do. We're starving."

"We were delayed at the print shop," Harriet explained.

"That's an understatement," Lauren said around a bite of sandwich.

Harriet set a small cucumber sandwich on her plate

"Unfortunately, we weren't able to get your printing." She went on to explain what they'd found at the printer's.

James stood up when she'd finished.

"I'm glad you two are okay. Not to disrespect Daniel, but I need to go call the printer in Port Angeles. I'll wait and see what the business association wants us to do about the Christmas tickets, but I've got to have tea menus ASAP."

Lauren picked up another sandwich.

"Harriet did try to get Morse to let us take them, but it was a no-go. You might see if anything's changed. Maybe you can get them now."

"I'll do that," he said, and smiled. "And I'll send out more sandwiches."

"Do that," Lauren told him.

A little later, Harriet wiped her mouth after finishing a bite of cake.

"I only had a quick glance at Daniel, and I could be mistaken, but even though there was a stool tipped over under him, to me it didn't look tall enough for him to have jumped off of."

"What do you mean?"

"I would think that, to hang yourself, you'd need to be standing on a stool with the noose around your neck, and then you kick the stool out of the way so you drop down and hang. If you were to put the stool I saw back in place, I don't think his feet would have reached it."

Lauren chewed another cookie thoughtfully.

"So, you think someone hanged him?"

"Like I said, I only got a quick look, but the proportions looked wrong to me."

"Hard to imagine Daniel having those kind of enemies."

"You never know," Harriet mused. "My aunt told me he's from around here, but he moved to New York for about twenty years when he was younger. Anything could have happened there."

"Morse will be happy."

Harriet set her teacup down harder than she'd intended.

"Why should she be happy?"

Lauren smiled.

"For once, we don't have a dog in this fight. Other than finding him, we have no reason to do anything but watch from the sidelines."

"That's true." Harriet relaxed back in her chair. "I wonder how this will affect the downtown Christmas activities?"

"If it was suicide, we'll do a moment of silence for him and continue on, I would guess. If someone killed him, I imagine it will depend on how quickly they catch the killer."

"On that happy note, we better get going."

✂ --- ✂ --- ✂

Luke was sitting at the kitchen table when Harriet got home. Fred the cat opposite him, staring at his empty plate. Fred jumped to the floor and raced upstairs as soon as he saw Harriet. Her dog Scooter lay curled up in Luke's lap, while Cyrano the mini-dachshund was draped across his feet.

"You'd better run," she called after the cat.

Scooter looked up at the sound of her voice, wagged his tail, then put his head back down and closed his eyes.

"Don't trouble yourself, you little traitor. How was school?" she asked Luke.

"It's pretty lame right now."

"How so?"

"The school band and choir are doing next week's Christmas program downtown, so they have to keep missing class to practice. A lot of kids are involved, so the teachers are giving the rest of us busy work to fill the time."

"Do you belong to any groups at school?"

Harriet had wondered about this since September, but given his rough home life prior to moving in with her and James, she'd not wanted to make him feel bad if he didn't. Her own parents' almost total disinterest in her own day-to-day school life had not prepared her for how much normal parents were supposed to ask their kids about school. Their only interest had been grades. She was pretty sure there was more to it than that. She made a mental note to ask Robin or DeAnn or Connie what was appropriate at the next Threads meeting.

"Not really. Most of them meet after school, and before, I had to work. Besides, most clubs require money at some point."

"You know if you decide you want to join anything, James and I are happy to fund it."

Luke's face flushed, and he jammed his fists into his pockets.

"What?"

"I don't know how to say this without sounding like an ungrateful jerk."

Harriet put her hand on his arm.

"Whatever it is, you can tell me. James and I won't judge you, and maybe if there's a problem, we can help."

He looked at his feet, and she was worried he wasn't going to say anything.

"Before I lived here, the kids at school didn't have the time of day for me or any of the other kids at my foster home. In fact, they made fun of our clothes and stuff."

"That's terrible. I thought Foggy Point High School had an anti-bullying program."

"Yeah, well, I'm sure they do. Anyway, now that I live with you guys, and have nicer stuff, the same people are sucking up to me. Suddenly, I'm good enough to sit at their table at lunch when I wasn't before."

"I'm sorry."

"Yeah, well, it is what it is, as they say. I can't control their behavior, but I'm not going to pretend it's okay."

"That's very wise of you. It makes me a little sad that you don't have friends at school, though."

"Don't worry about it. I just need to get through the rest of this year, and then I don't have to see those people if I don't want. Besides, living here is giving me a chance to focus on my classes. I missed some stuff freshman year because of my living situation, so my counselor arranged for me to do independent studies during my free period to make it up. They're letting me retest in a couple of subjects I got Ds in back then to help bring my GPA up."

"That's great, and it will help with your college applications. Speaking of schoolwork, do you have any homework tonight?"

"No."

"I was thinking of going to visit Becky."

"Who's Becky?"

"Remember the horse I told you guys about? The one Lauren and I are supporting for the month."

"Oh, yeah."

"I got to thinking. Jade was so low on funds she couldn't pay her stable fee, so I wondered if she was able to get Becky's feet done."

Luke gave her a quizzical look.

"What's that mean?"

"Horses hooves grow like people's fingernails, so every month or six weeks they need to be trimmed. I have a feeling if Jade is low on funds she might not be taking care of Becky's feet like she should. Suffice it to say, a horse with bad feet is a big problem. Anyway, I was wondering if you wanted to go with."

"Sounds fun, but I don't know anything about horses."

"You don't need to know anything. We'll just have a look at her feet, and if they need trimming, we'll get the stable to schedule it."

"Is there a dress code at the stable?'

Harriet laughed.

"Maybe at the fancy ones back East or in Europe, but not a typical place around here." She looked at his jeans and flannel shirt. "You might want to add a sweatshirt or down vest or even both. We'll be outside, and it's pretty nippy today. I'm going to go change myself. See you back down here in five?"

Luke smiled and dashed to the stairs, taking them two at a time on his way to his room.

✂ --- ✂ --- ✂

The stable Becky boarded at was located on the back side of Miller Hill on a large shelf of land that cut into the hillside. It was surrounded by woods that had trails crisscrossing through them, which provided lots of trail-riding opportunities for the people who kept horses there. A long driveway took Harriet and Luke past multiple white-fenced enclosures, each with two or three horses in them.

49

"Wow, I had no idea Foggy Point had anything like this," Luke said as he swiveled in his seat to look out each side of the car in turn.

"I've never been back here, either."

Harriet slowed the car as the driveway widened into a parking lot. Directly ahead of them was a large barn. To the right and farther back was an enclosed riding arena with a smaller, covered, open-sided riding area attached to it.

"I'm going to go into the barn and see if I can find the manager. You can come along or wait here."

"I'll come with," he said and opened his door.

A young woman was leading a tall dark-bay horse out of the barn as they reached the door. She directed them to where they could find the assistant manager in the main riding arena.

Two people occupied the large arena. A girl on a white Welsh pony rode in a circle around a tall woman in Lycra riding pants and a green oversized sweatshirt with *Miller Hill Equestrian Center* printed on the back in white letters. The arena consisted of a large oval surfaced with twelve inches or more of footing, a mix of dirt and synthetic material that protected horses and riders from impact injuries. It was surrounded by a waist-high barrier with gates on each side. Harriet and Luke walked over to the open gate closest to them and watched as the woman directed the young rider.

"McKenzie, you're confusing her. Your legs are saying one thing, and your hands are saying the opposite."

The woman had barely finished speaking when the pony hopped sideways and bucked. McKenzie dropped the reins and held on to the front of the saddle. The pony took the opportunity to bolt for the open gate. Before anyone else could move, Luke stepped into the opening and grabbed one of the flapping reins, stopping the pony in its tracks.

McKenzie was crying, and he put his hand on her leg to steady her.

"You're okay," he said in a soft voice. "You're okay."

The riding instructor strode toward them at the same time the young woman they'd seen earlier ran in from the opposite direction and took the pony's reins from Luke.

"Are you okay, McKenzie?"

The child's face was white, and her bottom lip quivered, but she nodded.

"I'm fine," she finally managed.

Luke backed up a few steps as the tall woman reached them.

"Thank you," she said to Luke, and then turned to Harriet. "I'm Marcia Hamilton, and this is Emily Roberts. Did you need some help?"

"I was hoping to talk to you about Jade Meyer's horse, Becky." Harriet told her.

"Ahh, okay. Give me a minute." She turned back to the little girl on the pony. "How about you walk Snowflake around the arena a few times so you can both settle down." She looked at Emily. "Shut the gates, and stay in here to keep an eye on her. You can sit in the bleachers, but don't leave her alone."

Emily unlatched the latch that kept the gate open and swung it shut. She smiled at Luke as he moved out of the way.

"Now, how can I help you?" Marcia said and guided Harriet out of the arena. She paused a moment when Harriet finished her story and then blew out a breath.

"'To be honest, we've been worried about Becky ourselves. Jade *hasn't* had Becky's feet done—she's overdue by a couple of weeks. We were debating whether we should go ahead and have them done when the farrier comes out later this week."

"I'll let Jade know, but go ahead and do that. I'll pay for it. I can't stand the idea that any horse would have its feet ruined for lack of money, but it's especially bad for such an expensive breed."

"I agree. I didn't want to have to turn her into the county humane society, and Becky certainly isn't in that bad a condition yet, anyway."

"I know Jade wants to take care of her. Apparently, her parents are willing to help with her own living expenses, but they only grudgingly pay anything for Becky, and will contribute nothing toward Jade's business, which is how she pays for Becky. Or would if she was making any money. I suspect they want her to sell the horse," Harriet said.

Luke stood with his hands in his back pockets looking toward the arena.

"Have you ever met Becky?" Marcia asked.

Harriet shook her head.

"Would you like to?"

"Sure." She turned to Luke. "I'm going to go meet Becky. I'm sure it would be okay if you would rather watch…McKenzie and Snowflake."

Luke grinned and jogged back toward the arena.

✂ --- ✂ --- ✂

Marcia led Becky out of her stall and clipped cross-tie ropes to each side of her halter, securing her in the barn aisle. Harriet slowly circled the horse.

"She seems a little thin, but other than her feet, she looks healthy enough," she said.

51

"Until about three months ago, Jade was out here all the time, and no expense was spared as far as horse care went. She's not abusing her, by any means, but she's feeding a cheaper food blend and has dropped her vitamins. Her outdoor blanket has a big tear in it and needs to be replaced. I tried to talk to Jade about it—offered to work with her—but she shut me out."

Harriet patted Becky's neck.

"She didn't tell me much, either. I know she's hoping to have a big Christmas season to help her catch up financially. I have no clue as to what caused her sudden decline of fortune."

Marcia stood on Becky's other side and ran her hands through the horse's mane.

"I guess she'll tell us when she's ready. Or not. On another subject, your son was pretty good with McKenzie and her pony. Does he ride?"

"I don't think so."

Marcia raised an eyebrow.

"He's only been my foster son for a few months, but he's never been around horses."

"His instincts seem good. I'm asking because we have some volunteer positions opening up, for students to work in our horse-therapy program."

"Given his background, he could probably use a little horse therapy himself."

"The way we train our volunteers is to put them through a short version of the program, so it might work well for both of us."

"I can't speak for him, but I'll ask."

✂ --- ✂ --- ✂

"You moved pretty quick back there when that pony ran away with its rider," Harriet said to Luke as she drove back down the long driveway. "Have you ever been around horses before?"

Luke smiled and widened his eyes.

"Are you kidding? Drug dealers don't do horses, or anything else besides drugs." He paused. "Well, there was one time my dad dumped me off at a carnival with a bunch of little kids and a handful of cash. Some of them may have been my half-siblings, I'm not sure. Anyway, I took the littlest ones to the pony ride. I did that because they couldn't run off when they were on a pony." He laughed. "Does that count?"

Harriet smiled, too. She was glad Luke was beginning to be able to talk about some part of his past without withdrawing into himself and closing down.

"It wasn't exactly what I had in mind, but I guess anything counts." She turned onto Miller Hill Road. "Marcia asked me if you had horse experience. She said you were good with the pony when it ran away."

"It seemed like the thing to do," Luke said. His cheeks pinked.

"Well, she also asked me if I thought you'd be interested in volunteering for their horse-therapy program. I told her that was up to you."

"Emily asked me the same thing," he said, his cheeks turning a darker shade of red. "She said you have to go through the program—or a short version of it—so you get used to the horses and stuff."

"What do you think?" Harriet was trying to tread lightly after their discussion about his disinterest in afterschool activities.

"Sounds fun. If it's okay with you and James."

"Of course it's okay with James and I. If you *want* to do it—and are still able to keep up with your schoolwork, of course."

"No problem."

Harriet fiddled with the heater knobs, trying to coax a little more heat from the car. She glanced over at Luke, who was gazing out the window with a little smile.

"Emily seems nice. Does she go to your school?"

"She *is* nice, and she's homeschooled. I guess she didn't get along with the kids at school, either."

Harriet couldn't think of what to say to that, but was saved from having to answer when a deer darted across the road in front of them. She slammed on the brakes and stopped just in time.

She sat back in her seat.

"Whew, that will take a few years off your life. Are you okay?"

Luke gave her a little smile.

"I'm okay. My heart's beating a little fast, but I'm good."

"I don't know about you, but I think a stop at the cupcake shop might be in order."

Luke grinned.

"Sounds good to me."

Chapter 10

Harriet and Luke stopped in front of the shop window that displayed Connie's cupcake quilt.

"Connie did a nice job on that," Harriet said.

"They should make some cupcakes that are decorated just like the ones on the quilt," Luke said and craned his neck to see around it into the bakery.

Harriet laughed and opened the door.

"Can I get one of everything?" Luke asked as he went inside.

No one was tending the counter, but they could hear loud voices coming from the bakery in back.

"It doesn't matter that it isn't me, they have pictures," a woman said.

"But you didn't kill anyone," a second woman shot back.

Harriet coughed loudly, and the voices abruptly went silent. A moment later, Sunny Mason, the owner of Sunshine Bakery, appeared, removing her white apron as she approached the counter.

"Hi, how can I help you?" she asked, looking from Harriet to Luke and back again.

Luke was staring at the display case. There were samples of at least twenty different cupcake varieties.

"How am I supposed to choose?"

Sunny slid the door of the case open.

"What's your favorite flavor in the world?"

"Chocolate," he answered without hesitation.

"Okay, that cuts the choices by half. Do you like your chocolate more fudgy or more cake-y?"

Luke thought a moment.

"Fudgy," he said with a grin.

Sunny continued offering ingredient and flavor choices until they'd narrowed it down to four possible cupcakes.

"Okay," Harriet said, interrupting their game. "Let's get one of each of the last four contenders." She looked at Luke. "Is four enough?"

"I think four will do it," he said with an attempt at a straight face.

"We'll take his four, and I would like a lemon blueberry and a gingerbread."

"I'll bring them out," Sunny said. "Would you like anything to drink? I have peppermint hot chocolate in addition to the usual stuff."

They both ordered the hot chocolate and settled in at a bistro table near the window. Lauren came in as Sunny carried a tray with their cupcakes and hot chocolate to their table.

"I'll have what she's having," she told Sunny.

"What are you up to?" Harriet asked as she drew a chair up from another table so Lauren could join them.

"I had to get an ink cartridge for my printer, and ever since we first saw Connie's cupcake quilt, they've been on my mind. I thought I was going to slip in here and indulge in a guilty pleasure with no one the wiser."

Harriet filled her in on their visit to the equestrian center.

"You're getting in deeper and deeper with that horse." Lauren commented.

"I just hate to see her suffer because her owner is in financial trouble."

Harriet took a bite of her lemon blueberry cupcake as Sunny delivered Lauren's.

"So, where did you get your ink cartridge?" she asked. "Don't you usually get them from Daniel?"

"Indeed I do," Lauren said around a bite of cupcake. "Fortunately, Keystroke Computer Repair also carries a variety of printer cartridges. He also sells printer paper by the case."

"Good to know," Harriet said. She looked over at Luke, who was midway through his third cupcake—a chocolate brownie number with strawberry filling, strawberry frosting dribbled with chocolate, and with a chocolate-dipped strawberry on top.

"We heard an interesting argument from out back when we first got here," Harriet said in a quiet voice.

"Do tell," Lauren encouraged her.

Harriet repeated what they'd heard.

"Given today's events the 'Yeah, but you didn't kill anyone' caught my attention."

"Could you tell if one of them was Sunny?"

Harriet looked at Luke. He shrugged.

"I think the one who said 'It doesn't matter that it isn't me, they have pictures' could have been Sunny."

"Do you think we should tell…" Lauren stopped mid-sentence and put both hands up. "Wait, didn't we just discuss how Daniel's murder was none of our business and we were going to stay out of it?"

"If it turns out Daniel was murdered, Morse would want to know we heard someone talking about someone being accused of killing someone," Harriet argued.

Lauren shook her head.

"First, that's a big *if.* Second, we have no idea who they were talking about, and third, all you heard is someone didn't kill someone. I'm not sure how any of that helps Morse."

"I suppose," Harriet said, and sipped her chocolate.

The string of Christmas bells on the door jingled as Connie came into the shop.

"Are we having a Loose Threads meeting?" she asked.

Lauren laughed.

"Your quilt is making everyone cupcake-hungry."

"It's been great for business," Sunny said from the counter. "I think your whole quilt group has been in, plus a lot of other people. And we can use all the sales we can get."

"Isn't Christmas usually a pretty good time, business-wise?" Lauren asked her.

Sunny's expression darkened.

"You would think so," she said.

Connie went over to peruse the cupcakes.

"What can I get you?" Sunny asked.

"I would like a dulce de leche and a peppermint chocolate," she said. "And a small coffee." She slid another chair from a nearby table and joined them, then leaned forward and gestured with her hand for Lauren and Harriet to do likewise.

"Does anyone else find this whole business-is-bad story that we've heard from several shops to be a little strange?" she asked in a quiet voice. "I talked to Marjorie, and she said business at the quilt store is up twenty percent over last year. Beth got a similar story from Serena at the kitchen store."

"James says the restaurant is up, also," Harriet said in the same tone.

The doorbell jingled again, and Chris Baker from Keystroke Computers came in. He was a lanky blond who looked like he could use a good meal.

56

"Are you following me?" Lauren asked him with a grin.

"You did mention you were stopping here. Once you left, I couldn't stop thinking about…" He paused for dramatic effect. "…cupcakes," he finished with a laugh. "Besides, I needed to deliver Sunny's laptop." He held up an older model Sony Viao.

"Did it get a virus?" Lauren guessed.

"No, just came in for a routine check-up. It takes a lot of TLC to keep these older models alive." He looked over what was left of their cupcakes.

"You guys have any recommendations?"

"Anything chocolate," Luke said

"Works for me," Chris said, and strolled to the counter.

Chapter 11

*H*arriet shivered when the cold air hit her shower-damp hair as she got in her car the following day. She'd run two extra miles that morning in hopes the extra endorphins would protect her from whatever it was her aunt wanted to discuss with her. They'd just seen each other two days ago at the Loose Threads meeting, and everything had been fine then.

Aunt Beth had called the previous night after dinner and asked to meet at the Steaming Cup—a more formal invitation than the usual "Let's go to coffee" invite Harriet was used to. It was made all the more ominous by the public setting—her aunt usually preferred grocery-store coffee prepared in a home coffeemaker.

Beth was alone at a two-person table when Harriet arrived. Possibilities streaked through her mind as she ordered her latte and watched while the barista prepared it. Could her aunt have contracted a terrible disease? Surely, if that were the case, she would have mentioned symptoms or doctor appointments before this. Had she and Jorge had a falling out? Again, Harriet couldn't imagine that happening with no warning; they'd been fine two days ago.

She sucked in her breath. Her parents. Something had happened to her parents. But would her aunt ask her to meet in a public place for that sort of news?

The barista pushed her latte across the counter. Time to face the music.

"I hope you don't mind meeting here," Beth said as Harriet set her cup on the table and shrugged out of her coat. "Connie and Mavis wanted to meet for coffee after we're done. You're welcome to stay on when they get here."

Harriet relaxed a little at that announcement. Maybe the location wasn't strategic.

"What did you want to talk about?"

Beth took a deep breath.

"Jorge and I were talking about Christmas last night. I mean Christmas Day. If you remember, last year, Julio went to his girlfriend's parents' house. Well, this year they are coming to Foggy Point."

"I've only met him once or twice, but he seemed like a nice guy," Harriet said carefully, wondering what Jorge's son's holiday plans had to do with her..

"He's very nice," Beth said and smiled briefly.

Harriet sipped her latte in silence, waiting for her aunt to continue. Beth reached across the table and took her hand.

"You're making me nervous," Harriet said.

"I don't mean to. I just don't want you to get upset."

"For crying out loud, would you just say whatever it is you're trying to say."

"Jorge wants to invite Aiden to dinner."

Harriet got a sinking feeling in the pit of her stomach. Having her ex-boyfriend at her first Christmas dinner with her new husband and newer foster son seemed like a recipe for disaster. Especially given Aiden's refusal to accept Harriet and James's relationship.

Beth held up her other hand.

"If it's too upsetting, I'll tell Jorge, and we won't try to combine our families. He's been like a father to Aiden since his father died, and Julio *is* Aiden's best friend."

Harriet leaned back in her chair and stared at the ceiling.

"Why does this have to be so hard? Most people break up with their boyfriend and never have to see him again. I can't seem to get away from Aiden."

"That's small town living at its finest."

Harriet sighed.

"I don't want you to have to be apart from Jorge. That's not fair. James and Luke and I can do Christmas dinner at our house, and then have dinner the next night or any other night with you and Jorge."

Beth frowned. Clearly, this wasn't the outcome she'd hoped for. She sat in silence.

"It's not a problem for me," Harriet said. "But I won't have any of our relationship drama go on around Luke."

59

"I can have Jorge talk to Aiden. Explain about the boy."

"Do that, but I can't make any promises until I talk to James and Luke. If they aren't up for it, we won't be able to come."

Beth brightened.

"We'll cross that bridge when we come to it."

"You two look serious," Connie said as she approached. Beth and Harriet had been so engrossed they hadn't noticed the arrival of the others. "Shall we move to the big table?"

Beth and Harriet stood up and followed her to the bigger space. Mavis joined them a moment later.

"Is everyone ready for the holiday?" she asked as she hung her coat on the back of her chair and sat down.

Beth gave Harriet a long look before answering.

"We're getting there. Julio is bringing his girlfriend home for Christmas, and although he hasn't said as much, Jorge thinks Julio is going to propose over the holiday."

"That's exciting!" Connie said. "He must be pretty sure of the answer if he's willing to do it with an audience."

"They've been dating seriously for several years, so I think it will be fine," Beth told them. "Jorge is the one I'm not so sure about. He wants everything to be perfect. He's recarpeting his living room and having all the family pictures on his photo wall reframed. Now he's talking about painting pretty much the whole house."

"Wow," said Harriet. "Does he have time for all that?"

Beth gave a small laugh.

"Not really. Aiden volunteered to help him paint, but I'm trying to get him to scale back his plan. Maybe concentrate on the dining room and living room where everyone will be gathering."

Mavis sipped her coffee and set her cup down.

"Good luck with that."

DeAnn came in, and Beth waved to her when she glanced their way after ordering her drink.

"Can anyone join this party?" she asked, drink and a cookie in hand.

Connie pulled out a chair for her.

"I just got back from Melnyk's," DeAnn continued. "I had an extra one of those Russian-doll blocks left over from the quilt, so I made him a pillow. He told me someone tried to break into the gallery last night. He thinks they tried to jimmy the lock, but he has that ornate door handle-and-lock set, and apparently, they couldn't get it open, so they broke one of the panes of glass to reach inside.

"He said nothing was taken or even disturbed as near as he can tell, so he thinks something or someone scared them off before they got far enough to trip the motion detectors—his security system didn't send an alarm. He did allow for the fact they may have *disabled* his alarm. He's having his security people come out and see what they can tell him."

Harriet leaned forward.

"That's interesting, given Daniel Muhler's sudden demise. And their two businesses being almost next door to each other."

DeAnn took a bite of her cookie thoughtfully.

"Didn't Daniel commit suicide?"

"I think the jury may still be out on that one," Harriet said.

"Do you know something?" Beth asked her.

"Nothing official, but the way he was hanging didn't look right to me. Not that I'm an expert on these matters, but the stool that was tipped over under him didn't look like it was tall enough for him to have stepped off it. But I could be totally wrong."

The group was so focused on Harriet and what she was saying they hadn't noticed Jane Morse approach their table.

"Don't sell yourself short," she said to Harriet. "It's going to be on the news tonight, so I guess I can tell you that Daniel Muhler's death has been determined to be a homicide."

"I knew it didn't look right."

"Is it okay if I join you for a minute?" Morse asked.

"Oh, honey, you know you don't have to ask," Connie told her.

Morse sat down with her latte and chocolate croissant.

"Someone went to a lot of trouble to make it look like a suicide." She turned to Harriet. "You were right about the stool. When you set it up right under him, his toes barely touched it."

"Did you hear what DeAnn said about the attempted break-in at Melnyk's?" Harriet asked.

Morse sipped her latte.

"No, I didn't. What happened?"

DeAnn recounted what she'd learned from Valery Melnyk.

"That's interesting, especially given their proximity and the fact that both stores share an alley."

Harriet wiped her mouth on her napkin.

"That's what we were thinking."

Morse pulled her spiral notebook from her jacket pocket and made a note.

"Anything else I need to know?"

Harriet put her hand over her mouth as she thought.

"Okay, whatever it is you're trying to decide whether to tell me or not, the answer is yes, you need to tell me and let me decide if it's important or not," Morse prompted.

Harriet dropped her hand.

"This truly could be completely unrelated."

Morse sighed.

"Okay, okay," Harriet finally said. "It's hard for me to imagine anyone cares, but Daniel had a drawer full of what Lauren says are antiretroviral drugs."

Morse made a note.

"So, Daniel had AIDs?"

"Or maybe he was HIV-positive. I don't know. We just saw a bunch of drugs."

Beth picked up her spoon and twirled it in her fingers.

"Could Daniel's death be a hate crime?"

Morse closed her notebook and returned it to her pocket.

"It's early yet. At this point, it could be anything." She stood up. "And given that, I think I'll go have a chat with Valery and see want I can learn from him."

"Can it wait until you finish your croissant?" Connie asked.

Morse looked at her plate and sat back down.

"I guess it'll keep for a few more minutes."

✂ --- ✂ --- ✂

Harriet had prearranged with Lauren to meet at the coffee shop after her aunt had had time for her announcement, and she arrived as Morse left. Jenny joined them a few minutes later.

"I thought I might find you all here," she said as she shrugged out of her coat. "Ignore the texts I sent a few of you. I had to come in to Rubie's and take the quilt down so they could redo their window. After they saw the quilt, they decided they needed to upgrade their display. I have to go back in thirty or forty-five minutes and re-hang it. I told them they could handle it, but they were afraid they would 'hurt' it, so I agreed to come do it for them."

Lauren sipped her mocha.

"Seriously?"

Jenny smiled.

"Remember, I put a lot of crystals on that baby. Since the back side was visible in the shop, I put crystals on the back side, too. They were afraid the crystals would tear the fabric when they folded the quilt."

62

"Want some help?" Harriet asked her.

"Sure, that would be great. It'll give you a chance to see the crystal work I did on the back. I was really torn about doing crystals at all. I'm with Connie—I kind of feel like the whole crystals-on-everything look has run its course. It just seemed to me that a quilt in a jewelry store should have a little bling."

Lauren glanced at her phone.

"I've got time to come, too, if you want."

"Sure, the more the merrier," Jenny said.

The front window of Rubie's Jewelry Store was finished and ready for the quilt to be hung when Harriet, Lauren, and Jenny arrived.

"Anthony, this looks great," Jenny said when she saw the new window design.

The store owner, Anthony DeMarco, had created a winter forest effect with animals made from a white rhinestone fabric under stylized flocked Christmas trees. The central tree was decorated with diamond and amethyst jewelry.

Anthony carefully handed Jenny her folded quilt. She, in turn, handed one corner to Harriet and held the other herself. Lauren caught the bottom edge as Jenny unfurled her creation.

"Whoa," Lauren exclaimed.

Harriet gasped.

"Jenny, this is fantastic. I wasn't able to get close enough to the window on viewing night to see all the detail."

The quilt design used a variety of sizes of stars made from white-and-silver small-scale prints on varying shades of lavender background fabric. The back of the quilt was a medium purple with metallic silver flecks. Jenny's liberal use of crystals on the front made the stars seem to twinkle. The back side resembled the night sky.

"You can see why I needed to redo my window," Anthony said. "I had gone with traditional Christmas colors based on what Betty had told me."

Jenny slid the hanging rod into the quilt sleeve as she talked.

"Unfortunately, with Betty's fire, nothing was salvageable from her original quilt. I already had the fabric I used in this one in my stash, which saved time."

"I appreciate everything you've done," Anthony said quickly. "And it really wasn't any trouble to change the window design. Believe me, this window with your quilt will sell a lot of jewelry."

Jenny's cheeks turned pink.

"I was happy to do it."

"Well, we appreciate it."

The door opened, and Detective Morse stepped in, rubbing her hands to warm them.

"Jenny, your quilt looks great. And I like the new window design."

Jenny dipped her head.

"Thanks. Since Betty's quilt was destroyed, I was able to start from scratch. I was just telling Anthony, I already had the fabric for this, so I was able to start cutting and sewing right away. I think it was harder for the people who had to pick up a project in process."

"Don't sell yourself short. Your quilt is spectacular, even more so given how quickly you had to make it," Morse told her. She pulled her notebook from her pocket as she spoke. "Have you ladies noticed anyone coming in or out of Melnyk's gallery while you've been standing here?"

"I didn't," Lauren said. "I was focused on the quilt and the window."

Harriet shook her head.

"Why? Is something going on over there?"

Morse made a note.

"I'm not sure. Someone called the station on the non-emergency line and said they'd gone in to pick up a painting, and Melnyk wasn't there. The door was open, but no one was in the place. They thought it was odd, since they had an appointment. I guess they waited for thirty minutes, and when he still didn't show, they called it in. Given recent events, I decided to check it out myself."

Anthony had gone to a glass display case at the back of the store to show a ring to a customer. Now, he locked the case and returned to the group.

"Valery would never leave his shop unattended. He locked all the doors when he took his trash out to the back alley. He was very paranoid about art theft. In fact, to say he was paranoid would be an understatement."

"So, where do you think he is?" Morse asked the jeweler.

Anthony spread his hands wide.

"I have no idea. Like I said, I can't imagine any circumstance where Val would leave the gallery unlocked without him being there."

Morse made another note and put her pad back in her pocket, then pulled out a business card, handing it to him.

"Call me if you see or hear from Mr. Melnyk, or if you see anyone else over there. In the meantime, I'll send an officer over to put one of our locks on his door."

"Do I need to be worried?" Anthony asked.

Morse blew out a breath.

"I'd like to say no, but given your proximity to both the print shop and the gallery, you would be wise to exercise a little extra caution. Don't let anyone, including you, work alone. Make sure you double-check your door locks when you leave, and set your alarm even if you're only gone for a few minutes."

"I'll let my clerks know about doubling up on our shifts. We already have a robust security system, given the business we're in. We have video cameras inside and out as well as glass-break and motion detectors."

"Depending on what happens next door, I may need to have a look at your camera footage from out front."

"Not a problem," Anthony said. "We upload it to the cloud and keep it for two months at a time."

"I'll let you know if we need it." Morse turned back to Harriet, Jenny and Lauren. "Until we figure out what's going on, you ladies would be wise to shop in pairs."

Lauren gave her a mock salute then glanced at her phone.

"I better get going. Call me if you hear anything."

"Don't go looking for trouble," Morse cautioned them before leaving.

Jenny buttoned her coat.

"I think I'll see if I can catch up with Beth and Mavis and Connie and fill them in on what's going on and pass along the 'don't go downtown alone' warning."

"Good idea," Harriet said, joining her as she headed out the door.

Chapter 12

Harriet turned her long-arm quilting machine off when she saw Luke coming up the driveway after school and waited in her studio until he came in.

"Hey, how was school?" she asked.

Luke grinned and shook his head.

"You always ask, like it's going to magically get better. The best I can say is it wasn't any worse than usual."

"Hope springs eternal," Harriet said and smiled back at him. "James left you a plate of tea sandwiches when he was home earlier. After you eat them, would you like to come to the homeless camp with me? James also brought home a couple of boxes of food for them, and I need to run it out there."

"Sure. It'll only take a minute for me to eat."

"I'll take the dogs out while you're doing that."

True to his word, Luke had finished his plate of sandwiches and was just finishing a second plate of small desserts James had also left.

"I'm ready," he said around a mouthful of cookie.

"Take your time, we're not in that big of a hurry."

✂ --- ✂ --- ✂

Luke opened the back of the car and pulled out the large blue tote. Harriet grabbed a smaller one and set it on the pavement at her feet while she locked the car.

"Follow me," she said, picking up her tote.

"This is really cool," Luke said as he scanned the park.

"Haven't you ever been here?"

"We weren't really the picnic-in-the-park sort of people. My dad probably came here after dark to sell drugs, but he never brought us kids along."

Harriet smiled as she led the way toward the homeless camp.

"We'll have to add 'picnic in the park' to your life-experience to-do list."

Luke laughed.

"You're assuming I'm going to survive the sit-on-Santa's-lap adventure."

"Am I trying too hard?"

"Maybe just a little. You know, I've got a whole lifetime to make up for these early deficits. You don't have to try to recreate the perfect childhood all in the first couple of months."

"I know," Harriet said with a sigh. "I just feel so bad for what you had to go through. And I want things to be better for you."

Luke stopped.

"Harriet, things *are* better for me. Just waking up in my own room in your house with you and James and the animals and not being hungry is beyond my wildest dreams. Don't get me wrong, I'm enjoying all the new experiences, and I like that you're trying so hard, but you've already done the important stuff."

She set her tote down and hugged him awkwardly around his box. He set it down and hugged her back.

"You are the best son ever." She said, swiping at the tears in her eyes.

Luke picked up his tote again.

"Now, don't go getting all mushy on me."

She smiled.

"I'll try," she said and headed into the woods.

✂ --- ✂ --- ✂

Joyce Elias had her back to the trail as Harriet entered the homeless camp's eating area. She turned when Harriet set the box of food from James on the large table in the center of the clearing.

"Harriet," Joyce said in her soft, British-accented voice. "I was hoping I'd see you. And this must be the lad you were telling me about."

Harriet put her arm around Luke's shoulders.

"Joyce Elias, meet our foster son, Luke Harris."

"It's a pleasure to meet you, young man. Harriet and James have told me all about you—all good of course." Joyce said, and extended her hand. He shook it, his cheeks turning red.

"It's nice to meet you," he said.

"Can I make either of you a cup of tea?" Joyce asked then, her breath visible in the cold air as she spoke. She wore a plaid wool shirt under a green down vest, a jaunty Fair Isle beret covering her gray curls.

Harriet opened her tote.

"Thanks, but we can't stay. James was so busy with his afternoon tea service he didn't have time to drop these off earlier, so I told him we'd handle it while we were out doing errands." She lifted a foil-wrapped bundle from the box. "These are toasted ham-and-cheese sandwiches," She set it down and pulled out a round foil-covered pan. "Three of these pans are chicken piccata and three more of them are chicken fettuccini. And in the bottom, we have baked potatoes and two bags of rolls. He suggests you use the fettuccini first—it doesn't keep as well as the piccata does."

"We greatly appreciate everything he sends us."

"It works out well for him, too. I don't think a lot of people realize how much food waste restaurants produce. He's happy his leftovers can be put to good use." She snapped the lid back on the tote. "You said you were hoping to see me. Is there something I can do for you?"

Joyce sat on the wooden bench that ran the length of the table.

"One of our regulars has gone missing. I know homeless people tend to be a transient lot, but as you know, we have people who pass through here, and then we have the group that winters over. Smokey Joe is one of the latter. He has only been with us for a year or so, but he had no plans to go anywhere. Max has searched the woods as well as he can, and we've found no sign of him."

"Do you think he might be at the warming shelter?" Harriet asked.

"It's possible. He had a friend who stayed in town; I suppose he may be visiting. Or he may have gone to the clinic and been kept. He was having chest pains a week or so ago. The point is, he's been gone for two days, and it's not like him."

"Sure, we can check the warming shelter and the clinic, and I'll ask at the Methodist church. I know they make beds available on these cold nights. Would you like me to ask Detective Morse to look into it?"

Joyce pressed her lips together.

"Let's hold off on that for a bit. He's not been gone that long, and I don't want to cause him any problems if he's just staying in town with his friend. As you know, we don't ask too many questions when people come to live here as long as they follow the camp rules. If he's here trying to get away from something, that's his business."

"Okay." Harriet said. "Give me a contact number, and I'll see if I can find him." She handed Joyce her phone.

"I would appreciate it. I'm sure he's fine, but you know, in the winter we tend to worry a little more."

"Well, we better get going. I'll come by tomorrow and let you know what I find out, either way."

"Wow, do they live there all year around?" Luke asked as he followed Harriet out of the woods and back to the car.

"Indeed, they do."

"My dad sold drugs to the homeless people in Seattle when I was little, but they were a lot different than Joyce."

"I'm guessing they were a younger crowd?"

"Some of them, although there were plenty of old alcoholics. At least, they looked old."

"We made quilts for this group last winter and learned a lot about them in the process. An architect friend of mine worked on a project that included building showers in the park restrooms for them as well as the dining table and benches and secure storage boxes for their personal possessions."

"That's cool."

"I'm sure it helps. I think Joyce has had offers to move inside, but she likes living in the woods. Max, too."

"If I was still living with my dad when I turned eighteen, I'd think seriously about moving onto the streets. It would be safer."

"I'm glad you aren't in that situation anymore."

"Me, too," he finally said.

"Are you okay with doing a little looking for Smokey Joe on the way home?" Harriet asked when they reached the car.

"You're the driver."

Harriet paused before getting in the car.

"You do get a say in what we do."

"I know," he said, smiling. "I just need some time to get used to that concept."

"I don't know about you, but I'm freezing," Harriet said as she put the key in the ignition. "I say we go through a drive-thru and get some hot chocolate or something."

Luke shivered as he fastened his seatbelt.

"Sounds good to me."

✂ --- ✂ --- ✂

Thirty minutes later, Harriet and Luke got back in the car, parked in front of the downtown warming shelter, a location that had been a boutique hotel in a previous life.

"Well, we've checked the clinic and the warming shelter, and I have a call in to the friend," Harriet said. "Before we go to the church, how about we have a look in the little park by the Muckleshoot River bridge, since we're close. Sometimes, the homeless people congregate there when they come into town so they can catch up with people who live in other camps."

"As long as we're here, we might as well. That hot chocolate did warm me up a little."

Chapter 13

They could have walked to the park, but it was cold and a wind had kicked up to make it feel even colder, so Harriet drove.

"Let's follow this path to the left," Harriet suggested as she wrapped her knitted scarf more tightly around her neck. "There are several picnic areas along the river, and if we're going to find any homeless people out in this weather, it will be in one of them."

Luke stuffed his gloved hands into his vest pockets and cocked his head, listening.

"I don't hear anyone talking."

"I'm not sure you would over the sound of the river."

No one was in the first picnic area, or anywhere else. They continued along the path as it curved toward the river and the next set of tables, set on a small bluff overlooking a parallel bend in the river.

Luke went to stand on the edge of the bluff.

"Wow, this spot has a great view of the river."

Harriet went over to stand beside him.

"It *is* nice, especially on a sunny day when the winds are calm. In the summer, the water is so clear you can see all the way to the bottom."

Luke leaned forward and pointed.

"Wait, what's that white thing at the bottom of that area of rapids?"

"Where?"

He moved behind her and rested an arm on her shoulder so he could guide her line of sight.

"It kinda looks like a person."

Harriet trained her eyes on the spot he was pointing at.

"It does look like a person. Let's go to the next picnic area—I think we'll have a better angle."

They hurried back to the path and jogged to the next picnic area, crossing past the tables to stand on the edge of the steep river bank. This vantage point was closer to the river and a good ten feet lower. From here, they could see a human shape clad in a white shirt. The legs were underwater and appeared to be wedged between two large rocks.

Harriet pulled the phone from her pocket and dialed 911.

"There's a body in the river just below the rapids," she reported when she'd given her particulars to the operator. She paused and listened. "We're not close enough to see anything else."

After listening to admonitions to stay where she was until the police arrived, she hung up and put her phone back in her pocket.

"We'll have to wait until someone arrives."

"I wonder why they were outside without a coat," Luke said. "I mean, it looks like they're just wearing a shirt."

"We can't assume they went into the water without a coat on. If they went in above the rapids, and then went over the rocky area before getting hung up at the end, their coat could have come off and been swept down the river."

"You'd think they'd have it zipped up tight in this weather, though."

Harriet smiled at him. She liked his analytical reaction to what was clearly a disturbing situation. His questions were good. She had a thought he would make a great detective, but she wasn't sure how she'd feel about his putting himself in harm's way. This parenting business was tougher than it looked.

✂ --- ✂ --- ✂

A uniformed officer joined them near the picnic tables ten minutes later. Harriet was thankful that, for once, it wasn't Officer Nguyen. This guy's name tag said *Smith*. He looked to be in his thirties, with dark hair and a muscular build.

"Are you the woman who thinks she saw a body in the river?" he asked her as he pulled a notebook from his pocket.

Luke didn't wait for Harriet to answer. He pointed to where the body bobbed at the base of the rapids. Officer Smith scanned where Luke pointed until he found it.

"Oh, geez, it really is a body."

Harriet put her hands on her hips.

"What did you think it was going to be when we called in and said we saw a body in the river?"

Smith's face flushed.

"I'm sorry, but you can't imagine how many dead-body-in-the-river reports we get that turn out to be bags of garbage, large stuffed animals, dead real animals, and all sorts of other stuff."

Harriet sighed and shook her head.

"You're right, though," he went on. "You do have a reputation around the station for finding dead people."

"Not on purpose," she protested.

"Still, most people never see a dead body outside a funeral home, and you've found more than one or two, according to the talk at the station." He pushed a button on the radio clipped to his shoulder and began his report.

"Sorry about all this," she told Luke.

"Hey, it's not your fault. And we *were* looking for a guy."

"We didn't find our guy, though. If Smokey Joe wore a white shirt in the winter, jacket over it or not, I'm sure Joyce would have mentioned it. White shirts aren't something you see among the homeless, given their lack of laundry facilities in the camps."

"Is there any reason I should keep the two people who spotted the body?" she heard Smith say into his radio. "No, we're quite a distance away. The kid spotted the body from the lower picnic area in the park."

They couldn't hear the reply, but Smith listened, then turned the volume down.

"You two are free to go, but depending on what they find, someone might want to talk to you again later."

"Do you need my contact info?" she asked.

"We know where to find you," he said with a smirk.

Down below, people in wetsuits had arrived on the opposite bank of the river and were preparing to go into the frigid water.

"Is there any way we could be notified about the identity of the person?" Harriet asked.

"Why? Are you missing someone?"

"As a matter of fact, we are. Or rather Joyce from the homeless camp in Fogg Park is missing someone. She asked us to look for him in town. It's a guy they call Smokey Joe. That's what we were here doing."

"You can call the station tomorrow. Depending on how long the vic's been in the river and how far the body traveled, it could take a while to identify."

"Thanks, we'll do that. Come on, Luke, I think we're done here."

She spun on her heel and headed for the car; Luke mimicked her motion and followed her.

Chapter 14

W eak sunlight attempted to warm the still-frigid air the next morning. Harriet stood, her upper body bent into the open door of the tool cabinet in her garage.

"I know my uncle had a tree saw," she said over her shoulder to James, who was at the back of the car winding a coil of rope.

"I'm sure they'll have saws at the u-cut place," he told her as she continued to rummage around.

She straightened finally, a worn bow saw in her hand.

"This one will cut through our Christmas tree trunk like butter."

James put his rope in the back of the car and took the saw.

"Wow, that one has cut a few trees." He turned it from side to side. "The paint is almost completely gone from the handle."

"Uncle Hank changed the saw blade regularly, and he taught me how to do it. I put a new one in last year, so it should be sharp."

James smiled and pulled her into his arms.

"You've gotta love a girl with a sharp saw," he said and kissed her.

"Let's go see if Luke's had any luck wrestling the dogs into their coats," Harriet said, and headed for the kitchen door.

Scooter was running from the stairs, across the kitchen to the studio door, and back again, barking the whole time; Cyrano sat at Luke's feet, his quilted Christmas coat strapped around his long body, a look of disgust on his face.

"How's it going in here," James asked with a laugh.

"Cyrano was fine, but Scooter is being a little jerk."

74

Harriet tried not to laugh, without much success. She opened the dogs' treat jar and held it out to Luke.

"Try a little bribery," she suggested.

He took a dog biscuit and held it out for the little dog and, when Scooter was in reach, grabbed him with one hand while giving him the treat with the other. Scooter sat down beside Cyrano, looking more miserable than his buddy if, that were possible.

James pulled his phone out of his pocket.

"We've got to get a picture of this."

Harriet folded her arms across her chest.

"They might not like their new coats while we're in the kitchen, but they're going to appreciate the wool batting I quilted into them when they get to the tree farm."

Luke shook his head.

"I'll have to see it to believe it."

James took Harriet by the hand and positioned her next to Luke, then picked the dogs up, handing Scooter to Harriet and Cyrano to Luke. He stood between the two of them and held his phone out in front of them.

"Okay, let's get a family picture to document the start of our adventure."

Luke and James started down one row of trees at the farm while Harriet walked down the next row over, looking at the same trees from the opposite side.

"Watch where you're going," a familiar voice said. Lauren was standing in the same row as Harriet, one tree away.

"Fancy meeting you here," Harriet said with a smile. She held a dog leash in each hand; the dogs were out of sight under the lowest branches of the tree in front of her.

"My parents sent Les and I out to find them a tree, or I wouldn't be here. I have a very nice potted Norfolk Island pine tree that doubles as a Christmas tree for my house."

Lauren's twin brother Les joined them when he realized Lauren had stopped.

"Hi, Les, Merry Christmas," Harriet said.

"Hi, Harriet. Are you having any luck finding a tree?"

"I'm letting James and Luke do most of the searching. I'm just making sure whatever they find doesn't have a flat spot on this side."

"Our parents want a Noble fir, and my mom has a specific spacing between whorls of branches in mind," Les sighed. "This is our third tree farm."

Lauren sighed, sounding just like her brother; and Harriet once again noticed how much they looked alike, especially with their hair tucked up in knitted caps. They were, of course, fraternal twins, but with the exception of Les's pale facial hair, they looked identical. She had to force herself not to stare.

"We ran into Morse at the coffee shop on our way here," Lauren said, "and she said they haven't positively identified the body you and Luke found in the river yesterday, but they're pretty sure it's Valery Melnyk. The face and hands are too damaged, so they're going to have to do DNA testing, but the clothes and wallet say it's him."

The tree in front of Harriet shook.

"No, this side isn't good," she called to James and Luke. She stepped down the row a couple of trees, pulling her little charges with her. Lauren moved with her while Les went back to checking trees on the opposite side of the row.

"I wonder what happened?" Harriet finally said.

Lauren shuddered.

"I wonder if its connected to Daniel's death," Harriet continued.

"Hard to imagine how, although I guess we don't know either of them well enough to know."

"They could be friends or even lovers or have business dealings…"

"Or they could run Foggy Point's drug cartel," Lauren added, getting into the spirit. "But let's get real. The most likely scenario is either a psychopath picking random victims or their deaths are unrelated. I mean, I don't think they've even determined that anyone killed Valery. He could have fallen in the river."

Harriet raised an eyebrow.

"Seriously?"

Lauren chuckled.

"I guess not. Not very many people walk along the river in this weather."

A tree started shaking to Harriet's left. She examined the foliage on her side of the tree.

"This one looks good," she called.

"You realize the people in this row don't know James and Luke are on the other side. To them it looks like you're talking to a tree."

Harriet looked around her and did notice an older couple staring at her. She smiled and turned back to her tree.

"Do you have time to take a few pictures of James, Luke, and I cutting the tree?"

Lauren looked at Les across the aisle.

"Sure, we're good. I'm pretty sure we're going to have to go up in the hills to find what my mom wants, in any case."

Harriet reeled the dogs in, and they walked down the aisle to the opening between rows.

✂--- ✂--- ✂

James held the saw against the trunk of their chosen tree, and Luke crouched on the opposite side of the tree pulling the trunk toward him. Harriet was behind Luke, holding the dogs, one in each arm.

"If we don't stop with the picture-taking it's going to be the new year before we get this tree home," James said through his fake smile.

Harriet set the dogs down.

"Okay, fine, go ahead and cut."

Lauren scrolled through the pictures on her phone.

"We do have twenty-some pictures to choose from."

Harriet went to check for herself, or she would have seen Aiden approaching.

"Getting a tree with the little family, I see," he said, stopping in front of her. He spread his arms out. "And here we are at the same farm where we got our first Christmas tree together. Is this where you bring all your boyfriends on your first Christmas tree date?" His voice grew louder as he spoke. "Oh, wait, I should have said husband. You two skipped right over the boyfriend stage."

"Aiden, please, can we not do this now?"

James and Luke had started to carry the tree back toward the parking area, but James set his end of the tree down and rejoined Harriet when he heard Aiden's voice.

"Is there a problem here?" he asked, looking from Aiden to Harriet and then Lauren.

Lauren looped her arm through Aiden's.

"Aiden was saying hello, but he's going to find his tree now, aren't you Aiden?"

Les came over and stood on Aiden's other side.

"Come on, man, you're starting to draw a crowd."

Several groups of tree hunters had stopped what they were doing and were watching the drama. Aiden started to say something, but apparently thought better of it. Finally, he shook his head and stomped down the aisle in the opposite direction from the parking area. Lauren followed him for a few yards to be sure he wasn't going to come back and then returned.

"Boy, he's a stubborn one."

"That's one way of putting it."

James stood behind Harriet and put a hand on each of her shoulders.

"And we get to have Christmas dinner with him at Jorge's," he said with a grin.

Lauren laughed.

"Sounds like fun."

Luke waved at them.

"Everything okay?" he called to Harriet and James.

"Be right there," James called back.

Lauren tapped the face of her phone.

"I sent the pictures to your phone." She paused for a moment then looked at Harriet. "You're going to have to do something if he keeps this up."

"Didn't you say Jorge was like a father figure to him?" James asked Harriet.

She nodded thoughtfully.

"Maybe it's time we talked to him. I mean, we could try talking to Aiden, but that's what he wants. He wants to stay connected. Assuming Jorge agrees that he needs to back off, he's probably the only one who can convince him."

Lauren dropped her phone back into her messenger bag.

"My work here is done. And I need to go light a fire under Les."

"Thanks for taking our pictures," Harriet told her.

"Go enjoy your family," Lauren said and left to find her brother.

Chapter 15

Harriet walked up her driveway after her morning run the following Monday, stomping her feet to restore feeling in her frozen toes. Her aunt's silver Volkswagen Beetle sat next to the garage, and she could see Aunt Beth's white hair above the cafe curtain in the kitchen window.

"I hope it's okay we came early," Beth said as Harriet came into the kitchen from the garage. Mavis and Connie were seated at her kitchen table, mugs of steaming tea in front of them.

Connie took a cellophane-wrapped cookie from a plate in the center of the table.

"The steamer machine at the coffee shop was broken. They gave us free cookies and sent us on our way. Beth figured you wouldn't mind if we came early."

"As long as you don't mind waiting for me to shower."

Mavis sipped tea and set her mug down.

"You take your time, honey. We've got things to talk about, anyway."

Harriet wondered what that might be. She hadn't had a chance to talk to any of them about her encounter with Aiden at the tree farm yet. She was tempted to hide just out of sight on the stairs but thought better of it. She was cold and sweaty and would feel foolish if they caught her.

She came back down stairs thirty minutes later wearing a fleece sweat-shirt over a long-sleeved plaid shirt and jeans.

"Do we have time for me to have a quick cup of tea before we go?" She shivered. "I got really cold running this morning. It doesn't seem any colder than it has been, but I'm freezing."

Beth felt Harriet's forehead when she sat down at the table.

"You're not getting sick, are you?"

"No, it just felt really damp, and even though I was running, I got cold. I'll be fine once I have something warm to drink."

Connie set a mug of steaming tea in front of her.

"Thanks," Harriet said and smiled when her aunt slid the honey jar to her.

"Honey's good for what ails you," Beth said, and she knew better than to argue when her aunt went into medicine-woman mode.

Mavis handed her one of the wrapped cookies.

"Do you know Sunny Mason?"

Harriet took a bite and chewed thoughtfully before answering,

"You mean the cupcake lady? I know her from ordering cupcakes, but I don't 'know her' know her."

"Do you know anyone who does?" Connie asked.

"Not really. Why?"

Mavis picked up her cup and sat back in her chair.

"Jenny was in getting cupcakes for her master gardeners meeting yesterday, and she was the only customer in the store. When she came in, Sunny had her back to the counter and had a paper in her hand she was staring at. Jenny could see over her shoulder it was like an old-fashioned ransom note like they have in vintage movies."

"You know—the kind where someone cuts out the letters of each word from different magazines," Aunt Beth added.

"Jenny said Sunny folded it up as soon as she realized a customer had come in, but Jenny got a good look."

"Could she read what it said?" Harriet asked.

Beth picked up the honey dauber and added a little more honey to Harriet's tea.

"She said with the way the letters were glued at all different angles, she couldn't read what it said before Sunny folded it."

Harriet stirred the additional honey into her tea.

"It could be completely unrelated to Daniel's death—and Valery's, if it really is Valery who was in the river."

"What?" Beth and Connie said at the same time.

"We saw Lauren yesterday, and she ran into Morse in the coffee shop. Morse told her they aren't sure, but evidence indicates it's him."

Mavis tapped her spoon rhythmically on the table.

"I don't like it. All of a sudden, shops in town that have always been thriving are struggling to keep their doors open."

"But not all shops," Beth interrupted.

"True," Mavis continued. "Some shops are suddenly struggling, and now two business owners are dead. I don't like it."

Harriet made a face as she sipped her now too-sweet tea.

"It does seem like something might be going on. On the other hand, running a small business can be rough. I think the statistic nationwide is ninety-five percent of all small businesses fail in the first five years. A few months ago, I went into the gallery, and Valery had some visitors who didn't appear to be customers and were speaking Ukrainian with him. Whatever they were talking about was not making Valery happy."

"So, what are you saying?" Beth asked.

"Valery might have enemies that have nothing to do with Foggy Point, the businesses might be having business troubles at the same time by co-incidence, and Daniel...I don't know. I also can't explain the mystery letter Sunny had, but there could be an innocent explanation for that. I mean, back in California, Steve and I went to one of those mystery dinner parties one time, and the invitation was made from cut-out magazine letters."

"From what Jenny said, whatever Sunny was reading, it wasn't anything fun," Mavis said.

Harriet made a face as she drank the last of her tea and carried her mug to the sink.

"Okay," she said. "Who's ready to go shop?"

✂ --- ✂ --- ✂

Harriet drove the group to the Walmart out on the highway to get wrapping paper before returning downtown to park in front of the quilt store. Beth and Connie crossed the street to the kitchen store and the outdoor store, while Mavis and Harriet headed to Ruby's Jewelry store. They agreed to meet in an hour at the quilt store.

Anthony DeMarco met Harriet and Mavis at his door.

"I'm still loving the quilt in the window."

"Jenny did a wonderful job," Mavis said with a smile.

Anthony rubbed his hands together.

"What can I help you ladies with?"

Harriet walked over to a display in a glass case near the cash register.

"If it's possible, I'd like to get my foster son Luke a class ring. He's a senior this year but hasn't had the opportunity to get one."

Mavis joined her.

"And I'm looking for a watch for my son."

"Okay," Anthony said and went behind the counter to retrieve a catalog. "Here's the class jewelry catalog. You can look through it while I show

81

Mavis a few watches. When you've looked at all the options, I can show you samples of the styles you like. Does that sound good?"

Harriet and Mavis agreed and immersed themselves in their respective tasks. Mavis chose a watch; Anthony gift-wrapped it for her and then turned to Harriet.

"I've picked a couple of styles, but can you tell me which ones are most popular at Foggy Point High School?" she asked him.

Anthony looked at the catalog page she was looking at.

"You've found them," he said. "These are the ones the kids are ordering."

"I don't want him to have the most common one, but I don't want him to have something no one else chooses, either. I'm walking a fine line here."

"I understand," Anthony said. He pulled a tray from the glass case and showed her a ring. "This might be the one you're looking for."

She slid it on the tip of her finger and held her hand out, turning it from side to side.

"Mavis, what do you think?" she said and held her hand toward her friend.

"It looks good. It's simple but has all the relevant information."

Harriet handed the ring back to Anthony.

"How long will it take to get here?"

He glanced at a calendar by the register.

"I can have it here before Christmas."

"Whew, I was worried you were going to say it would take a month."

"No, these people are pretty quick. I'll call you when it's in."

"Can I go ahead and pay for it now?" she asked.

"You can wait until it arrives if you want," he countered.

"No, I'll just pay now. Once Luke is out on break, it will be harder for me to get away without him knowing where I'm going."

Anthony pulled out an order pad and handed it to Harriet to fill in.

"Have you heard anything about Valery?" he asked while she wrote. "I've been told that lady detective is a quilter."

Mavis laughed.

"We are friends with her, but she mostly tells us to stay out of police business. Have *you* heard anything?"

Anthony rubbed a hand over his face, clearly torn.

"I don't know anything official," he finally said. "But Valery used to stop in for a cup of coffee when business was slow." He paused.

"And?" Mavis prompted him.

"The other day he came in, and he seemed troubled."

Harriet looked up from her form.

"What do you mean?"

"It's hard to describe. He's one of those people who usually talks a lot and tells jokes and gossip, and he wasn't doing any of that. I asked him what was wrong, and at first he tried to brush me off but I persisted. Finally, he told me someone had sent him a blackmail note. He wouldn't tell me what they were blackmailing him about, but he said they were serious. He asked me if I'd received a note or if any of the other shop owners had said anything about receiving notes. I told him I hadn't received anything and hadn't heard anything."

"Have you told the police?" Harriet asked.

"No. I wasn't sure if they'd take me seriously. Besides, I don't really know anything useful. He didn't show me the note or say who it was from or even what sort of thing they were blackmailing him over."

Harriet handed him the completed form and her debit card.

"You definitely need to tell the police. If you want, I can text Detective Morse and ask her to stop by here to talk to you."

Anthony looked relieved.

"Would you?"

Harriet pulled her phone out and sent the text while he completed her transaction. An answering text came almost immediately.

"She'll be here in a few minutes."

"Thank you," he said. "And thank you for your business, and I'll call you when the ring is in."

✂ --- ✂ --- ✂

"Well, that was interesting," Harriet said to Mavis as they headed for the quilt store. "We think someone is blackmailing Sunny, and now possibly Valery, who appears to be dead."

Mavis held the shop door open for her.

"And Daniel was killed, plus several of the shops are suddenly not doing as well as they should be. Makes you wonder if they're being blackmailed, too."

Beth and Connie were waiting for them. Marjorie was counting the change in the cash register.

"I just heated the kettle if you ladies would like some tea. No one is in either of the classrooms."

Beth smiled at her.

"Thank you, that sounds real nice."

Harriet filled her aunt and Connie in on what they'd learned at the jewelry store.

83

"That's interesting, but connecting everything is pure speculation," Beth cautioned.

"I might be able to answer the question about whether the shops doing poorly is connected to the deaths," Harriet offered.

Mavis sipped her tea and set her mug down.

"What do you have in mind?"

"I'm going to go by Jade's shop and ask her."

"Do you think she'll tell you?" Beth asked.

Harriet thought for a moment.

"I think she will. I'm helping her keep her horse, so hopefully, she'll offer something up as a reason why she can't afford to do it herself. I'm going to flat-out ask her how things went so bad so quick."

"When are you going to do it?" Connie asked.

Harriet took another sip of tea.

"Are you all coming to our Threads session tomorrow?"

Connie, Mavis, and Beth all nodded.

"I'll stop by on my way to quilting, then," Harriet told them.

"Do we have time for me to stop at the yarn store before we go home?" Beth asked, changing the subject.

✂ --- ✂ --- ✂

Mavis led the way across the street to the Wool Merchant. They all stopped to admire her quilt in the front window. She had done a wool appliqué quilt featuring a flock of sheep, a shepherd, and the Star of Bethlehem. Millie White, the store owner, had arranged yarn in complementary tones under the quilt, accenting its colors.

"This looks real nice," Beth said, and the others agreed. She opened the shop door, and they immediately heard loud voices arguing.

"If I'm not here, the problem goes away," a male voice said.

"I will not negotiate with terrorists," Millie shot back.

"It's not negotiating. It's removing the incentive," the male voice replied, quieter as the bell on the door signaled the arrival of customers.

Mavis hurried across the shop and stepped up to the counter, where Millie and her male employee, an older man with graying hair and a days growth of beard, were standing.

"Is everything all right?"

The man gave Millie a dark look before spinning on his heel and disappearing into the storeroom. Millie stared at his back before turning to Mavis.

"We're fine. We're having a little difference of opinion about how to handle a problem."

84

Harriet had caught up to Mavis.

"Are you being blackmailed?" she asked Millie without preamble.

The color drained from the shopkeeper's face, and Harriet thought she wasn't going to answer.

"No, nothing like that. Why would you even think that?"

"No reason, really. I just heard something that made me think Foggy Point might have a blackmailer, and I thought…never mind."

Millie looked past Harriet to Beth.

"Can I help you find something?"

"I'm hoping to find some red worsted," Beth replied, and Millie came around the counter to lead her to a display of red wools by various vendors.

Mavis gave Harriet a *we'll talk later* look and went to the other side of the shop to check out the baby yarn.

✂ --- ✂ --- ✂

Harriet and her friends waited until they were back across the street before saying anything.

"Does anyone else feel like they've been dropped into the middle of *The Invasion of the Body Snatchers*?" Harriet asked. "You know, the one where everyone in town is replaced with a duplicate that looks just like them but doesn't act like them at all."

"I don't know what you've been watching on TV," Beth said. "But it does feel like something is going on below the surface in our town that we know nothing about."

Mavis folded the top of her bag of baby yarn and tucked it into her tote.

"It's a good thing Detective Morse is on the case and we don't have to worry about it."

Harriet smiled at her.

"Are you trying to tell me you aren't the least bit curious about that drama we just witnessed?"

Mavis sighed.

"Of course I'm curious. But that isn't a reason for us to stick our noses into police business."

A familiar black Bronco drove by on the cross street, and Harriet watched it until it was out of sight.

"You're right, we've got enough drama without borrowing someone else's."

Chapter 16

Harriet was stitching on a customer quilt when Luke came home from school. He'd entered through the garage, which was his habit as that entrance got him into the kitchen more quickly. She smiled as she heard the dogs yipping with excitement at his arrival. He came into the studio a moment later, an apple in one hand and a chocolate chip cookie in the other. Both dogs followed him closely, hoping he would drop a crumb of food.

"How was school?" she asked.

"It was okay," he replied, and took a bite of apple.

"Who are you and what did you do with Luke?"

He grinned. "I think I might be getting used to it."

Harriet clipped her thread and turned her machine off.

"Good."

He watched her put her tools away, eating as he did so. She looked up at him.

"Something on your mind?"

"I was just wondering…well, if it's not too much trouble…" he stammered.

"Luke. Just spit it out. The answer is probably yes."

"Well, Emily texted and wanted to know if I could come to the stable this afternoon and start my orientation for the therapy horse program."

"I think that will be fine. It'll give me a chance to check in on Becky." She watched as the smile left his face. "Don't worry, I'll check on her and then leave. Just call me when you're done."

The smile returned, and his cheeks pinked.

"You're the best. I'll be ready in a flash."

Harriet pulled her phone from her pocket and touched Lauren's name on her favorites list.

"Hey," she said when her friend answered. "You want to meet at Annie's for a warm drink?"

"Is there a reason for us to meet? I mean, we *are* going to see each other at Threads tomorrow morning, right?"

"We are," Harriet replied. "Luke wants to go to the stable and start his therapy horse training. Surprisingly, he doesn't want me hanging around while he works with his new friend Emily. It makes no sense for me to drive home and then back again, so I thought I'd stay in town."

"Imagine that. Sure, I'm done with anything useful for work. When will you be there?"

"I need to check on Becky, so how about thirty minutes?"

"It's a date," Lauren said and rang off.

✂ --- ✂ --- ✂

Harriet watched Luke until he reached the entrance to the large riding arena, where Emily was waiting for him.

"Don't worry, we won't let anything happen to him," Marcia Hamilton said.

Harriet turned to face the assistant stable manager.

"I'm not worried. Luke has been taking care of himself for most of his life."

"Hopefully, he'll benefit from working with the horses."

"Speaking of horses, I wanted to check and see how Becky is doing."

"Come see for yourself," Marcia said and led the way to the barn.

Becky was wearing a blue blanket, but what Harriet could see of her coat was shiny and healthy-looking, and her feet had been trimmed and reshod.

"She looks good," Harriet said.

"She is, other than lacking exercise. I haven't had a chance to take her out. Jade had asked me if I could take her out now and then when she wasn't able to. I agreed, but then we had a change of ownership of another horse, and the new owner asked if we could exercise his, so it's getting hard to keep up."

"Does that happen often? Horses switching ownership but continuing to live here?"

"Not very often. There seems to be an epidemic among Foggy Point business people lately, though."

"Who besides Jade?"

"Valery Melnyk, for one. You know, the guy who owns the art gallery downtown. He had a Thoroughbred and a Warmblood until he sold them. The Thoroughbred's new owner doesn't live here, hence the request for exercising."

"I didn't know Valery kept horses."

"His daughter took riding lessons here for years, and when she was skilled enough to move from a pony to a horse, he bought the two horses. She wasn't very interested, but he kept hoping that would change.

"Did his daughter move away or something?"

"In a manner of speaking. She died about a year and a half ago."

"Oh, I'm sorry to hear that. I didn't know. Of course, I've only been back in town about that long."

"He was devastated. He lost all interest in the horses, and from what I hear, pretty much everything else. He told me he couldn't afford them anymore, so I'm guessing he lost interest in his business, too."

"That's so sad," Harriet said. "At least he found someone to buy them."

"I've never met the guy who bought the Thoroughbred, but Valery said it was a family friend who lived back east. He said the guy was traveling overseas and would make arrangements to have him moved when he returned."

"I'm sorry to hear that."

"He's a nice horse and never any trouble, but I've got a waiting list, so the stall will be filled within a week of his departure."

"That's good."

"Do you want to come watch Luke?" Marcia asked.

Harriet smiled.

"I think Luke would be very disappointed if I hung around while he's trying to get to know Emily."

"Emily did seem to have a little extra spring in her step when Luke said he could come out today. Tell you what, I'll observe from the judge's booth above the arena floor. I need to make sure she's teaching him what he needs to know, but I won't interfere unless I need to."

"Sounds good. I'm going to have coffee with a friend. How soon should I be back?"

Marcia glanced at her watch.

"I think an hour and a half should be about right. That will give them time to groom and feed the horse when they're finished. Part of the program is learning to care for their assigned horse."

Harriet turned to leave.

"I'll be back in an hour and half, then."

Lauren was waiting in Annie's when Harriet arrived, two steaming mugs of hot cocoa in front of her.

"I took the liberty of ordering for you," she said, sliding one of the mugs to the opposite side of the table.

Harriet shrugged out of her jacket and hung it on the back of her chair with her purse. She sat down and cupped her hands around the warm mug.

"Thanks for this." She closed her eyes and took a sip, savoring the warm liquid.

"How is Becky?" Lauren asked when Harriet opened her eyes again. "That is, if you're done doing whatever it is you're doing with your chocolate and can speak."

Harriet set her cup down and grinned.

"Sorry, it's really cold at the stable. Becky seems to be fine. She'd had her feet done, and they've upgraded her food."

"Well, good for Becky. Have you heard anything from Jade?"

"Still nothing. I called her this afternoon, but no answer. I'll go by there on the way to Threads tomorrow. I did learn something interesting at the stable, though."

"What's that?"

"Did you know Valery Melnyk had a daughter? And they kept horses at the stable?"

"I remember reading something about him having a daughter who died a couple of years ago. A kayaking accident or something like that."

"Apparently, he and his daughter were regulars at the stable. He hasn't been back since and, in fact, recently sold the horses."

"That's interesting. Isn't selling off your precious belongings a sign of impending suicide?"

Harriet sipped her cocoa.

"I think I've read that somewhere. Do you think he committed suicide?"

"If he did, he wouldn't be the first distraught parent who couldn't go on after the death of a beloved child."

"That's sad."

"It is. And, if I remember the local gossip right, his wife left him some years ago to go back to the old country. Something about a sick relative. Only, she never came back, and we're talking maybe eight or ten years ago. She just left him with his kids."

"Wow, that's rough."

"On a happier note, are you looking forward to Christmas dinner with Aiden?"

Harriet put her head in her hands.

"I don't want to think about it. I've decided I'm going to have a heart-to-heart with James and see if he thinks we should expose Luke to what is sure to be family drama."

Lauren stretched her legs out and leaned back in her chair.

"When you were first dating Aiden, when things were good, did you have any idea he had this obsessive side?"

Harriet thought for a minute.

"No. Well, maybe a little, I guess."

"From what I've heard, his family thought the sun rose and set over his head."

Harriet sipped her cocoa.

"Aiden was young when his dad died, and according to Aunt Beth, his mother bent over backward to make up for him not having a dad. Losing her, too, was really hard on him. And I suppose with everything else that's happened in the last year or so, our breakup was one too many losses for him to handle."

"So, what? He's had a rough time, so he gets a pass on his behavior? I think not."

"That's the tough part. I do understand why he's acting the way he is. I just can't be in a relationship that's all about him. Months at a time with no communication is not a relationship."

Lauren wiped her mouth on her napkin.

"You'd think a smart guy like him would be able to figure out that the silent treatment wasn't going to be good. Especially when you hadn't done anything wrong."

"If you can figure out why people do what they do in relationships, you can write a book and get rich."

Lauren sat up and drained the rest of her cocoa.

"We've still got an hour before you have to go get Luke. Why don't we walk up to Blood Moon and check in on Jade?"

"For one reason, it's freezing out there."

"Oh, come on. The walk will warm us up."

Harriet finished her drink and stood up.

"Fine."

Lauren took their cups back to the counter, and they bundled up and headed out the door.

✂ --- ✂ --- ✂

"It's possible Jade is trying to avoid me because she isn't making enough money this month to take care of Becky," Harriet said as she and Lauren walked up the block. "But with two store owners dead, both of them within two doors of Blood Moon, I'm really worried."

"It's hard to see a connection between Valery and Daniel, and even harder to see a connection between them and Jade," Lauren countered.

"There is the obvious fact that they all three own business in Foggy Point and in close proximity of each other. Have you heard anything about anyone wanting to develop that part of downtown?"

"No, and besides, that scenario would make more sense if they were all on the same side of the same block. They're on three sides of an intersection. I'm not sure how a developer could work with that."

"Unless they're planning on taking over the whole downtown," Harriet argued.

"Hard to imagine a developer who would think killing the current store owners was the best way to obtain the property."

Harriet rubbed her gloved hands together as they stood on the street corner in front of the sandwich shop.

"It is hard for me to believe the deaths, the downturn in business, and the possible blackmail notes are all connected to some wild takeover of downtown."

Lauren stepped into the crosswalk ahead of her.

"It is hard for *me* to believe that much is going on in Foggy Point and it's *not* connected. I'm not so sure about the developer idea."

"I suppose. There was that case in Eastern Oregon almost forty years ago where that religious cult tried to take over a whole town. There was a documentary on it a few months ago. The group went around town poisoning salad bars and water systems or something like that.".

Lauren shook her head.

"Whatever."

They walked the next block in silence, lost in their own thoughts, before crossing the street. Harriet peered in the darkened front window while Lauren rattled the door handle.

"Nobody home," Lauren announced.

"And her quilt is down." Harriet shaded her brow with her hand to better see the dark interior. "Look," she said, and pointed.

Lauren joined her and struggled to see inside.

"Is that a note on the quilt?"

The shop Christmas quilt was neatly folded on a stool near the window with a folded piece of paper on top, Harriet's name written in large block letters on it.

Harriet sighed.

"It is, and that sure looks like my name on it."

Lauren looked at her.

"So, now what?"

"I'd like to pick the lock and go in and read the note."

"But?"

Harriet laughed.

"Morse would kill us, but the main problem is the fact that I don't have a set of lockpicks."

"Are you implying you could use them if you had them?"

"Maybe, maybe not."

Lauren pulled out her phone.

"We call Morse, right?"

"Unless we walk away and pretend we didn't see anything."

Lauren tapped the number into her phone and quickly explained the situation to Detective Morse.

"She'll be here in a few minutes. She wants us to remember not to touch anything."

Chapter 17

*H*arriet's feet were completely numb by the time Detective Morse opened the door to Blood Moon. Officer Nguyen had arrived along with a second detective Harriet had never seen before and whom Morse had introduced as her new partner, Jason Martinez. Multiple calls were placed to the assistant district attorney and Morse's lieutenant. She couldn't hear everything that was said, but the words *exigent circumstances* seemed to be central to the discussions. Eventually, it was decided that, given the situation, entering the store in the absence of the owner wasn't violating anyone's Fourth Amendment rights.

Once inside, she immediately reached for the note, but Morse grabbed her wrist.

"Since we don't know what's going on here, let's put gloves on you before you touch that." She pulled a pair of black latex gloves from her pocket and handed them to Harriet. "Hold the gloves by the wrist edge while you slip your hand in so you don't contaminate the finger areas."

Harriet donned the gloves and opened the note from Jade. She read it out loud.

> I'm sorry to dump my mess in your lap, but I have to leave the area. I'm afraid what happened to Daniel will happen to me, so I've decided to join my parents in South America.
>
> I explained the situation to them, and they sent me a ticket. They also agreed with me that giving Becky to you was the best solution for her. I can't bear to sell her to a stranger, and they don't want me to stay around Foggy Point

to deal with her. Their lawyer will be sending you all the paperwork, transferring ownership to you along with her registration papers. I'm so sorry to surprise you with this, but I hope you will keep her and give her a good home.

My parent's lawyer will pay the rent on my shop until we figure things out, but I don't expect to be back in Foggy Point any time soon.

Thank you again,
Jade

PS—The soap and lotion I owe you and Lauren are in boxes on the back counter—Merry Christmas.

Officer Nguyen stood with his hands on his hips.

"Is Becky a dog or a cat?"

"Actually, she's a horse," Harriet told him.

"She gave you a horse?"

Morse glared at him.

"Why don't you check around the back and see if anything's disturbed."

Morse watched until he'd crossed the room and disappeared into the back room. She turned to Harriet.

"She gave you a horse?" she echoed Nguyen's question.

"It's a little complicated. Lauren and I paid the horse's board bill this month, and I paid for a few more services for it. Jade is having money trouble. She was hoping this Christmas season was going to put her back in the black, but apparently that wasn't happening. As you heard, she was spooked by the merchant deaths.

"And before you ask, I don't know why her parents will pay her shop rent but won't pay her horse bill."

"She told us just the opposite before," Lauren said. "So, that's weird. Makes you wonder what she's really telling them."

"I wish we knew what's going on with our merchant community," Morse said, more to herself than to them. "I suppose you're going to want the quilt."

Harriet rubbed her hand over the folded quilt.

"No, I *would* like to see it hung back up again, though."

"I think we can do that. Let me see if the powers that be want us to do any processing, given that I can't see that a crime has been committed here."

Lauren shivered.

"Can we get going? Harriet needs to pick up Luke, and I need to get home."

Morse looked around.

"I guess so. And thanks for calling instead of going inside yourselves."

"We would never do that," Harriet said.

"Yeah, right," Morse said with a wry smile. "And I suppose there's no harm in you taking the gift boxes she left you. I *would* like a peek inside before you do, however."

"No problem," Lauren said and headed for the back of the shop.

Luke was in the barn with Emily when Harriet arrived to pick him up. He was standing next to a large unkempt gray horse that was cross-tied in the aisle.

"I need to finish brushing Major before I leave," he told her.

Harriet walked over and patted the large horse on the neck.

"No problem. I need to talk to Marcia. Is she around?"

Emily ducked under the horse's neck and joined her.

"She's in the feed room preparing the evening meal. It's the last door on the left."

"Thanks," Harriet said and headed down the aisle.

The door was open, and Marcia was bent over a large bin of grain.

"Knock, knock," Harriet said.

"Hang on a minute," Marcia said, and poured two scoops of feed from the bin into a small bucket before straightening up and turning around. "How can I help you?"

"I just came from Jade's shop. It seems she's joined her parents in South America."

"What about Becky?"

Harriet pressed her lips together, as if keeping the words in would mean her new horse ownership wasn't real. She blew a breath out.

"She left a note giving Becky to me. She said in the note that her parents' attorney would be sending legal documents and the horse's papers in a few days."

Marcia was quiet for a long minute.

"Is she doing drugs again?" she finally asked.

Harriet's eyebrows raised.

"Again?"

"Yeah, she had a bit of a drug problem. Used a little, sold a little. That was a while ago, though. When we were just out of high school. I thought she'd been clean since then. And she was not a big player in the drug scene, anyway. It seemed like the typical teenage rebellion. Her parents overreacted and sent her to a fancy rehab in California, and she stayed gone for a few years."

95

"I haven't seen any evidence of her being on drugs when I've dealt with her, but you never know."

"Like I said, she was never a heavy user. Her parents just went nuts. Sounds like maybe they are again."

"I'll know more about Becky's situation when I receive the documents from the attorney, and if she really is giving me the horse, I'll need to talk to my husband and Luke about whether they're on board with us becoming horse owners."

"As you've noticed, Luke and Emily are interested in each other, them both being red-blooded American teenagers and all."

Harriet chuckled.

"Having said that," Marcia went on, "he did well for his first time with a horse. He seemed to bond with Major."

"Good. He seems so world-weary at times, and he hasn't really been interested in any of the activities at school. I'm hoping the horse program will help him let his guard down and enjoy life a little."

"Major is a bit of a special case himself. He came to us from the Seattle Mounted Patrol. He was injured in the line of duty and came here for a well-earned retirement and a little therapy of his own."

"What happened to him?"

"He was stabbed in the shoulder. He stepped between a mentally ill person with a knife and a young woman. Had she taken the blow Major took, she probably wouldn't have survived."

"Wow."

"He's lucky nothing vital was hit. He's been a little wary of strangers since he got here, which as you can imagine will limit his usefulness as a therapy horse if he can't get over it."

"He seems to be doing okay with Luke, from what I saw."

"I watched them a while, and he's doing better with Luke than he has with anyone here so far."

"This could be good for both of them. Maybe they're kindred spirits."

"That's what I'm hoping. I got to get back to feeding. Feel free to come watch Luke with Major anytime."

"Thanks, and I'll let you know about Becky when I know."

✂ --- ✂ --- ✂

"How did it go?" Harriet asked Luke when they were back in the car with the heater blasting on high.

Luke held his hands in front of the vent.

"Major is amazing. He used to be a police horse."

"So I've heard. I guess this means you want to go back again."

He smiled. "Can I?"

"Of course you can. As long as you keep your schoolwork up."

"No problem. Could we go to the store and get some carrots for next time? Emily said he likes carrots."

"I think that could be arranged. James usually has a few dozen carrots in his big refrigerator at the restaurant."

"Oh, yeah. I always forget about that."

"How would you feel if we had a horse of our own?"

"That would be cool."

"I have to talk to James and see what he thinks, but Jade is apparently going to give me Becky."

"Would you keep her at the stable?"

"We would have to, if we keep her."

"I guess we'd have to go there a lot, then."

Harriet fought to keep a smile off her face.

"Would you mind if we did?"

Luke rubbed his hands together.

"I think we'd have time. I mean, I'm going to be volunteering with the therapy horses anyway, so I could keep an eye on Becky."

"That could work very well, then."

✂ --- ✂ --- ✂

Luke sat at the kitchen table, his face tense. He looked from James to Harriet and back again as she explained the horse situation. James in turn watched Luke's face as he spoke to Harriet.

"If you want to keep the horse, go for it. You've been around horses, so I'm sure you know what you're getting into."

Luke grinned. "Can I tell Emily?"

"You can tell her we're willing to take Becky, but it's not a done deal yet. I think I'd like my lawyer to look over whatever Jade's lawyer sends. I'd feel more comfortable if they'd let us buy the horse. It feels a little weird being given such a valuable gift from a virtual stranger."

"May I be excused?" Luke asked and started to stand.

Harriet put her hand on his arm, stopping him.

"This will only take a minute."

He sat back down.

"Lauren and I were talking about Christmas dinner, and it made me think about the possibilities."

James shook his head.

"Wait, don't dismiss my worries," she continued. "You know with Aiden coming to dinner, there will very likely be some sort of drama."

"Sweetie, it's only one day and one dinner," James said. "We can have our own holiday dinner another night if it's really bad."

Luke started laughing and then tried without success to be serious.

"I'm sorry. I know you're worried, but in my world, there's drama every time a group of people get together. And if it doesn't end up with knives, guns or the police, it isn't really drama. And you know Aunt Beth and Jorge are going to make amazing food. James is right, it's one night, and we can do our own holiday celebration if we want."

Harriet slumped in her chair.

"You guys are right. I just wanted everything to be perfect for your first Christmas."

Luke now put his hand on Harriet's arm.

"It already is perfect. I'm here with you and James." He looked down at the begging dogs. "And the pets. I've never had a pet. Besides, as my social worker always said when she'd send me back to live with my dad, 'Luke my boy, life is messy.'"

James chuckled.

"That's awful."

"Yeah, well, that's the system for you."

"I still wish your first holiday didn't have to include my ex-boyfriend drama."

Luke shook his head.

"Can I go call Emily, now?"

"Sure," Harriet and James said at the same time.

Chapter 18

Old-fashioned foil stars with small white twinkle lights in their centers festooned the quilt store's windows and doors as the Loose Threads arrived for their weekly meeting. Beth entered the classroom wrapped in wool from head to toe. Snowflakes dusted her knitted cap and the shoulders of her plaid wool jacket.

Harriet set a mug of steaming gingerbread tea in front of her.

"When did it start snowing?"

Beth unwrapped her scarf and stuffed it down the sleeve of her coat, which was now hanging on the back of her chair.

"While I was in the yarn shop."

"How are things going over there?"

"No new inventory, and the tension between Millie and her employee was so thick you could have cut it with a knife. And Millie looks like she's aged overnight. I wish she would tell us what's going on. She's going to have another heart attack if she's not careful."

Harriet made herself a cup of peppermint tea.

"I've got news, but let's wait until everyone else gets here so I don't have to say it twice."

"What don't you want to say twice?" Lauren asked as she came in and settled into her favorite spot next to Harriet. Harriet slid her an empty mug along with a basket of holiday teas she'd brought from home.

"You already know."

Lauren filled her cup with hot water from the carafe on the table.

"Oh, the horse thing."

"What horse thing?" Mavis asked as she and Connie came in shedding their outer garments.

Harriet laughed.

"I'm trying to wait for everyone to get here before I tell my story. It's not that big a deal, so don't get your expectations up."

Connie unwrapped a plate of Christmas cookies and set it on the table.

"Carla is parking, and she has more cookies." She smiled. "She's becoming quite the baker. We made extra to take to the homeless camp."

DeAnn came in, followed by Carla and two more plates of cookies. Harriet took a chocolate krinkle when Carla had removed the plastic wrap.

"I hope you two didn't think we were going to eat three plates of cookies today."

Lauren took a Russian teacake from Connie's plate.

"I'll do my share."

Carla took a box of sandwich bags from her quilt tote.

"I was hoping you would all take some of mine home and critique them for me." Then, her cheeks turned pink, and she looked away.

"Carla is being modest," Connie said. "She made up several of the recipes herself."

"I'm impressed." Harriet said. "And I'll have James try them."

"Do you think he'd be willing to answer some questions about them?" Carla asked. "The texture isn't quite right on my gingersnaps, but I don't know how to fix it."

"There isn't much James likes to talk about more than food, so I'm sure he'll be happy to tell you whatever you need to know," Harriet told her.

Aunt Beth bit into a gingersnap. "Now that everyone's here, I'd like to hear Harriet's news."

Robin set her mug on the table.

"What news."

Harriet held both hands up in front of her.

"As I said earlier, it's not that big. It's mostly curious."

Lauren rolled her eyes. "Just spit it out already."

"Lauren and I went to see Jade yesterday, and she wasn't at the store. In fact, she's not in Foggy Point or even the country. Her shop was locked up and her Christmas quilt was folded on a stool in the window with a note on top with my name on it."

"And before you ask," Lauren said, making eye contact with Robin, who had started to interrupt. "We didn't break in, we called Morse, and she let us in. Something about exigent circumstances."

"Anyway," Harriet continued. "The note said Jade was joining her parents in South America, and she's giving me her horse."

DeAnn brushed cookie crumbs from her hands.

"Can she do that? I mean, without telling you first?"

"Sure," Robin said. "And I'm guessing she had some reason to believe Harriet would be receptive to the idea."

"She does," Lauren answered for Harriet.

Harriet sipped her tea.

"When I picked Luke up at the stable the other day, I was talking to Marcia the assistant manager, and she said Jade has had drug problems in the past. Using and selling. Marcia says her parents overreacted and sent her to an out-of-state rehab, and she wasn't seen in Foggy Point for several years."

"Wow, she must have been in deep," Carla said.

"According to Marcia, she wasn't. She says it was typical teenage experimentation. She said the parents overreacted big time. And apparently, they're doing so again."

Lauren stirred her tea. "Unless she's in danger staying in Foggy Point."

Beth pulled a wool appliqué block from her bag.

"Are you keeping the horse?"

"James and Luke and I talked about it, and I think we are. I'd like to pay Jade, however. Becky is an expensive horse, and I'm not really comfortable taking her for free.

"I wonder what has Jade so panicked she would abandon her horse, her business, and just leave," Robin said.

Harriet selected a Linzer cookie.

"What I wonder is if Millie and Sunny are being threatened by whatever scared Jade out of town."

"And Daniel and Valery, too?" Lauren asked.

"That would be a pretty big conspiracy, don't you think?" Robin asked.

Harriet chewed and swallowed a bite of her cookie.

"On the other hand," she said, "it's a pretty big coincidence that two people are dead, one's been driven out of town' and two others are obviously having business problems and are being threatened. I mean, how can that all be random?"

"Let's not forget Vern. He seems to be having money problems, too," Lauren added.

Robin pulled a yellow legal tablet from her oversized bag.

"I think we need to write this all down. Maybe it will make sense if we lay it all out."

Mavis stopped stitching on the Christmas ornament she was making.

101

"Do I need to remind you all that Detective Morse and her colleagues at Foggy Point PD are quite capable of solving crime in this town without our help."

Robin went to the door and closed it. "Normally, I'd be the first one to agree with you."

"But?" Mavis asked.

"But," Robin continued, "it's unusual for someone to give someone they barely know an expensive horse, and when you couple that with the information about Jade being a former drug user and dealer—"

"If it's true," Connie interrupted.

"Yes, assuming it's true," Robin agreed. "I think before Harriet accepts the admittedly unusual gift, we should see if we can learn a little bit more about what's going on. It may be completely above board. On the other hand, Jade could be involved in the drug world more deeply than it appears on the surface, in which case, I'd like to confirm she legitimately owns the horse. I mean, we need to be sure there isn't someone else in town who thinks *they* own it and maybe used it for collateral against their latest fix, not really intending to permanently give the animal away."

Harriet sipped her tea thoughtfully. "She seemed pretty torn up about the idea of losing the horse when I talked to her."

Robin sat back down.

"Unfortunately, drug users can be very proficient liars if it means they can feed their habit."

Lauren pulled her tablet computer from her messenger bag. "I can see what I can find about our friend Jade."

DeAnn popped a thumbprint cookie into her mouth and ate it before speaking.

"This is only slightly related, and I'm not sure what the rules are about things you learn at a trial when you're a juror and the person on trial has gone to jail and then gotten out."

Robin twirled her pen in her fingers.

"Jurors are allowed to talk about their trial as long as they stick to the truth. If you make stuff up, the usual rules about slander apply, but otherwise, you can tell all if you wish once the verdict is in."

DeAnn gave a sigh of relief.

"A number of years ago, I was on the jury of a murder trial. In the end, we found the guy guilty of manslaughter. He had gotten in a fight with a drunk guy, completely started by the drunk, but he punched the victim, and the victim went down and hit his head and died."

"And?" Lauren prompted.

"And the guy we sent to jail for six years now works at the knitting store."

Harriet leaned back in her chair. "Wow."

"Wow is right," Mavis said.

Carla plucked a shortbread cookie from Connie's plate.

"Is it possible that all the shopkeepers who are having trouble now are involved in a drug ring? Maybe they were all selling drugs and accidentally got into someone else's territory or something like that?"

"Or maybe they double-crossed their distributor," DeAnn suggested.

Robin made a note on her pad. "Anything's possible."

Lauren stirred honey into her tea. "I thought you were going to say DeAnn's been watching too much television."

Robin sighed. "You'd be amazed how many otherwise ordinary citizens get involved in crime. Especially drug crimes. Somehow, little old ladies on a fixed income get involved in distributing or selling drugs to make a little extra money, and because they don't have a gun and their distributor doesn't look like a street thug, they don't think it's a real crime. They disconnect from the effects the drug they're handling have on the users."

Harriet set her cookie down.

"So, you think Jade, Daniel, Valery, Sunny and Millie are involved in drugs?"

"No, not for sure. I'm saying it's a possibility. I represented a bunco group that was growing and distributing pot. Granted, they weren't hardened criminals, but their activities were illegal, and it turned out they were all Master Gardeners and so successful their profits qualified them for hard time. And all of them were over sixty-five."

"Wow, hard time? Really?" Harriet said.

"It was complicated. Some of them were snowbirds," Robin explained.

Carla looked confused.

"They spent their winters in Arizona," she continued. "They got involved in a bunco group there and got some of their friends there involved, so then they were trafficking drugs across interstate lines. It was a mess. And through it all, they couldn't seem to grasp how much trouble they were in."

Mavis threaded a needle with green pearl cotton.

"Let's hope we don't have anything like that going on."

Lauren pulled her stitching project from her bag—a mat for her mother to put their centerpiece on for Christmas dinner. She'd opted for a wool felt penny rug with small candy canes, fir trees, wrapped packages, and other Christmas symbols on black wool circles surrounding a plain oval center.

"Whatever's going on, it's bad enough for two people to be dead and one driven out of town."

Harriet picked her cookie back up and took a bite.

"I hate to say this," she said when she'd finished chewing. "But what if Jade is the mastermind, and she left town after she killed two people."

"Let's not go crazy here," Robin cautioned her. "But having said that, I *would* like more evidence the whole horse thing is legitimate. Have your attorney check things out, you need to make sure she legally owns the horse before you accept it. And do you have any evidence her parents actually agree with her plan? That could be important if they are the actual owners."

"I know Lauren is looking on the internet for background on Jade, but if there is anything you can access about any drug arrests or other trouble that could be helpful. And please charge me. I don't expect you to work for for free."

"This isn't work," Robin replied. "This is satisfying my curiosity."

Connie slid the cookie plate out of her own reach.

"I hope you'll let us all know what happens."

"I will," Harriet answered for Robin.

✂ --- ✂ --- ✂

"Did you all leave me any cookies?" Jenny asked as she breezed into the room. "Sorry I'm late. The tooth cleaner person was running late today. What did I miss?"

Robin caught her up on the speculations of the group while Carla moved the cookies to her end of the table. Harriet poured hot water into Jenny's favorite mug and set it and the teabag basket in front of her.

"Do you have any theories as to what's going on? As long as we're all making our guesses."

"I have more than a theory," Jenny said with a wicked smile.

Lauren leaned forward.

"Do tell."

"Sunny cracked." Jenny paused as the Loose Threads all stopped eating and stitching to stare at her. "Connie told me what Harriet heard at the bakery last week. I went in this morning, and no one else was in the shop. Sunny was sitting at one of the tables holding a piece of paper and crying. I went over, and she tried to fold the paper, but I could see it and she gave up. The words were cut from magazines and glued to a page of copy paper. It said, 'You are late. You now owe six hundred dollars. Pay by tomorrow or we go to the press'.

"It took a little coaxing, but I convinced her she'd feel better if she let it all out. She said someone has been blackmailing her. When she was younger, she was part of a group of goth kids that hung out and played fantasy role-

104

playing games. Two of their group members were involved in the murder of a child out in the forest. Sunny and the rest of the group were completely exonerated, but the blackmailer threatened to go to the press and claim insider knowledge implicating Sunny. She's afraid it will ruin her. Of course, paying the increasing amounts to the blackmailer *will* ruin her, but she's a single mother and doesn't want her daughter to know about her past."

Connie picked up her cup of tea. "Poor Sunny."

"Does she have any idea why now?" Harriet asked. "I mean, hasn't she had the shop here for a while?"

"Six or seven years," Beth answered.

Jenny dunked her teabag up and down and removed it from her mug.

"Sunny is pretty sure Millie is being blackmailed also. She tried to get her to talk about it, but Millie wouldn't go there. The only thing she can think of is someone wanting to take over the downtown area for a development."

Lauren bit the leg off a gingerbread man and chewed thoughtfully.

"Harriet and I thought of that, but it's hard to imagine Foggy Point's downtown generating enough income to interest a developer."

Harriet pulled the crazy-quilt ornament she was working on from her bag and set it on the table while she dug for her needle and thread.

"I read about this sort of thing on the internet. The developer doesn't make money on the shops—in fact, in some communities, they don't even bother with the commercial spaces. They put in a lot of low-cost apartments over the shops. They get a tax break and other considerations as well as the rent."

Mavis set her stitching down and reached for another cookie.

"Wow. So, we either have a drug ring or a real estate scam operating in our otherwise peaceful community."

"Or it could be something else entirely," Harriet said.

Robin scribbled another note on her tablet.

"I have a friend at the courthouse who works in the building permit department. I can ask her if anyone new to town has been asking about permits for the downtown area. She and her co-workers usually have a good idea who is trying to do what, building-wise, in this county."

"I can check with Morse," Harriet volunteered. "She might be willing to tell us if there has been an increase in drug activity lately."

Connie reached for the basket to make a second cup of tea.

"On a lighter note, who has their Christmas shopping done?"

Her query was met with groans all around the table.

Chapter 19

Harriet picked up the empty dinner dishes and stacked them before carrying them to the sink.

"I hope you guys won't think this is too corny, but since we're getting our pictures taken with Santa this evening, I thought we could have them taken in matching sweaters."

James groaned.

"Please tell me you didn't. My mom used to make my sister and me wear these terrible matching Christmas sweaters for our holiday pictures. They had bells and bobbles and I don't know what all hanging off them."

Luke looked up from his phone.

"I want to see them. The pictures, that is."

"I'm sure my mother will be happy to show you. And don't try to tell me you're excited about being dressed up like a Christmas clown."

Luke's face burned red.

"Harriet wouldn't do that to us? Would she?"

James smiled and watched Harriet as she crossed to the stairs and picked up a shopping bag she'd left on the first step.

"You better hope not."

Harriet opened the bag and handed the red sweaters to James and Luke and pulled out a green pullover for herself.

"This isn't bad," Luke said.

"Don't sound so amazed," Harriet said indignantly. She reached back into the bag.

James tried to look inside, but she pulled it away.

"You may have spoken too soon," he warned Luke.

"O, ye of little faith," Harriet said, and pulled two dog sweaters from the bottom of the bag, one green and one red. "I figured the boys should be in our first Christmas together picture."

"What about Fred?" Luke asked.

"As much as I like the idea, there are many problems with that. He hates clothes—don't ask how I know that, just trust me. Then, there's the problem of taking him downtown. I like my fingers too much to attempt that. He's miserable to take to the vet; I can't imagine taking him out in a crowd."

Luke reached down and petted the cat, who had appeared at the mention of his name.

"Maybe we can put ink on his feet and let him walk on the matting for the picture."

James patted him on the back.

"Not a bad idea. You're kind of a clever kid, you know that?"

Luke blushed.

Harriet folded up her now-empty shopping bag.

"Let's get into our sweaters and round up the dogs."

"It's a plan," James said and led the way upstairs.

A light snow was falling as James parked the car and Harriet and Luke put leashes on the two dogs. Today was the shortest day of the year—winter solstice—and at six o'clock it was already full dark. The white twinkle lights on the storefronts of Main Street lent a festive touch to the downtown area.

Harriet picked Scooter up.

"I'm going to carry him until we get to the photo booth. I don't know how Cyrano does with the cold, but if Scooter's feet get cold, he'll start whining; and then there will be no hope of getting a good photo."

James patted Scooter's head.

"Cyrano is tough. He'll be fine as long as he's got his sweater on."

Harriet looked back at the dachshund just as Lauren bent down, petting him. Les was a few paces behind her.

"Are you two here for Christmas pictures?" Harriet asked.

Lauren rolled her eyes and gave a dramatic sigh.

"Unfortunately, we are. Our mother has insisted on a twin picture every Christmas since we were born."

"And she buys us hideous matching outfits for the occasion," Les added. Even his tenor voice was remarkably similar to Lauren's husky contralto.

James smiled.

"Let's see them, then."

107

The twins looked at each other and sighed again before flashing their coats open. Harriet and James tried to keep from laughing.

Les's sweater featured a traditional red-suited Santa complete with sack of presents over his shoulder, while Lauren's featured a female elf in a green fur-trimmed dress holding a festively wrapped package.

"I feel so much better," James finally said.

Lauren and Les busied themselves zipping their coats.

"Can anyone come to this party?" Connie's husband Rod asked as he, Connie, and Carla's daughter Wendy joined them on the sidewalk. Connie wrapped Wendy's scarf tighter around her neck.

"Have you seen Carla?" she asked. "We're supposed to meet her here."

Harriet shifted Scooter in her arms.

"We just got here, and other than Lauren and her brother…"

Lauren shoved her hands into her coat pockets.

"We saw Jenny and her family earlier, but I think they were headed home."

Les glanced at his watch.

"Can we get this over with?" he asked his sister. "I'm supposed to meet some friends in half an hour."

The group moved up the block to where the photographer had set up her camera on the sidewalk in front of Kitchen Kouture. The store had replaced its display of table covers with a queen-sized holiday quilt Aunt Beth had made several years ago. It had an off-white background with appliquéd images of gingerbread men, Santas, reindeer, and Christmas trees surrounding a center medallion that portrayed a side view of a winking Santa.

They joined the waiting line of two families. Aunt Beth and Jorge were delivering small paper cups of Mexican hot chocolate advertising Tico's Tacos. Harriet took one from the tray and looked at the logo on the cup.

"Nice touch. Since you and Jorge are here, how would you like to be in a group photo with James, Luke and I?"

Beth beamed.

"Oh, honey, I think that sounds wonderful."

✂ --- ✂ --- ✂

They posed for multiple pictures, some with Santa and some without. She stuffed Scooter inside her coat when they'd finished.

"Do you guys mind if we walk up to Blood Moon and peek in the window? I'd like to see if the quilt is still there."

James put his arm around her shoulders.

"If you think Scooter is warm enough, I'm game."

Luke picked Cyrano up.

"We're good."

The trio made their way up the block through the falling snow. Harriet sniffed and turned her head from side to side.

"Do either of you smell smoke?"

James tilted his head up and sniffed.

"I do."

Luke pointed up the block.

"There's smoke is coming out of that building."

Harriet hurried up the block, unable to run because of the slick sidewalk.

"That's Blood Moon. Luke, call nine-one-one."

James matched her pace.

"Don't even think about going in."

"My quilt was on a stool just inside the window. If the fire isn't too bad, I'd like to rescue it."

James grabbed her arm.

"We need to let the firemen do their job. No quilt is worth risking your life over."

Sirens already blared as they reached the store. A red ladder truck pulled up to the curb, and several firefighters jumped out dressed in their turnouts, boots, and helmets and headed for the door. One of them came over to where they stood.

"I'm going to need you to leave the area," he said.

"I have a quilt on a stool inside the door. If it's possible, I'd like to have it."

James tried to guide her away. The fireman tilted his helmet up and took a better look at Harriet.

"You're that quilter lady, right?"

Harriet nodded her head.

"You did some nice work on a quilt for my wife. She won a prize at the fair with it." He looked toward the building. "No promises, but if I can get the quilt, I will. Now, I really do need you to leave the area."

Harriet smiled.

"Thanks," she said, and joined Luke and James, walking back down the block. She pulled her phone from her pocket. "I need to call Morse. She's going to want to know about this."

James took Scooter from her so she could make her call.

✂ --- ✂ --- ✂

Morse pulled up next to where they'd stopped to watch just as the fireman brought Harriet her quilt. She held her badge up.

"Do you know the cause of the fire yet?" she asked. She had on a red sweater with metallic gold trim and dark-green leggings. Her hair was neatly coiffed and sported a clip with a sprig of fresh holly. She'd clearly been at a holiday gathering of some sort.

"I've called the arson team," the fireman said. "They'll make the official determination, but the fire was in the office, and it looks like someone ransacked the place before lighting a wastebasket." He exchanged a look with Harriet.

"No, Harriet can't take the quilt with her," Morse told them. "I'll tell you what. When they finish processing the scene, if it turns out all the action was in the office, and the quilt wasn't involved in any way, I'll bring it to you. Are you going to be around town?"

Beth and Jorge, empty tray dangling from his hand, had joined them as Morse finished speaking.

"We could go back to the restaurant and warm up while you wait," Jorge offered.

"That'll work," Morse said. "I'll call you if we discover the quilt is not going to be available."

✂ --- ✂ --- ✂

Harriet settled Scooter and Cyrano in Jorge's office with Beth's dog Brownie before rejoining James and Luke in the back room at Tico's. Connie and Rod were already there, sitting opposite them; Lauren was at the end of the table.

Jorge brought out a steaming pot of Mexican hot chocolate and a dispenser of whipped cream. Aunt Beth followed him with a tray of warmed mugs. Harriet wrapped her hands around her mug as Jorge filled it.

"It's hard to understand why anyone would want to burn Jade's store now she's gone," she said."

Lauren sipped her chocolate.

"You're assuming she is actually gone. Maybe she never left. And just maybe, she burned her own store to make it look like someone else was after her when she's been behind the problems in town all along."

"I realize I may be slightly biased due to the whole horse thing," Harriet said. "But she just didn't strike me as a criminal mastermind."

"That's what's so diabolical about it," Lauren said, her voice rising.

Jorge went to the kitchen and returned with a plate of Christmas cookies. Connie took a dark brown crinkle cookie from the plate.

"Are these Mexican-style?" she asked.

Jorge put his hand over his heart.

"I'm injured. How can you believe I would serve anything else?"

Connie laughed.

"Well, you do have Italian night once a month, so we never know what you're going to do."

Jorge held the cookie plate in one hand and pointed at each of the selections.

"These are *polvorones de canela*, a type of cinnamon-sugar cookie. The round ones are *hojarascas*, or Mexican shortbread." He moved to the next selection. "These are *galletas de Navidad*, which are like a blackberry Linzer cookie. Connie is eating a Mexican mocha crinkle, which is self-explanatory, and we finish with chili chocolate cookies."

Lauren took the plate. "These look delicious."

Jorge set a *galleta de Navidad* on a Christmas napkin and handed it to Beth. She savored a bite then set it on the table.

"I can't believe anyone in our town is so evil they would burn down a small business mere days before Christmas."

"Murdering people at Christmas *is* pretty Grinchie, if you ask me," Harriet said.

Luke ate one of the shortbread cookies and picked up a Mexican crinkle.

"Criminals don't think like that. They don't think about anything but where to get their next score, whether it's money or drugs or whatever."

James sipped his hot chocolate.

"On a happier note, I'm doing a land-office business on the Christmas tea. I'm thinking about adding a late-afternoon sitting the last few days before Christmas Eve."

Luke got a confused look on his face.

"What's a land-office business?"

Connie, the retired teacher, sat up straight in her chair.

"After the War for Independence, the US was very poor. They sold public land to the highest bidder. By the mid-eighteen hundreds, there was a backlog of some ten thousand land-grant applicants. 'Land-office business' became a metaphor for brisk business, and has been used ever since."

"How do you know all that?" Luke asked her. "I thought you taught kindergarten." His face turned red as he realized how he'd sounded.

Connie reached over and patted his hand.

"It's okay, honey. It's a valid question. When I went to college, I knew I wanted to teach little ones, but I also wanted to learn about my adopted country, so I double-majored in American history and education."

Harriet clicked on her phone and glanced at the time. She hoped Morse wasn't going to be too much longer, as she had a last-minute Christmas quilt project on her machine calling her name.

111

By the time Detective Morse finally arrived at Tico's Tacos, Connie had reviewed the process for college admissions from start to finish with Luke while Jorge, Rod, and James had analyzed the upcoming college bowl games. Harriet and Lauren scoured the internet on Lauren's tablet for any information on the murders of Anthony and Valery, but found nothing new. They were sipping their second hot chocolates in morose silence when the front door chime rang. Morse appeared in the back room moments later, Harriet's quilt folded over her arm.

James pulled out a chair while Jorge handed her a mug of steaming chocolate. Connie slid her the plate of cookies. Morse gave Harriet her quilt before sitting, and the group waited in silence while she sipped her drink and ate a cookie.

Finally, she set her mug down.

"It appears that someone was looking for something in Jade's office. All the files were dumped. Pretty much everything was trashed. I'm guessing when they didn't find it, they decided to burn the place as a precaution, maybe to destroy evidence. Or maybe they were interrupted. In any case, it looks like they lit a wastebasket on fire and set it in the footwell of the desk."

"What happens next?" Beth asked.

Morse blew out a breath.

"We'll keep trying to get in touch with Jade, which might be a problem, and then, we'll figure out who did it and arrest them."

Harriet wiped her hands on her napkin.

"No offense, but how likely is that?"

"None taken," Morse said. "And you're right. Given we have two unsolved murders, and no one was hurt here, plus there's not a lot of damage…it's not going to be high on our list. Her insurance company will undoubtedly investigate." She stared off toward the far end of the room, lost in thought.

"Would we be able to go in and do some clean up before Christmas?" Beth asked. "It would be nice if we could straighten it up a little and get the quilt back in the window. It doesn't sound like Jade's going to know what happened for a while and our holiday visitors shouldn't have to look into a burned-out shop. Jade's not likely to come back, in any case, even if you do manage to reach her."

"When her attorney sends me the papers for the horse, I might be able to get contact information from him," Harriet offered.

"Let me know," Morse said. "That would be useful." She looked down at her soot-smudged sweater. "I was thinking I should go back to my party, but maybe not."

Jorge handed her the cookie plate again.

"Have another cookie."

Connie pulled her scarf from her purse.

"We better head home. I've got things to do yet." She wrapped the scarf around her neck. "Do any of you want to come out to the homeless camp tomorrow? I'm taking the Christmas cookies Carla and I made to them."

Harriet wiped crumbs from her hand.

"I can come."

"I can send a few dozen brownies, if you want," James added as he tossed his crumpled napkin onto the table.

Connie smiled. "They would like that."

Jorge stood up.

"I have something for them, too. Wait here." He disappeared into the kitchen, returning a few minutes later carrying a shopping bag with a box inside. "I was buying some replacement Christmas lights, and I saw these solar powered ones. They claim to work even on cloudy days."

"That was nice of you," Connie said. "I think they'll like that, too."

"Should I go get the dogs?" Luke asked.

"Sure," James said, getting up and taking Harriet's coat from the back of her chair, holding it out so she could slip her arms into the sleeves.

Luke hurried to the back and returned with the two dogs, already wearing their sweaters. Harriet put her knit hat on and picked up her purse.

"Where shall we meet tomorrow?" she asked Connie.

"I'll come get you," Connie replied.

"I think I'll go, too," Beth decided.

Lauren began bundling up in her coat and knitwear.

"I have to work, but let me know if they need anything."

With the next day's plan settled, they all departed into the frozen night.

Chapter 20

The next morning, Harriet dressed the dogs in their coats and took them out to walk in the grassy area inside her circular driveway. The snow had begun to melt, so islands of green poked through the white crust. Connie pulled up as the dogs jumped from island to island, finally completing their business as she and Beth got out of the car. Mavis pulled in behind them.

"I hope it's okay I'm joining the party," she said as she got out of her car.

"The more the merrier," Harriet said as she tried to keep the dogs from jumping on her visitors. "Let me get these guys in the house, and then I'm ready to go."

Mavis carried two large shopping bags over to Connie's car.

"I went to the Costco in Sequim yesterday, and I was getting some of their baked chickens to put in the freezer for when the kids come, and I thought I'd get a couple for the homeless camp."

Harriet slid into the back seat and rested James's brownies in her lap.

"That's a good idea. All we're bringing them is sugary treats."

Connie moved a tissue box off the front seat so Beth could get in. "Hey, they need their treats, too."

Beth held up her box. "I'm bringing food for their soul—Christmas lights."

"That's nice, too," Mavis said. "So, tell me, how did picture night go?"

They discussed the pictures and the fire that followed. Mavis crossed her arms over her chest.

"What is going on in our town?"

Beth shook her head.

"I wish I knew."

✂ --- ✂ --- ✂

Joyce Elias was sitting in the common area with long-time camp resident Max and two people Harriet had never seen before.

"This is all so wonderful of you," Joyce said.

Beth handed her the Christmas lights. "Jorge thought you might like to decorate for the holiday."

Joyce's face lit up in a broad grin. "This is wonderful. We have a tree back here…" She pointed down the trail. "…but we don't have much to decorate it with."

She led them back to the main trail and then off to the left to a small clearing that surrounded a blue spruce tree. Several hand-carved deer hung from the branches, along with foil stars that were made from salvaged food wrappers.

"This is festive," Harriet said.

Joyce held her hands out. "We try."

Max led them back to the common area.

"Let's get our treats stashed before the animals come snooping around."

Harriet handed him the package of brownies.

"These are from James."

"And these are from Costco," Mavis said, handing him the bags of chicken.

Connie set her box of cookies on the wooden table.

"Carla and I made cookies for you. And Wendy decorated them."

"Could we convince you to stay for a cup of coffee and a cookie?" Joyce asked.

Harriet was starting to get cold, but she knew it was important they accept the hospitality.

"I think we have time for one cup."

Max fetched a large coffeepot from the edge of the fire pit where it was keeping warm and set it on the table, while Joyce opened a storage box and brought out pottery mugs and plates. Harriet examined her mug when Max filled it with coffee and handed it to her.

"These are really nice."

Joyce smiled.

"They *are* nice. The pottery group at the Angel Harbor Folk Art School made them for us."

"They made us plates, too," Max added. "We're living in tall cotton these days."

Connie started the box of cookies around.

"Carla would like feedback on the cookies, if you would care to give it. She's developing some of her own recipes. I think she has it in her mind to write a cookbook if people like them."

Joyce asked after everyone's families as they ate their treats and drank the coffee. Harriet was surprised at how good the coffee was, give it had been brewed over an open fire. She savored it before setting her mug on the table.

"Did you ever find Smokey Joe?"

Joyce frowned. "It's strange, now that you ask. We haven't seen him, but Max has checked on his camp—"

"He lives on the outer edge of our territory," Max interjected.

"And it appears he's been staying in his tent," Joyce continued.

"Is that usual?" Mavis asked.

"Yes, and no," Joyce answered. "He's not as social as Max and I, for instance, but he does come around at mealtimes, usually."

Max's bushy white eyebrows drew together.

"There *has* been food missing from the box. About the amount a man might eat. Of course, we don't lock the box, so anyone in camp can help themselves any time. It's just we haven't seen anyone doing so. Most people eat at our usual meal times."

Joyce carried the coffeepot around and topped off everyone's mug.

"I guess what we're saying is we think he's around, but we haven't seen him. I can't imagine who else it would be, if not him. I'm just not sure why he's not showing himself."

Max shook his head. "Can you not think of why he might be in hiding?"

Joyce set the coffeepot back on the fire.

"Just because he's had trouble in his past, there's no reason to think he does now. He told me he left all that behind a long time ago, and I believe him."

Joyce stared at Max, and Harriet waited until they broke the stare.

"What sort of trouble are we talking about?"

Max looked at Joyce before speaking.

"Joe was married to a gold-digging tart, and when he wouldn't or couldn't keep her in the style she wanted to become used to, she was done with him. She got a shyster lawyer and took him to the cleaners. They lived in a house that had been in his family for a hundred years. The courts gave it to her, and he decided he'd rather see it burn than see her in it."

"So, he set it on fire?" Mavis asked.

"That he did," Max said. "He burned it to the ground. And did his jail time for it."

116

Beth sipped her coffee.

"Why do you think he'd be hiding now? Has he burned something else?"

Max shook his head.

"I couldn't tell you. He seemed like he was in a good place. He's reconnected with a daughter he'd been estranged from for twenty years. If he's gotten himself in trouble, he hasn't said anything."

"I'm sure he'll make himself known when he's ready," Joyce said, effectively ending the discussion.

"Are you all staying warm enough in this snowy weather?" Beth asked.

Joyce stirred the fire with an iron rod.

"We keep the fire going all day, and with the quilts and tarps you all made us, everyone has plenty of warm bedding."

Max smiled.

"And we're taking a page from the pioneers' playbook. We've collected some bricks that we warm in the fire and then wrap in flannel your friend Marjorie gave us. We put them in our beds, and they keep our feet warm all night."

Mavis stood up and slipped her purse strap over her shoulder. "Is there anything else we can bring you?"

Joyce and Max stood as well.

"You are very kind," Joyce said. "I think we're set, for the time being. The church has offered to bring their bus and fetch us for Christmas Eve services and a meal, so we are well taken care of."

"And we thank you," Max added.

Beth led the way back to Connie's car. "Anyone want to go by the Steaming Cup on the way home?"

They all did.

✄ --- ✄ --- ✄

Harriet ordered a large peppermint hot chocolate and a frosted cookie in the shape of a Christmas tree.

"Does anyone else find it interesting that Smokey Joe is avoiding people and is an arsonist?" she asked when the rest of the group was seated with their drinks and snacks.

"You mean, since we had an arson fire last night?" Mavis asked.

Beth stirred a packet of sweetener into her tea and took a sip to test it for sweetness.

"It's hard not to make the connection. I mean, we haven't had an arson fire in this town in I don't know how many years."

117

Connie broke her molasses cookie in half and dunked a corner into her tea before biting it.

"Do you think he could be our killer?"

Harriet leaned back in her chair and blew out a breath.

"Anything's possible, I guess. You have to wonder what his motive would be."

Lauren arrived, and after getting her drink and a scone came over to the Loose Threads table.

"Did you guys just get back from the homeless camp?"

Harriet nodded.

"I thought you had to work."

"I had a client call, but it finished sooner than I thought it might. I've got a little time before my next client, so I snuck out for a snack."

"Do you know Smokey Joe's real name?" Harriet asked her.

"Smokey who?"

Beth laughed. "I guess not."

Harriet put her hands around her mug to warm them.

"He's that guy Joyce asked Luke and I about the other day. He was planning on wintering over in the camp, and now he seems to be absent."

"But," Connie added. "They think he might be staying there, but keeping out of sight."

"And," Mavis finished, "he has arson is his past."

Lauren took a bite of her scone and thought.

"Do you know his real name?" She looked at Harriet. "Of course you don't. That's what you want me to do. Have you asked Morse? They have databases of street names."

Connie sipped her tea. "We just found out about the arson."

Lauren took in a big breath and let it out slowly.

"I need to go out to the camp anyway—I bought them a solar-powered stove for Christmas, and I need to deliver it. If they know his real name, I have a chance of finding out who he is and maybe if he might have an axe to grind with our dead people."

"That *would* help us confirm whether he might be involved," Mavis said.

Harriet chewed on a bite of her tree.

"At this point, all we have is a bunch of theories and no way to confirm or eliminate any of them."

"I'll see what I can do."

✂ --- ✂ --- ✂

Harriet needed to finish stitching a table runner for James's mother, and Connie and Beth both had holiday projects that needed to be done; so they all decided to stay at Harriet's to work on them. Mavis didn't have a critical project, but she decided to stay. too, and work on her wool appliqué.

Beth filled and plugged in the electric kettle, and Mavis dug around in Harriet's kitchen cupboard, finally coming out with a box of ginger-snaps.

"I know none of us need any more cookies, but we should have a few available in case of emergency."

"Good idea," Beth agreed.

Connie brought a floor-stand Ott light to her chair and settled in to stitch.

"I appreciate that we're having winter weather at Christmas time, but I hate these days where it never really gets light all day."

"I hear you," Beth said as she threaded her needle.

Harriet focused on the table runner in her lap, and the next time she looked up, an hour had passed. She stood up to stretch and saw Robin's car pulling into the driveway.

Moments later, Robin came in and immediately made herself a cup of tea.

"I know it's supposed to be warmer today, but with the drizzle it feels so cold."

Harriet slid another chair over to the table.

"What brings you our way?"

"I had an errand out this direction and thought I'd take a chance at finding someone home. I had to file some papers at the courthouse this morning, so I stopped by the planning department and then the building permits desk. None of them know about any active plans to redevelop the downtown area."

"What does that mean—active plans?" Mavis asked.

"According to them, at any given time there are entities scheming on redeveloping downtown. They said most of the time nothing comes of it. Either their financing falls through, they require variances the city won't give them, or they can't get key building owners to sell."

Harriet set her table runner down.

"So they might not know if someone was trying to drive the current business owners out."

Robin set her mug down.

"That's what I got out of the discussion. So, we still don't know if that's the motive for the murders or the blackmail or both."

Beth handed her the box of gingersnaps. "Thanks for checking."

While Robin fished out a cookie, Harriet explained what they'd learned at the homeless camp. Beth and Connie had texted the Threads who hadn't been in town the night before, letting them know about the fire.

"That's an interesting development," Robin said. "Do we know if Smokey Joe's conviction was in Washington?"

Beth frowned. "No, we don't. I didn't think to ask."

Harriet's phone rang, and she stepped away from the table to answer.

"That was James," she said when she came back. "He needs me to go pick up some dill for his tea sandwiches. He said his small private dining room is available if we want to come have tea sandwiches and soup for lunch."

Beth stuffed her stitching back into her bag. "I'm in."

"Me, too," Connie quickly added.

Mavis put her stitching away. "I'll take your dogs out while you unplug the kettle."

Chapter 21

*H*arriet drove, and her aunt rode in the passenger seat. Harriet smiled to herself as Beth leaned forward to check for traffic, completely blocking her own view of the street to her right.

"Is it clear?" she asked.

Beth continued looking a moment longer before answering.

"Have you noticed that gray car before," she asked, gesturing at a sedan that was pulled off the road halfway into Harriet's neighbor's hedge.

Harriet turned onto the street and drove past the car in question.

"Now that you mention it, I saw a car that looked like that one yesterday when I went for my morning run. It wasn't parked there, though. It was on the other side of the road down the hill a little way."

"Does it belong to one of your neighbors?" Beth asked.

"As I'm sure you know, Detective Morse's grandmother owns the house next to mine through the hedge. She's a snowbird, so nobody is there this time of year. Jane comes about once a month to check things over, but she's the only one. The people on the other side of me have already left to visit relatives in the Midwest for the holidays, so I doubt they're having many visitors."

Beth adjusted the heater.

"Given what's been going on, you might mention it to Detective Morse."

"I'll mention it to James and Luke so they can keep an eye out, too, but Morse has bigger fish to fry right now."

Beth turned in her seat and shared an exasperated look with Connie and Mavis. Harriet ignored her and drove on to the grocery store to pick up the dill.

James met them at the door and gave Harriet a quick kiss and a smile be-fore taking the bundle of dill and whisking it away to the kitchen. Connie stopped in the foyer to speak to a group of retired teacher friends who were waiting to be seated while Harriet, Beth, Robin, and Mavis went on to the small dining room. A waiter dressed in a festive holiday-patterned vest over his usual white shirt and black pants came in immediately and took their orders, returning with a stack of small plates and a tray of tea sandwiches.

"Where did James learn to make these delicious little sausage rolls?" Mavis asked.

Harriet finished eating her own roll before answering.

"Who knows? He's always getting cookbooks and then experimenting. He found an old British cookbook at the thrift store, and it had a lot of re-cipes for tea treats, so it probably came from there."

"As a matter of fact, it did," James said as he came in carrying another tray of savory treats. "I hope you don't mind not having the usual selection of tea sandwiches. I mix them up a little from one sitting to the next, since some people come here with more than one group, and I don't want them to have to eat the exact same thing. You're getting some from the earlier batch and the rest from the upcoming selections."

Beth squeezed his hand when he set the tray down.

"Honey, anything you make is wonderful. We don't care what sitting they come from."

He stood aside as his waiter brought a tray laden with small soup bowls.

"Before I forget," he said to Harriet, "I'll be home a little late tonight. Valery Melnyk's family is having a service for him tomorrow, and of course, they want food."

"I guess that means they confirmed his identity," Harriet said. "The last we heard, his face was so battered they weren't sure."

James took a crustless smoked cheese sandwich from her plate and popped it into his mouth.

"The guy that came by here, his great-uncle, I think, said the police tried to put him off, but he told them the family came from Ukraine, and they have to go back Friday. He identified the body. I guess Valery had a dis-tinctive tattoo on his shoulder, and that was good enough for the police."

"Can I do anything to help?" Harriet asked.

"No, he doesn't want anything too complicated. He did ask me to spread the word about the service, since they don't know anyone locally, and they don't really have time to put it in the paper."

Harriet looked from her aunt to Mavis and Connie. "Shall we go?"

Robin had an appointment, but the rest agreed.

"I'd hate to have his family hold the service in an empty church," Mavis said. "Especially when they've come this far."

"And he *was* an important part of our downtown business association," Beth added.

"That's settled, then," Connie said. "I'll find out what time it is. I know Valery attended the Catholic Church; I'll call when we're done here."

Harriet sat at the kitchen table opposite Luke, a notepad and pencil in front of her. James had come home from the restaurant late and exhausted and had gone upstairs to shower and go to bed.

"Okay, who do you still need to shop for?"

"I still need to get something for my half-brother." Luke ran a hand through his hair. "I don't know what kids that age like."

"Music? Video games? Clothes?" Harriet suggested.

"But how do I know which one of those things?"

"You never know for sure what a person wants unless they tell you, so you just make your best guess. And we can look on the computer for the most popular gifts for boys that age."

"He has two younger half-sisters he lives with."

"It might be nice to get them something, too. I can help you with that."

"I'd like to get something for Aunt Beth, too. She's always doing nice stuff for me, like the flannel pajama pants she made and the hat she knitted for me."

"That's very sweet of you. She's easy—she likes fabric and yarn and pretty much anything crafty."

Luke took the pad and started a list.

"Who else?" Harriet asked.

The house phone ringing interrupted them; he got up and answered. He listened a moment and then held the receiver out to Harriet, covering the mouthpiece with his hand.

"It's for you. It's Marcia from the horse barn. Something happened, but she's talking so fast I can't tell what she's saying."

Harriet took the phone from him and listened.

"Marcia, slow down…Okay, we'll be right there." She hung up and turned to Luke. "I'm still not sure what she was saying. Apparently, the horses are okay. It sounds like someone broke in and something happened involving Becky and Major." She tore Luke's list off the pad and quickly wrote a note to James. "I doubt he'll wake up while we're gone, but we'll leave a note just in case."

Luke already had their coats out of the closet. He handed Harriet hers and got into his, pulling his hat from one pocket and gloves from the other. Harriet followed suit and grabbed her purse and keys on the way to the garage.

"I wonder what happened that would involve Becky and Major and not any other horses?" she said.

Luke slid into the passenger seat and fastened his seatbelt.

"Major's stall is next to Becky's," he said.

Harriet backed out of the garage and pointed the car toward the street.

"Whatever it is may have to do with those specific horses, or they may just be located in part of the barn that someone needed access to. Have you noticed anything they keep in the barn that would be worth stealing?"

Luke thought for a moment.

"The tack room, I guess. Emily told me some of the saddles are pretty pricey."

"Seems like a weird thing to steal. I mean, where would you fence them?"

"People who steal stuff to fund their drug habits aren't mental giants. They don't think very many steps ahead when they're doing this stuff. This guy, if it was a robbery, probably planned on showing up at his usual pawn shop with a bunch of silver-trimmed bridles and saddles."

"Maybe. I don't remember where the tack room is, but I don't think it's close to Becky, is it?"

"No, you're right, it's at the front of the barn where you cross-tie the horses. Becky and Major are in the middle of the row of stalls."

✂ --- ✂ --- ✂

The equestrian center was lit up brighter than downtown Foggy Point when Harriet pulled into the driveway. Several police cruisers were parked outside the barn, and an SUV with *K9* printed on both sides was parked farther away. Its back door was open, an officer holding a Belgian Malinois search dog straining at its leash, nose to the ground, anxious to start tracking.

Harriet zipped her coat and tugged her gloves on.

"Let's go see what's going on."

Marcia Hamilton was just inside the barn door, holding Becky's lead rope. Emily held Major farther back in the aisle. The big horse whinnied when he caught sight of Luke. Luke strode over, and Major began rubbing his large head on Luke's chest. Emily handed Luke the lead rope and joined Marcia and Harriet.

"Should Luke and I take these two for a walk in the arena?"

"Is that okay with you?" Marcia asked Harriet and, when she nodded, handed the lead rope to Emily. Emily motioned for Luke to join her.

"So, what's going on?" Harriet asked as they watched Emily and Luke lead the horses away.

"We're not quite sure at this point. The police are in the office reviewing the security camera footage. Someone was familiar enough with this place to black out the camera in this main aisle. You can see a dark figure drive up, and when they got to the barn, they pulled out a stepladder we keep over there…" She pointed to the front corner of the barn. "…for some of the kids who have tall horses. Anyway, they got on the ladder and spray-painted the camera lens."

"What are the police looking at?"

"There's a camera at the other end of the aisle. It doesn't have a clear view to this end, but you can see a little. Plus, there's another camera in the cross aisle midway down. You can't see much on that one, either. And they're looking at all the outside cameras and the arena cameras, just in case."

"What happened after the camera got painted?"

"That's where it gets fuzzy. What we know for sure is the dogs started barking, and I came out to see what was going on. I live in a cottage behind the arena.

"Becky and Major were in the aisle. He was sort of herding her, keeping her in the barn. He was all wound up, snorting and prancing."

"Why Becky and why Major?"

"Someone had put Becky's halter and lead on, but Major had no halter or lead or anything."

Marcia led the way down the aisle toward Becky's stall. Two police officers were taking pictures, and a small blonde woman with a pixie haircut was dusting the stall door for fingerprints. She looked up.

"Hi, Harriet." Darcy Lewis said. She was a criminalist for the Tri-county Forensic Task Force but, more important, when her schedule permitted a Loose Threads quilter.

"What's going on?" Harriet asked.

"That's what we're trying to figure out," she said without looking up. "This is off the record, but if I had to guess, I'd say someone let *this* horse out, then the other horse kicked its way out. I guess it didn't like its friend leaving without him or her."

Harriet chuckled.

"He's a retired police horse. I guess he still thinks he's on the job."

Marcia was pacing the aisle behind Harriet.

"Do these type of horses get stolen?" Harriet asked her.

"They do. All horses can be subject to theft. I read in an industry magazine that forty thousand horses a year get stolen in America. Of course, most of those are not expensive show horses. It seems like most of the show horses you hear about are taken from more populated areas and usually from pasture situations, not from a barn. All the horses here are microchipped. And both Becky and Major have tattoos inside their lips."

Darcy stood up and picked up her box of tools. "Do they take a horse like this and hold it for ransom?"

Marcia though for a moment.

"Yes, it seems like I've read about something like that. That was a couple of years ago, though."

They all turned and looked as another car drove up and parked by the barn. Harriet recognized Detective Morse's sedan.

"What brings you here?" she asked when the detective had joined them.

"Darcy called me. And she was right to do so, with what's been going on downtown, and especially with Jade's shop being burned last night. Now someone attempts to steal Jade's horse." Morse held her hand up before Harriet could speak. "I know she says she's giving you the horse, but not many people know that, and you don't have the paperwork yet, in any case, do you?"

Harriet shook her head. Morse continued.

"To my way of thinking, someone is after Jade, and what better way to get her to show herself but to take her horse and hold it for ransom?"

Harriet rocked back on her heels.

"Wow. Someone really doesn't like her."

"Don't forget Anthony and Valery. I don't know what's going on, but this isn't a coincidence. This has something to do with whatever is happening in town."

"Do you need me for anything?" Marcia asked. "The stable owners are out of town for the holidays, so I need to go deal with all this."

"What are you going to do?" Harriet asked her.

"First, I'm going to get the security company out here to repair the cameras and maybe add a few more. Then, I'm calling the company we use to provide guards when we do horse shows here. Until they find out who did this, or at least till the owners get back, I'm going to have someone patrolling twenty-four/seven."

"That sounds like a good plan," Morse said.

"Do you have another stall for Becky?" Harriet asked. "I'm guessing the police don't want her back there tonight."

Marcia looked down the aisle and tapped a finger on her lip.

"I think I'll put her down at the other end, in clear view of that camera. I can move the horse in the stall next to that one around the corner so Major can be next to her. He seems to have strong feelings for her safety. If you can go take Becky, Emily can get the stalls ready."

"I can do that," Harriet said and headed for the arena.

Chapter 22

We aren't going to do anything important at school today," Luke pleaded with Harriet. "It's the last day. The teachers are showing movies and stuff like that."

He slid into his chair at the kitchen table. Harriet set a box of cereal in front of him and glanced at the wall clock.

"If I drive you—and you don't take too long eating—we've got just enough time to go by the barn and check on the horses on the way to school."

Luke had poured cereal and milk into his bowl before she'd stopped speaking and began shoveling it into his mouth.

She laughed. "You've got time to chew. I'll take the dogs out and warm up the car."

Outside, she tapped a two-word text into her phone and sent it to the Threads while the dogs attended to their business. *Coffee? Nine?* it read.

Something happen? came Lauren's reply.

Yes, Harriet wrote back and took the dogs inside. Replies came in one after another as she and Luke got in the car and headed for the barn.

"Do you want me to check your messages?" he asked her.

"It'll be the Threads. If you want, you can tell them we'll meet at the Steaming Cup, if that's what they're asking."

Luke picked up her phone, and she smiled to herself when he tapped in her security code without asking her what it was; she'd told it to him once before.

"Aunt Beth and Connie both asked where coffee will be and said they'd tell everyone else." He wrote a group text to the two of them and told them

128

coffee would be at the Steaming Cup and thanked them for telling the rest of the group.

"Are you writing a novel over there?" Harriet asked him as he kept typing.

His cheeks turned pink.

"They think it's you, so I'm being chatty like you would be."

She looked over at him. "You think I'm chatty?"

He laughed.

"You and your friends do talk a little." He typed another reply. "Jenny has a master gardener meeting and will stop by after that. You told her that would be okay and if she didn't make it, you'd call her and tell her what you talked about."

Harriet shook her head.

"You are too funny." She made a mental note that Luke was much more observant than she'd given him credit for.

She stopped the car at the end of the drive that led to the Miller Hill Equestrian Center. True to her word, Marcia had brought in security guards. A uniformed man stepped over to the driver-side car window and asked her name. She gave him hers and Luke's. The guard held a clipboard with a list of approved names. He found both of them and noted the time they were arriving.

"Go ahead," he said and stepped back.

"Wow, that's pretty serious security," Luke said and looked back at the guard as they approached the barn.

Harriet pulled into a parking spot and turned the car off.

"It's serious business trying to steal an expensive horse from a boarding stable."

Marcia came out of the barn as Luke and Harriet walked toward it. He spotted Emily in front of Major's stall and hurried to join her.

Marcia raised an eyebrow.

"I'm guessing he wanted to make sure Major was okay?"

Harriet smiled.

"He wanted to skip school and sit by his stall all day. Our compromise was to come by this morning to reassure him the horses are okay and everything is secure."

"As you can see, Emily was here at the crack of dawn. She needs to go home and do her schoolwork, too." Marcia blew out a breath. "I sat up most of the night watching the security cameras, but everything was quiet. With two guards on the property, whoever it was tried to take Becky would be foolish to come back. And the police were here for a few more hours after you left."

"Did they figure anything out?"

"Not that they told me." She looked down at her boots. "They took tire impressions, dusted half the barn for fingerprints, and ran dogs around the property several times. The dogs followed a trail to where they think the car was parked and then stopped. The video wasn't clear enough to identify the person or the car that drove up last night." She looked up at a new camera on the side of the barn. "I asked the security company to install upgraded cameras, and they did first thing this morning."

"That only helps if the person doesn't spray-paint the lens," Harriet said.

"True, but maybe we'd have been able to identify the car. The driver was careful enough to not give the camera a look at either license plate."

"Sounds like someone who was familiar with the layout here and the camera placement."

"That's what I'm thinking. It would be hard to tell who, though. When we hold riding clinics, lots of people come who aren't regulars and who could have scoped the place out."

"I haven't heard from Jade's lawyer yet, but it's only been a few days. I don't even know if Becky is my problem to worry about."

Marcie visibly tensed, and Harriet rested a hand on her arm.

"Don't worry, I'll still take care of her needs until we hear one way or another. Hopefully, that won't be too much longer."

"Good. With all of this, I can't deal with much more. I emailed the other owners about the new security protocols, and they've all been calling to find out what's going on and wondering if their horses are at risk. Fortunately, there aren't a lot of other options in the immediate area, or I'm sure some of them would be moving out."

"It's pretty clear Becky was the target, don't you think?"

"That's what I've been telling them all. I hope it's true." She looked at Harriet. "I'm sorry. I don't want anything to happen to Becky."

"I understand. Do you think *I* should consider moving her?"

"Since we don't know what's going on, how could you be sure the thief wouldn't follow her to her new home? And like I was saying, there aren't any other stables with an arena in this area. You'd be farther away from her if something did happen."

"I guess we'll have to hope the police figure this out." Harriet glanced at the time on her phone. "I'd better get Luke to school."

She walked down to the center of the barn where Becky and Major were now lodged. Luke was in Major's stall, and the big horse had his head pressed into Luke's chest. Becky nickered and hung her head over the stall door as Harriet approached and took a moment to scratch the horse's ears.

"Let's go," she called to Luke, and with a last pat for both horses, they left.

✂ --- ✂ --- ✂

The Loose Threads were seated around their customary table in the Steaming Cup when Harriet arrived. Beth pushed a mug of hot cocoa in front of her, and Connie handed her a small scone.

"So, are you saying someone tried to steal the horse that might or might not be yours last night?" Mavis asked her when she'd finished telling them about the break-in at the stable.

"That pretty well sums it up." She sipped her cocoa.

Lauren arrived, shrugging out of her jacket and putting the strap of her messenger bag over the back of her chair before heading for the counter.

"But not very many people know the horse is yours, so I think we can assume someone is continuing to attack Jade." Beth pointed out.

Carla was at the end of the table, quietly sipping her latte; she set her cup down.

"Unless it's Jade that has been doing the stuff to herself."

Robin pulled her legal pad and a pen from her purse.

"Continue," she said.

Carla's cheeks turned pink.

"I was just thinking. Jade is having money problems, and with two murders in the downtown area, what if she burned her own shop? Everyone would assume it was whoever killed the other two guys, right?"

Lauren, settled into her chair, took a bite of croissant and set it back down on her plate.

"She's got a point."

"I figured," Carla continued, "she probably has fire insurance on her shop, and if her horse is so expensive, it's probably insured, too."

"So, you think she tried to steal her own horse?" Harriet said.

Robin scribbled notes on her pad.

"Do we have any proof she actually left the country?" she asked without looking up.

Harriet sipped her cocoa thoughtfully.

"Other than the note she left me, no."

Mavis took her stitching from her bag and set it on the table.

"Didn't you say her lawyer was going to send you some papers about the horse?"

"Yes, but I haven't gotten anything yet. It's only been a few days."

Beth stirred her tea.

"Do you know who her attorney is?"

131

"Not a clue," Harriet answered. "And I think it's her parents' lawyer."

Robin made another note.

"Let me see if I can find out anything. If the lawyer is local, I should be able to figure out who it is."

"Are her parents working through a church program?" DeAnn asked no one in particular.

Carla wrapped her hands around her mug as if she needed to warm them.

"I could call all the local churches and see if anyone knows."

Connie patted her hand.

"That would be very helpful."

"What about the horse, in the meantime?" Robin asked.

Harriet explained about the enhanced security at the equestrian center and also about how Major, the retired police horse, had defended Becky.

Robin sat back in her chair.

"Sounds like security is covered. At whatever point the horse becomes yours officially, you need to get her insured. It might not be a bad idea to go talk to your insurance people, so they're prepared."

Connie wiped her mouth on her napkin.

"If I haven't told you yet, Valery's funeral is at two o'clock at the Catholic Church. Is everyone still planning on going?"

"I am," Harriet said.

Lauren glanced at her schedule on her phone.

"I'm in."

Robin and DeAnn did the same, and both agreed they'd be there.

Carla frowned. "I can't go. Wendy has a holiday party at the church playgroup at two."

Connie patted her hand.

"I'm sure that's fine. You and Wendy don't need to be going to a funeral for someone you don't even know."

Carla looked relieved.

Harriet stood and gathered her empty dishes.

"I better get home and get some things done before two, then."

Lauren swallowed the last of her latte and joined her.

"Me, too."

✂ --- ✂ --- ✂

Harriet shivered as she entered St. Alexander's Catholic Church beside her aunt. She had looked up *Ukrainian Catholic Church* on the internet to make sure basic black didn't violate any traditions (it didn't); and as a result, she was dressed in a modest black wool skirt with black tights and a coordinating silk blouse.

Lauren and Connie stepped through the carved double doors. They were similarly attired in black skirts. Lauren leaned forward and whispered to Harriet, "We look like chamber musicians."

"This is the warmest black dress outfit I have," Harriet whispered back.

Beth put her hand on Harriet's arm.

"Behave yourself," she said quietly and led them into the third row of pews from the back, sitting down next to Anthony De Marco. Harriet leaned forward to set her purse under her seat, and Lauren followed suit.

"Check out the young guy in the front row," Harriet said quietly.

Lauren raised her head up slightly and peered at the front of the church.

"Valery's son?"

"Looks just like Valery. He's a lot thinner, though."

The officiants entered, and the service began, eliminating any possibility of further conversation.

Harriet looked around as she listened to the Latin recitation of the Beatitudes. Two large men in black suits sat next to the slender man she assumed was Valery's son. That seemed to be the extent of Valery's family. There were several empty pews between them and a group of people Harriet assumed were the church's regular funeral attendees. Two of the women were customers of her quilting business, and she knew they were part of a group who were called on to fill pews when the church didn't think the dearly departed had enough family or friends to be seemly.

An hour and a half later, the last prayers were chanted, a litany was said, and then a prayer of dismissal. They were all invited to repair to a small reception hall in a stand-alone building behind the church.

"Are we done?" Lauren asked.

Harriet buttoned her black wool coat. "Since there wasn't any mention of a graveside service, I'm assuming he's being cremated. I'd like to go by the reception." She pulled an envelope from her purse. "Donations to the parish were suggested, and I thought I'd make one. I'd like to offer my condolences to the son, too."

Lauren sighed. "I should have known."

The two large men in dark suits flanked the younger man when Harriet, Lauren, Connie, and Beth entered the reception hall. Mavis and several more of the Loose Threads had come to the service but left immediately after due to family obligations.

Beth made a beeline for the coffee and the tastefully done tray of finger foods James had delivered. Harriet headed for the son.

"I'm so sorry for your loss," she said and held her hand out to the young man.

He took it. "Thank you. It was quite a shock."

The man to his left glared at him and stepped closer. Connie had joined the group, and craned her neck to make eye contact with the man.

"Are you family?" she asked with a smile and angled herself between the son and his guard.

"I'm Harriet Truman," Harriet said to the young man. "I'm one of the quilters that made quilts for the downtown shops.

"I'm Valery's son Oleksander. People call me Ole."

Lauren came up beside Harriet, standing close enough to the second 'guard' that he had to take a step back to avoid a scene if she took exception.

"I'm Lauren Sawyer, Harriet's friend. Do you live locally?"

"Not anymore," he said and looked away. "It's really awful. I came to town because my friend Danny passed away. His memorial service is the day after Christmas. I thought I'd spend Christmas with my dad..." He trailed off.

"You mean Daniel Muhler?" Harriet asked.

"You knew him?"

"Lauren and I both did. We weren't close friends, but my husband owns a local restaurant and has...had Daniel do his printing."

Ole's face turned red.

"It was such a shock. Everyone loved Danny."

"He was working so hard to stay healthy," Lauren said. "I'll bet he never imagined his life would be taken from him. It's sad."

Harriet's eyes widened, but she didn't say anything. She felt Connie brush against her back as her friend moved to keep herself between Harriet and Ole and the man in the dark suit she was blocking.

"That was how Danny and I met, you know," Ole said. "We were in an HIV support group. I still am, I guess, although it won't be the same without him. He had to drive to Seattle to find support. Foggy Point is too small for some things."

Connie's man put his hands on her upper arms and picked her up, turning and setting her down behind Harriet.

"We need to go," he said to Ole.

"Thank you for coming to my father's funeral. It really means a lot to me."

Harriet patted him on the back.

"If there's anything we can do for you while you're in town, let me know."

"Thank you," he said and let the men lead him away.

Aunt Beth joined them when Ole was out of the room.

"Annie's, anyone?"

"Why not?" Harriet said.

✂ --- ✂ --- ✂

Annie herself sat down with them after asking her barista to bring a pot of her special Christmas tea blend and five mugs.

"I'm guessing you ladies are here to talk about the funeral we all just attended. Do you mind if I sit in?"

"You're always welcome to sit with us," Beth said.

Annie leaned forward with her elbows on the table.

"That was a weird funeral. I mean, they followed their script, but it seems like someone at some point would get up and say something personal."

Connie accepted a cup of the spicy tea from the barista.

"I was thinking the same thing. It was very impersonal. And who were the two men in suits. Are they supposed to be relatives?"

Harriet sipped her tea.

"James was told there were Ukrainian relatives who had to leave town before Christmas. They seem like the only possibilities."

Annie set her mug down.

"If they were related, they must have been from the other side of his family. I mean, they must have been at least a foot taller than Valery."

"They seemed more like bodyguards than relatives, if you ask me," Harriet commented.

Annie gestured to her worker, and a moment later, a tray of biscotti was delivered. She took one and passed the tray to Harriet.

"I saw you talking to the son. Did he have anything interesting to say?"

Harriet plucked a tea biscuit from the tray and passed the tray on.

"He said he no longer lives in the area, and he actually was in town for Daniel Muhler's funeral, which is planned for after the holidays. He said they met at an HIV support group in Seattle."

"Did he know if Daniel had any enemies?" Beth asked.

Harriet shook her head.

"I didn't get to ask. One of the thugs-in-a-suit interrupted and took Ole away before I could ask."

Annie dipped her biscotti in her tea and took a bite.

"I feel sorry for the boy. I know he wasn't very close with his father after he came out, but after his sister died, Valery was all he had left. Valery told me once that his wife had cut off contact after she went back to Ukraine. He said they'd never divorced, but from what he heard from friends, she's moved on."

Harriet sat back in her chair.

"What are you thinking?" Lauren asked her.

"I'm thinking Valery's wife might have decided to end their relationship in a more permanent way. Maybe the two thugs are her family, sent here to take care of Valery and make sure Ole didn't raise any suspicions at the funeral."

Lauren sipped her tea thoughtfully.

"I wonder if she benefits financially. Be nice to know if she had an interest in the gallery. And before anyone asks, given the current political climate, I'm not going to hack anything remotely near Russia."

"Can't we check his business license at the courthouse?" Connie asked.

"Good thought," Beth agreed.

Lauren blew across the top of her steaming tea.

"I'm not sure it would do her any good, given what we know about business in Foggy Point lately."

Harriet sat up straight.

"Let's think about that. Valery might not have many sales of his European artwork in Foggy Point, but maybe his inventory is worth more if she took it back to Ukraine."

Lauren pulled out her tablet and made a note. "That I can look up."

Harriet finished her cup of tea.

"I better get going. Luke still has a little shopping to do."

Beth reached out and stopped her. "Have you noticed that gray car parked on your street again?"

"No, why?"

"I'm pretty sure it was in the church parking lot when we came in."

"Did you get the license number?" Lauren asked.

Beth hung her head.

"I was focused on getting into the funeral. I'm sorry."

"We don't know if it was the same car—a lot of people have gray sedans —so it doesn't matter if you got the license or not," Harriet reassured her.

Chapter 23

Harriet had just finished making a sandwich for Luke when he came home from school. His cheeks were rosy from the cold and he smiled when he saw Harriet set the sandwich at his normal place at the table.

"Can we go to the barn?" he asked around a bite of his sandwich.

Harriet sat down opposite him.

"I have an alternative. We both have a little more shopping to do, and it turns out the shops are open late every night until Christmas." She glanced at the kitchen clock. "I think we have just enough time to get our shopping done after you've eaten, and then tomorrow you'll be available whenever works best for the horses."

Luke set his sandwich down. Harriet could see he was disappointed.

"I'm worried about Major. He's really sensitive, you know?"

"Why don't you call Emily or Marcia and ask how he's doing? If he's upset, I'll take you out tonight. If he's okay, you can wait until tomorrow."

He picked up his sandwich.

"That works," he said, and took a big bite. Both dogs sat at his feet begging.

"I'll take these two clowns out while you finish," she said and picked up a dog in each arm.

✂ --- ✂ --- ✂

Luke stopped in the middle of a toy aisle in Walmart and turned slowly around.

"How am I supposed to figure out what to buy?"

Harriet pulled a folded piece of paper from her back jeans pocket.

"Lucky for you, while you were at school, I did my homework. I looked up the most popular Christmas gifts in several age ranges." She held the list out to him.

"Whew," he said. "This'll help a lot." He took the list from her and scanned it. He was quiet for a moment.

"What do you think?" she asked.

"I'm kind of torn. It would be good for him to get the electrical circuits kit because educational stuff would help him. I'm just not sure if he would be interested enough to use it, or if anyone would help him with it." He looked from the paper to Harriet. "I don't want to sound all judgmental now that I live in a better place, but Ta'Shawn's mom isn't the sharpest knife in the drawer."

Harriet laughed.

"It's not judgmental if it's true. You're probably right—if you don't know your brother's interests or the amount of help he'll get, it's probably safer to give him a toy or game this first time."

"I was thinking maybe I could get him a Razor scooter. It's twenty-eight dollars."

"That sounds good. I'll get a few smaller things for any younger siblings. If there aren't any living with her, we can donate the stuff to the church toy drive."

They agreed to meet in fifteen minutes at check stand seven, and each set off to their target aisles.

✂ --- ✂ --- ✂

Harriet was waiting at the designated checkout with a shopping cart half-full of toys, pet gifts, wrapping paper, ribbon, cellophane tape, and a couple of decorations that were too cute to pass up. Luke walked up carrying the boxed scooter.

"Should I go get wrapping paper for this?"

"No, I've got enough for you, me, James, both dogs, and Fred, should they all decide to buy us gifts."

He laughed. "I wouldn't count on them for anything."

"You're right. Here, you go first, since you only have one thing."

✂ --- ✂ --- ✂

Harriet parked in front of the Outdoor Store, two doors down from Millie's yarn store. She scanned the parked cars up and down the block. There were three gray sedans; any of them could have been Aunt Beth's suspicious car. Even if one of them was the same car her aunt had seen, she wasn't sure what she was supposed to do about it. Perhaps call the police and tell them she'd seen the same gray car three times? She could imagine Officer Nguyen hanging up on her.

Luke still needed to buy yarn for Aunt Beth, and Harriet decided she would pick up a couple of skeins for James's mother. She'd just taken up knitting and was pretty anxious to build her skills to the point she could make herself a shawl.

A bell dangling from the inside doorknob jingled as they came in. Harriet looked to the checkout counter on her left but didn't see Millie or her employee, William.

"Hello?" she called out. Luke started to go past her toward the back of the store. She held her hand out, stopping him. "Did you hear that?"

He shook his head.

"Hello?" she called again and moved quietly to her right. An L-shaped yarn case defined one side of the front area of the store. Behind it were a series of small rooms with closed doors. A storeroom shared a wall with Millie's office, with stairs to the basement and then a restroom taking up the rest of the wall.

Harriet entered the office. The chair behind the desk was tipped over, and papers were scattered around the floor.

"Millie?"

Luke came up beside her.

"I heard it that time. Sounds muffled. Like someone is trying to talk through a gag or something."

Harriet backed out of the office and opened the door to the basement.

"Wait here," she told Luke and started slowly down the stairs. She stopped to listen, and Luke bumped into her back. "I told you to wait up there," she whispered, glancing up at the landing.

Luke's eyes were wide, but he had a determined look on his face.

"If you're going down, I'm going down."

"Millie?" Harriet descended two more steps.

The muffled response was louder here. This time, it sounded like Millie saying . "Down here."

Harriet hurried down the last few steps, Luke on her heels. The scene they stumbled into was terrifying.

Millie sat in a chair facing the foot of the stairs, her hands and feet bound tightly, shiny gray duct tape wrapped several times around her head, covering her mouth. William lay motionless on the dirt floor a few feet to her right; blood seeped from a nasty indentation that started on his forehead and continued into his gray hair. More blood pooled around his head.

Harriet started toward William.

"Take another step, and it will be your last," an electronically altered voice said.

She froze.

"Now, turn around," the voice said. "Slowly."

She did as she was told and sucked in a breath as she saw a tall figure clad in black, left arm pointing a nasty-looking gun at Luke, a smartphone held in the right hand. A black balaclava pulled over the face and black gloves on the hands made it impossible to tell if the figure was a male or a tall female.

The figure poked Luke in the side with the gun, indicating he should move to a dusty card table on Millie's left that had three more chairs pulled up to it.

"Bring two chairs." The distorted voice came through the phone.

Luke obeyed, pulling two chairs over and setting them in line with Millie's.

"Apart," the figure said, indicating he should space the chairs a few feet from each other.

When Luke had the chairs positioned to the satisfaction of their captor, he was handed several zip ties. The figure pointed the gun at Harriet.

"Sit." She did as instructed. "Restrain her," the distorted voice ordered Luke.

When that was finished, the figure inspected Luke's work to be sure Harriet was tied tightly, hand and foot. Luke was then instructed to sit in the third chair and was similarly bound.

With everyone secured, the dark figure slid the gun into their waistband and picked up a roll of duct tape from a workbench. He quickly wrapped several layers of tape around their mouths.

It felt like an hour had passed by the time the figure stood up and, with barely a glance at William, went up the stairs. Harriet realized it had more likely been less than five minutes.

They heard the door at the top of the stairs close, and the click of a lock.

Harriet looked from Millie to Luke. He was working his jaw up and down. She began doing the same, and within a few minutes, they both had slipped the lower part of their mouths free.

"Are you okay?" Harriet asked Luke.

He sighed. "That gun was scary."

She noticed that being bound up didn't seem to panic him nearly as much as it did her. She wondered if binding was a form of babysitting that had been used on him in the past.

She watched as he raised his hands above his head, elbows out, and quickly brought his arms down and toward his belly. The zip-ties broke apart.

"How did you learn to do that?"

His face turned red.

"On the internet. It's come in handy a few times. It takes a few tries to get the snapping motion just right. And it does hurt a little, but you can do it."

Luke was busy unraveling the bulky cord bracelet he wore on his left wrist.

"It's paracord," he explained.

She watched as he took the now long, single cord and slipped it under the zip-tie binding his ankles. He began sawing it back and forth.

"Are you okay?" she asked Millie as she picked the tape off her face with her still-bound hands.

"I'm fine," the older woman replied when she'd gotten the tape away from the bottom of her mouth. "But, William…" Tears ran down her cheeks.

Harriet stood and hopped over to Millie's chair, unwinding the tape from around Millie's head. It was pretty clear William was beyond anything either of them could do for him.

Harriet slid her phone from her pocket, but as she'd suspected, there was no signal in the dank basement.

"Who did this to you?"

"I don't know," Millie sobbed. Harriet rubbed her back. "Will and I were in my office going over inventory lists. This person burst in and grabbed Will around the neck, pointing the gun at him. He told me to head for the basement, or he would shoot us both right there."

"You say he," Harriet said. "Did he use the voice distorter the whole time or did you hear his real voice."

Millie pressed her lips together.

"I assumed it was a man. Why would a woman do this to us?"

Harriet imagined there could be an angry wife, mother, sister, or other female person related to William's victim who might bear a grudge.

"We can't assume anything. Did you notice anything about the person that might help us figure out who it is?"

Millie thought.

"He…I mean, they…walked funny. Like he was wearing a brace on one leg."

With a grunt, Luke pulled the paracord through the last bit of the weakened zip-tie.

141

"I'll go find scissors," he said and headed for the stairs.

"He locked the door on his way out," Millie reminded him.

He reached the top of the stairs and, raising his leg, kicked the door open.

"Call nine-one-one while you're up there," Harriet called after him, and she heard him speaking a moment later. He reappeared with a large pair of shears and cut the ties from her wrists and ankles. Harriet took the shears and did the same for Millie.

"Probably best not to touch William," she cautioned as Millie stepped toward him.

"Shouldn't we try CPR?"

Harriet stepped over and guided her away.

"I've been watching him, and his chest hasn't moved. Besides, that dent in his head is pretty deep. I don't think you survive that sort of blow." She led Millie to the chair farthest from William as Luke hurried down the stairs and came up behind them.

"Is he really dead?" he whispered.

"I'm afraid so," she whispered back.

The sound of approaching sirens forestalled their conversation. They heard the jangle of bells as police officers entered the shop.

"Down here," Harriet called.

Officer Nguyen let a parade of police officers, firemen, and paramedics down the stairs.

"Luke and I came here to Christmas shop," she said when she saw him.

He shook his head and walked past her and over to William. Detective Morse came down at the end of the initial rush. She stopped by Harriet.

"What's going on?"

"Luke and I came in to shop and walked in on this." She swept her arm in front of her from Millie to William. "He was on the floor, as you see him. Millie was tied in a chair at the bottom of the stairs, and someone all in black was in the shadows. I say 'someone' because they wore a balaclava over their face and gloves. They were tall and slender and walked with a limp. They also carried a big black gun. I'm not sure why William has a head wound instead of a gunshot."

Millie had been sitting in her chair, hands covering her face; but when Harriet finished, she looked up.

"I can tell you that. The robber came in when William and I were in the office. He used the gun to force us downstairs. William went for the gun when we got down here, and they struggled around until the robber grabbed a pipe wrench from the workbench and hit him in the head."

Morse looked at William's body, surrounded by paramedics standing around with nothing to do. She tilted her head at Luke, now sitting next to Millie.

"Why don't you take him and meet me back at the station. Millie, too, if you don't mind."

Harriet put her hand on Millie's back. "Can you walk upstairs?"

"Yes, just give me a minute," Millie replied. "Can we call my daughter?"

"Sure, you can call her from the car," Harriet said, then followed the shopkeeper up the stairs.

Chapter 24

arriet, Luke, and Millie sat in an interview room at the Foggy Point Police Department as James, followed by Robin, Aunt Beth, Jorge and Mavis and, finally, Millie's daughter, Amanda.

The desk sergeant moved Harriet and Luke to a conference room as their guests accumulated. Millie stayed in the interview room with Amanda.

Jorge arrived carrying two white bags. He gave one to the desk sergeant and took the other to the conference room.

"I figured after this trauma, you might need some sugar," he said. Harriet reached for the bag, but Jorge pulled it back and handed it to Luke.

"What?" she complained.

Luke looked at her and grinned.

"I'll share," he said. He pulled a handful of cookies out and then passed her the bag.

The door opened, and Morse came in. She took the bag from Harriet and helped herself to the cookies. James stood behind Harriet, his hands on her shoulders.

"Keep the cookies coming, and you all can stay—if you keep quiet," Morse said.

Beth raised her hand; Morse nodded.

"Do you have any tea?"

The detective sighed. She opened the door and spoke to someone they couldn't see. Moments later, a non-uniformed worker brought in a tray with tea, mugs, and a carafe of hot water.

Morse questioned Luke at one end of the large table while Beth distributed steaming mugs of tea. Harriet watched as Luke described the series of events and answered Morse's questions. He didn't seem to be as rattled as she was by what had happened, and she wasn't sure if he was in denial or if his life before coming to her and James involved so much violence this was ordinary for him. She made a mental note to talk to James about it. She made eye contact with him and was pretty sure he was thinking the same thing.

"If you're finished," James said, addressing Morse when she closed her notebook and stood, "can I take Luke home?" He turned to Harriet. "Beth and Jorge will bring you home, if that's okay."

Clearly, they'd all talked about this beforehand

"Sounds good," she told him. "You guys can feed the dogs, too."

James smiled at her.

"Lauren is already at our house with the dogs. And Connie."

Harriet shook her head.

"I guess that's that, then. I'll see you two at home."

She was pretty sure James was giving Luke a chance to talk about what had happened without an audience. Just having him in the same room had calmed her nerves. Not for the first time, she thought about how much better her life worked with James in it.

Morse waited until they'd gone before starting to question Harriet. Harriet's basic account matched Luke's.

"There was something odd about the attacker," she said. "I can't put my finger on it. Something about the limp. And maybe the proportions of their body."

Morse held her pen over her paper but didn't write.

"Do you think they had a disease? Parkinson's? Something like that?"

Harriet thought for a moment.

"It was more like there was something wrong with their hips, so they walked with a sort of rocking motion."

Morse made a note.

"Can I ask a question?" Beth interrupted.

The detective smiled and shook her head. "Could I stop you?"

Beth ignored the comment and continued.

"Did you know Millie's employee William was a convicted killer? And further, we think our local blackmailer was blackmailing Millie because of William."

"Do I want to know how you know that?" Morse asked.

Harriet replied as her aunt was thinking of how to answer.

"This is a small town, and one of us was on jury duty at William's trial. The blackmailing is a guess on our part. We've heard and seen a few things in our local shops that makes us think someone is harassing several of our local shopkeepers."

Morse picked up her pen again.

"Care to tell me who?"

"Millie, obviously," Beth said.

"Sunny," Mavis said, speaking for the first time.

"We think Jade," Robin told her.

"There could be more," Jorge said. "These are only the people the ladies have observed."

Morse made a note and set her pen down.

"I'll definitely check this out. Anything else?"

Harriet thought.

"For what it's worth, there were two large, mean-looking guys at Valery's funeral. They seemed like bodyguards or something, and they were very protective of Valery's son. I guess you probably know that. I assume some of the mourners were your people."

"Was one of them your captor?" Morse asked, ignoring Harriet's last comment.

"No, they were a lot heavier. Our person was thin. Which was why I thought it could be a woman."

"Could you tell from the voice?"

Harriet shook her head.

"With that voice-distortion program they used, it was impossible to tell. And they didn't say enough to pick out any sort of speech pattern."

Morse scanned her notes.

"Other than tying you up, the person made no attempt to harm you or Luke or Millie?"

"No. And William was already on the floor when Luke and I joined the party."

Morse closed her notebook and put it back in her pocket.

"If you think of anything else, let me know." She looked around the room. "Thanks for the cookies. Don't think you're always going to be able to take over my interrogation room. Cookies or not." She took another one from the bag. "You caught me at a weak moment." She turned to go out the door.

"Merry Christmas, Detective," Jorge said to her back.

She raised her hand in a wave and left the room.

✂ --- ✂ --- ✂

Robin left the group in the police department parking lot.

"Don't talk to these people again without me being there. I know Morse knows you didn't do this, but you were at William's crime scene, and you and Lauren found Daniel, and you and Luke found Valery, admittedly from afar, but still. Given no other leads, someone here…" She gestured back toward the police department. "…is going to decide you're a common denominator they can't ignore."

Beth started to protest, but Robin held her hand up.

"We know Harriet didn't have anything to do with these deaths or with the fire at Jade's, but again, she's been first at the scene in every case. They can't ignore that."

"Oh, great," Harriet muttered.

Beth put her arm around Harriet's shoulders. "We'll be sure to call you, don't worry," she assured Robin.

Jorge shivered and took keys from his pocket.

"Let's get out of here."

✂ --- ✂ --- ✂

James was stirring a pot of chili at the stove, Luke beside him at the counter grating a block of cheddar cheese into a bowl while Lauren placed napkins and silverware around the dining room table. Harriet came up behind James and wrapped her arms around him, resting her chin on his shoulder.

"When did you whip this all up?"

He set his spoon down and turned in her arms, hugging her.

"I'm sorry you and Luke had to go through what you did today. And to answer your question, I put chili, stew, and a few other easy meals in the chest freezer here. You never know when you're going to need a quick meal. Especially around the holidays."

"I wondered what those blue containers were," she said.

Beth dug around in the cupboard and came out with deep soup bowls while Jorge popped a pan of cornbread he'd taken from the refrigerator in the oven.

"Did you whip that up from scratch?" Harriet asked Jorge. "And by the way, when did you have time to do that?"

He laughed. "How else do you make cornbread? And it only takes a couple minutes. I did it while you were upstairs freshening up."

Harriet shook her head.

"Clearly, you all don't need me taking up space in my kitchen. I'll be in the dining room with Lauren."

147

Mavis and Beth followed her. Lauren had her tablet on the table in front of her.

"DeAnn just sent me a message. She said she tracked down the church program Jade's parents are working with and verified they *are* out of country but there's no information on whether Jade has joined them. For what it's worth, the program people sent a message asking if she's there, but with the holidays, they don't expect to get an answer until next week."

Harriet sat down beside her and closed her eyes, rubbing her hands over them.

"I wish I had recognized something about the person who killed William today. Whoever it was, was built oddly. They were tall and slender, but somehow they weren't built like most taller people, who tend to be all arms and legs. I don't know. I can't explain it."

Lauren opened a notepad app on her tablet. She typed the name of each of the people who had been killed in a column, made a line and then added the names of the people they thought were being blackmailed, and then Jade's name.

Opposite William's name she typed *convicted of manslaughter*. Beside Daniel's she wrote *AIDS*.

"What do we know about Valery?"

Beth opened Harriet's hutch and took out a cut-crystal set of salt and pepper shakers and placed them in the center of the table before sitting down.

"Didn't the jeweler say Valery told him he was being blackmailed?"

Lauren put that opposite Valery's name.

"He did," she said as she typed.

Next to Daniel's name, she wrote *knew Valery's son — AIDS group*.

Beside *Jade*, she put *sold drugs*.

Harriet looked over Lauren's shoulder, reading what she typed.

"Remember how I told you the manager at the stables was telling me that Valery sold his horses when his daughter died?"

Lauren sat back in her chair.

"Yeah, vaguely."

"She also said that Valery's wife had left him with the kids and gone back to the old country. What if she came back and was mad at him because their daughter died kayaking and their son got AIDS. That would give her a reason to kill Val and possibly Daniel, if she thought he had something to do with her son's disease."

Mavis absently toyed with the edge of her napkin.

"That leaves a lot unexplained. What about William? And why blackmail the other shopkeepers?"

Harriet sighed.

"I didn't say it was a perfect theory."

"Do we know who William killed?" Beth asked.

Lauren started tapping on her pad.

"We don't yet. Do we know his last name?"

"Crowe," Beth answered. "Millie introduced him when Mavis and I went there to talk about the shop quilt."

Lauren added that to her search.

"Nothing immediate comes up. There are a lot of people of note named William Crowe, it turns out. Including a former Chairman of the Joint Chiefs of Staff. I'll have to dig deeper, and that will be more easily done from my computer."

Harriet thought for a moment.

"What do we know about the death of Valery's daughter?"

Beth gestured toward Lauren.

"Look it up on your tablet. There was something about a wrongful-death suit."

Lauren tapped on her screen and flipped through a rapid succession of screens before stopping and reading one.

"Well, well, well," she said. "This is interesting. Anyone want to guess who the wrongful-death suit is against?"

"I'm going to make a wild guess here," Harriet said. "His daughter was killed in a kayaking accident. Could she have purchased the kayak at the Foggy Point Outdoor Store?"

Lauren turned her pad around so the others could see the screen.

"We have a winner. Vern was exonerated, but this could explain why he's being blackmailed, if he is."

The conversation stopped while Luke and James came into the dining room with bowls of grated cheese, sour cream, and chopped green onions. Mavis arranged her napkin on her lap.

"Do we think Vern is in danger?"

Lauren slipped her tablet into her messenger bag.

"As I said, the lawsuit *could* explain it, but we don't even know if Vern *is* being blackmailed, for one thing. For another, if he was exonerated at trial and the evidence clearly showed the kayak he sold them wasn't faulty, that may have satisfied the family."

Beth frowned. "Is anyone ever satisfied when their child has died?"

"Do we know what Mrs. Melnyk's full name is?" Harriet asked.

Lauren held her hand up.

"Before you ask me to look anything else up. I don't know her full name, but even if I did, I can't tell you if she's in Foggy Point, unless she's committed a crime or done anything else to get herself in the paper or on social media. The airlines aren't going to tell me or anyone else without a badge and a warrant whether she flew on a plane, even if we had any idea when she might have come, not to mention which airline she might have come on. And that wouldn't even cover the possibility that she might have come by cruise ship."

Beth cleared her throat.

"We haven't even considered how Sunny might fit into all this. It's pretty clear she's being blackmailed about something."

Jorge brought a basket of warm cornbread and a bowl of whipped honey into the dining room and set them on the table.

"You don't know for sure the blackmail and the murders are connected, do you?" he asked.

Harriet got up and went to the kitchen, returning with a stack of bread plates and the butter dish.

"We connect the blackmail and murders because we don't believe in coincidence."

Jorge went to stand in the doorway.

"But you can't rule out the possibility Daniel's death was a hate crime, Valery's was suicide, and William's was revenge for his light sentence for his manslaughter conviction. A horse thief tried to steal Jade's horse—arguably the most valuable animal lodged at the stable—and the blackmail is an anti-crime vigilante group."

Beth took some of the plates from Harriet and helped distribute them around the table.

"I'm with Harriet. That's a lot of coincidence." She looked at Jorge with an affectionate smile. "But, you're right, it's possible."

James handed Jorge two bowls of chili and returned to the kitchen for more. He carried them to the table, setting one in front of Beth and Mavis. Mavis sprinkled grated cheese on hers.

"This looks wonderful. Just the thing on a cold night like tonight."

Luke sat down beside Harriet when the food had been distributed.

"I've never had chili that didn't come from a can."

Jorge laughed.

"Prepare to be amazed."

✂ --- ✂ --- ✂

"May I be excused?" Luke asked when he'd finished his second bowl of chili. "I need to call Emily and find out what time we should come to the barn."

Harriet wiped her mouth on her napkin and set it on the table.

"Let me know when you find out. I need to drive over to the yarn store in Port Townsend, since I wasn't able to get the yarn I'd planned on getting for James's mom. I checked when we got home, and tomorrow being Christmas Eve, she's only open until one o'clock."

Luke looked at her expectantly.

"Oh, yes, you're excused."

"He's sure polite," Mavis commented when he was out of earshot.

"He's new to family life," Beth said. "Give him some time, and he'll be like any other teenager."

"I hope not," Harriet said. "I'm liking this version."

Jorge stood up, and James started to.

"You sit and enjoy the ladies," Jorge ordered. "You did most of the meal prep. I'll handle cleanup."

Chapter 25

Luke was sitting at the kitchen table eating his second bowl of oatmeal when Harriet came downstairs the next morning. The dogs were at his feet in their normal begging positions, the cat curled in his lap.

Harriet refilled the water kettle and set it on the stove to boil.

"Since I'm going to the yarn store in Port Townsend I could get that yarn for Aunt Beth for you, if you want."

"She'll know I didn't pick it out for her. Should I forget about the stable and go with you?" His face lost all expression while he waited for her answer.

"Aunt Beth will know that you tried to shop at Millie's, but due to extenuating circumstances, you weren't able to get her present. She'll understand. And she knows you need to go check on Major."

A grin lit up his face.

"You guys are the best."

He gave the dogs each a crust from his toast and scooped a little dab of butter from the edge of his plate onto his finger for Fred to lick. When they were all finished, he cleared his dishes and headed for the stairs.

"I'll be ready in a flash."

"Don't be too flashy—I've got to eat something before we go. Don't worry, I'll be quick about it."

✂ --- ✂ --- ✂

Harriet was thankful her drive to Bazaar Girls Yarn Shop in Port Townsend was uneventful. She found a pale-blue fingering yarn for Kathy, James's mother; it would match her eyes and make a lovely shawl. She bought a

152

pattern the shopkeeper assured would be good for a beginner. She chose a hand-spun, hand-dyed, Blue-faced Leicester wool for her aunt. She was pretty sure it was something Beth didn't already have in her stash.

James had just gotten home when she returned.

"Oh, good," he said. "I was afraid you'd pick up Luke on your way home. Since the restaurant is closed for the rest of the day, I thought I'd go out to the stable with you then tag along when you drop off the presents at Luke's...I'm not sure what to call his father's baby momma and her children."

Harriet slipped her arms around his waist.

"I'd call them his past. It's sweet that he wants to share his newfound prosperity with his little brother. I hope the kid appreciates it."

"I can't help resenting the mother for not taking Luke when she took his brother."

"So, you're thinking if you go and see that it's horrible, you'll feel better about that?"

He pulled her to him and buried his face in her hair.

"That sounds terrible, doesn't it?"

Harriet smiled.

"No, it just sounds like you care a lot about Luke."

She guided him over to the kitchen peninsula and a plate of tea sweets he'd likely set there when he came in. She took a tartlet and popped it into her mouth.

"Want one?" she asked as she chewed.

James stepped back.

"If I never see a tea cake or sandwich again, at least until next Christmas, it'll be too soon."

Harriet picked up a glazed miniature sausage roll.

"They're so good, though."

"How soon are we going to the stable?"

Harriet glanced at the kitchen clock.

"How's thirty minutes?"

"Perfect." He leaned in for a kiss. "Like you."

✂ --- ✂ --- ✂

Marcia was alone in the barn, sweeping and picking up debris left from people grooming their horses. She leaned her broom against a stall as they walked up to her.

"If you're looking for Luke, he's in the arena with Emily. Usually when people are in the therapy program, we spend a few sessions having them groom the horse, walk the horse on a lead, feed the horse, and generally

153

get used to being around them. Depending on how nervous they are, this is a longer or shorter process. We take things slow with the riding process, too. Luke and Major bonded so quickly, when he asked if he could start riding, I said okay. I hope that's all right with you."

"That's great," Harriet said. "How's he doing?"

Marcia smiled.

"Like a duck to water is the appropriate expression, I think. Go see for yourself."

James grabbed Harriet's hand as she started to head for the arena.

"How have things been going here?" he asked Marcia. "Security-wise."

She reclaimed her broom and leaned on it.

"No one who shouldn't be here has been near Becky. The cameras in the barn haven't shown anything. We put a camera out at the end of the driveway to see if anyone comes in but doesn't drive all the way to the barn. The security company suggested we do that in case someone parks and then comes in on foot."

"Has it shown anything?" Harriet asked.

"Yes, and no. No one has driven in that doesn't belong, but there's a gray BMW sedan that drives by more often than seems normal. Whatever normal is."

Harriet stiffened.

"Can you see who's driving?"

Marci began sweeping.

"Tinted windows. The security people don't think it's significant, but if you live out here, you know. No one who doesn't live on this road drives by that often. And I recognize all the neighbor's rigs."

Harriet glanced down the aisle.

"How's Becky doing?"

"You can go see for yourself. She's none the worse for the wear, and she's liking her improved diet."

James led the way to Becky's stall, pulling a bag with two carrots from his coat pocket. She whinnied and came to the front of her stall, hanging her head over the half-door.

"Okay, you can take it from here," he said and handed the carrots to Harriet.

"It's easy, just watch how I hold the carrot. She's going to bite it in half when you first give it to her. Hold the second half flat in your hand so she can use her lips to get it into her mouth." She demonstrated with the first carrot and handed the second carrot to James."

"Here goes nothing," he muttered.

Becky chomped the carrot loudly, and James smiled when her lips tickled his palm picking up the second half. Harriet patted him on the back.

"See, that wasn't so hard. We'll make a cowboy out of you yet."

"I think I might be one of those people who has to hang around the horse a few times before I try riding."

She put her arm around him and gave him a hug.

"But, see, you're talking about *when* you ride, not *if* you try it. I'll take that as a good sign."

"Yeah, well, we'll see. This might be a Harriet and Luke thing, not a James and Harriet and Luke thing."

"Let's not make any decisions about that yet. You never know."

When they reached the arena, Harriet stepped up on aluminum bleacher seats at the side of the ring and sat down. James slid onto the cold seat beside her. Luke and Emily were riding side-by-side on the far side of the ring.

Luke caught sight of them and steered Major across the arena, stopping in front of them.

"Hi," he said. "I hope it's okay I'm riding."

"Of course it is," Harriet assured him. "If you're comfortable with it, we're comfortable. Just be sure you listen to Marcia and Emily. He's a big horse, and you need to pay attention to the safety rules."

"Don't worry. I am."

Emily rode up behind him on a much smaller black horse.

"I'm keeping an eye on him. He's learning really fast."

"Just because he learns quick, he still needs to be told everything. Don't assume he knows anything."

Luke blushed at this.

"She's telling me everything, believe me."

"Okay, take another few turns around the arena so we can see how you're doing, and then we need to go deliver presents," she told him.

She watched him ride off, and when he was out of earshot, James leaned over and bumped her with his shoulder.

"So, how's he really doing?"

Harriet answered without taking her eyes off Luke.

"He looks good. He's holding his hands nice and low, and he's not putting too much pressure on Major's mouth. His balance seems good."

"I don't know anything about riding, but he's so athletic, I suspect he could pick up any sport and do it well," James said proudly.

Harriet laughed.

"I'm sure it's all because you feed him so well."

"I wasn't going to brag, but he does look better since I've been feeding him." He tried to keep a straight face, but he, too, started laughing.

Luke and Major came around the ring again, followed by Emily.

"Are you guys laughing at me?"

Harriet reached out and patted Major's thick neck.

"No, you're looking very good. James was just saying your riding skill was due to his excellent cooking."

Luke smiled. "I'm sure it helped."

Emily looked confused.

"James has a restaurant on Smuggler's Cove," Luke explained. "He's a really good cook."

The girl's eyes widened.

"We went there for my mom's birthday. It was…" She struggled to find the right word.

"I hope *fabulous* is the word you're looking for," James said.

Her face burned red.

"It was beyond fabulous. My mom said it was the best birthday dinner she'd ever had."

James smiled. "Now you're going to have *me* blushing."

Harriet stood up.

"Okay, we better end this love fest and get moving. I'm going to check on Becky again while you put Major away."

✂ --- ✂ --- ✂

James stood beside Harriet in front of Becky's stall.

"I'm glad Luke is enjoying this horse stuff so much." He glanced up at the newly installed security camera across the aisle. "But I have to say, I'm really nervous about him coming out here while someone is trying to steal a horse that may or may not even belong to us, not to mention may be connected to the murders downtown."

Becky nuzzled Harriet's chest, and she rubbed the mare's nose.

"If it would make you feel better, I can come with him."

James smiled and stepped behind her, wrapping his arms around her waist.

"I know you've taken care of yourself most of your life, but these are dangerous people. I don't know why they want Becky, but if they are the same people who killed Daniel and William and Valery, they won't let you and Luke stand in their way.

"That gray sedan you told me about, the one that keeps appearing where you are, just might prove they aren't done yet. I know you like Detective Morse, but she and the FPPD aren't making any headway on any of these crimes, as far as I can see."

"So, what are you saying?"

156

James stepped back and ran his hands through his hair.

"I don't know. Luke is really starting to blossom since he's been coming here. I don't want to take that away from him, but I can't come out here with you as often as he wants to be here; and besides, I'm sure he doesn't want us hanging around him as he tries to woo Emily."

Luke led Major into the barn and cross-tied him in the open area just beyond Becky's stall.

"You guys look serious," he said as he lifted off the saddle and carried it past them to the tack room. "Something going on?" he asked on his return trip.

Harriet picked up a brush and started grooming the big horse.

"James is worried about the gray car. We've seen it on our street a few times."

"It's probably nothing," James said. "I'm just a little paranoid with everything that's been going on in town."

Luke patted Major's neck.

"I can take care of myself. Besides, this one makes a good guard dog."

James blew out a breath.

"I hope it won't come to that."

Chapter 26

It turned out Luke's half-brother lived in a complex of newly renovated low-cost housing units. Luke looked around as James parked the car.

"Wow, Arinda's come up in the world."

Harriet got out and handed Luke the bag with the wrapped scooter in it; she and James carried the other packages.

"According to your social worker, Arinda lives in unit Twelve-D."

They located the appropriate door on the second floor of the third building. Luke knocked, and when no one answered, he knocked again. Arinda Washington finally answered, a baby on her hip and a shy toddler hiding behind her leg.

"Oh, it's you." She blew a strand of over-bleached blond hair from her face. "I told your social worker I still don't have room for you, so if that's what you're here for, forget it."

Luke's face burned red. He stood in the open doorway, unsure what to do.

Harriet stepped past him and held her hand out.

"I'm Harriet Truman, and this is my husband James. We're Luke's parents now."

Harriet could almost see the wheels spinning in Arinda's head. Now that the woman had established they weren't asking her to take Luke, she was pretty sure Arinda was trying to figure out what she might get out of their visit.

"Luke wanted to bring a Christmas present to his brother."

Arinda led them into a small living room. She set the baby down in a worn portable crib and scooped a mass of celebrity gossip magazines off the sofa and into a pile on the floor.

158

"Ta'Shawn," she screeched. "Luke's here."

Harriet looked around the apartment while they waited for Luke's brother to appear. None of them made a move to sit down on the stained and lumpy sofa. The carpet still looked new, although it was accumulating stains, but overall it appeared Arinda was attempting to keep the place clean.

After a second summons from Arinda, Ta'Shawn appeared in the hallway. A cheap set of earphones hung around his neck. His eyes got big when he saw Luke.

"Luke?"

"Hey, little bro," Luke said with a grin. He held out his arms and after a brief hesitation, Ta'Shawn ran into them.

"Hey, I've missed you," Luke said. "Are you okay?"

Ta'Shawn looked at Arinda, but she turned her back and went out on a small balcony to smoke.

"Things are a little better since we got into this apartment. It came with strings. To keep living here, you have to be working a program so you can get a job. Mom doesn't like that part. She got pregnant again, so she gets more time. She has to keep taking classes, but then she gets a year after the new baby is born before she has to get a job."

"Who's the dad?"

Ta'Shawn shrugged.

"Otherwise, are things okay? Are you getting enough to eat?"

"Yeah, we get SNAP and boxes of stuff from some food place. It's been a little tight since Grandpa disappeared.

Luke looked confused.

"What grandpa?"

"He's not really our grandpa,"

"I know—your grandfathers are in jail."

"I guess Joe lived with Mom's mom when she was little. He lives in the homeless camp, but he'd bring us food and diapers for the baby. I think he got some sort of check for something. Anyway, he hasn't been around. He went to get us a Christmas tree and never came back." Tears filled the boy's eyes.

Luke rubbed his brother's back.

"I'm really sorry," he said. "Hey, I brought you a present." He handed Ta'Shawn his Christmas present.

"Can I open it now?"

Luke looked to Harriet. "You probably should ask Arinda."

Ta'Shawn went out to the patio while Harriet picked through the wrapped presents she and James still had in their shopping bags, choosing

159

several that were appropriate for a toddler and a baby. She set them on the coffee table, and James put the bags by the apartment door.

"She said I can open it," Ta'Shawn said as he came back in, followed by Arinda.

"What's this?" Arinda asked, pointing at the wrapped packages on the table.

Harriet picked them up.

"We brought presents for the other kids."

"You think I can't take care of my own kids?"

"Not at all," Harriet said. "We just thought since Luke was bringing something for Ta'Shawn, we could bring something for the little ones. He told us you had younger children."

"Mom…" Ta'Shawn whined, dragging out her name.

"I suppose it's okay."

Harriet handed her the present for the baby and gave the other one to the toddler, a girl of about two with frizzy dark-blonde hair. The girl squealed when she tore into her package, revealing a baby doll. Arinda quickly opened the baby's present, a round object that had large buttons in primary colors that lit up when you pressed them, announcing their color before playing a song.

"Thank you," Arinda said quietly. "This was very nice of you."

"This is the coolest present ever," Ta'Shawn announced to the room. He looked at his mom. "Can I go outside?"

"Sure, honey," she said, and he ran for the door, holding his scooter.

"Hey," Luke said. "Put on a jacket." He grabbed a small sweatshirt from a peg by the door and followed Ta'Shawn out the door.

An awkward silence followed.

"Ta'Shawn was telling us his grandpa is missing." Harriet said.

The baby started crying, and Arinda dug a pacifier from under a magazine on the table and popped it into the child's mouth.

"I'm not sure you call it 'missing' when someone is homeless. He may have moved south for the winter. He does that sometimes. Usually, he tells us before he goes, though."

"Ta'Shawn said his name is Joe," Harriet said.

"That's right. Joe Smith. The people at the camp call him Smokey Joe."

Harriet looked at James.

"What?" Arinda asked. "Do you know something?"

"No." Harriet answered. "We deliver food to the camp at Fogg Park sometimes. The people there are looking for him, too. They said they've seen activity at his campsite, but no one has seen *him*."

Arinda looked worried.

"It's not like him to not stay in touch. He helps me out a little. Especially with the kids at the holidays. If he's not going to be here, he usually sends me a little money to buy their gifts with."

Harriet tried to focus on the idea that Arinda was worried about him, and not that she was worried about her source of income drying up.

"If I hear anything, I'll let you know."

"Do you know why people call him 'Smokey'?" James asked.

"My mom told me he was firebug. He used to set stuff on fire for people. She met him when he was on probation, and he told her he'd changed his ways."

Right, Harriet thought. Setting fires didn't seem like the sort of habit one just decided to give up one day.

James made eye contact with her, and she gave a slight nod.

"We better get going," he said to Arinda. "You have a Merry Christmas."

"Thanks," she muttered.

✂ --- ✂ --- ✂

"Do you guys mind if we make a small stop on the way home?" Harriet asked when they were back in the car.

James put the car in reverse and backed out of their parking spot.

"If you're thinking we should go by the homeless camp and see if Smokey Joe has turned up, I'm with you. If we swing back by the house, we can pick up some of the leftover tea sandwiches and desserts I brought home. I was going to take them over there tomorrow anyway."

Harriet smiled at him.

"Perfect."

✂ --- ✂ --- ✂

The denizens of the homeless camp were all gathered around a roaring fire in the common area of the camp.

"Merry Christmas," Joyce called out when James came into view, followed by Luke and Harriet.

"Merry Christmas to you," James answered and held up the tray of holiday treats. "I brought you a little snack."

Joyce peeked under the foil lid when he set it down.

"Ah, tea cakes. I'll put the kettle on."

James took a disposable platter from the pan and began arranging the sandwiches and treats on it.

161

"Have you had any luck finding Smokey Joe?" Harriet asked when Joyce had returned from filling the kettle. Joyce stirred the fire and then put the kettle on a grate over the coals.

"I've not seen him, but then I haven't gone looking, either." Joyce looked for Max among the gathered group. "Max, have you been to Joe's campsite?" she asked him.

Max got up and came over.

"What's your interest in Joe?"

She explained his relationship to Luke's half-brother's family.

"They're pretty worried. Arinda said he never leaves the area without telling her."

Max absently drew a circle with the toe of his muddy boot.

"I'm getting concerned myself. I went up to his camp this morning. He's been there. At least, someone's been there. His flannel shirt was there. Joe wore that shirt every day. He was like a kid with a blanket. When he washed it, he stood in front of the washer and dryer until it was clean again and he could put it on."

"That does seem suspicious," Harriet said.

Joyce poured hot water into teacups for people who wanted it. She held the pot up to Harriet. Harriet shook her head.

"I agree," Joyce said when she'd finished serving tea. "I can't imagine Joe without his shirt on, but on the other hand, he *is* living outdoors, and in our lifestyle, it can be a lot harder to keep track of your possessions."

James looked around the clearing.

"Is there anything else we can bring you to brighten your Christmas?"

Joyce patted him on the arm.

"You're so kind to think of us, but we're doing fine. The Methodist church is sending a bus for those of us who want to go to the evening program tonight. The Lutheran church is doing the same in the morning for people who want to have turkey lunch at their place. We're well taken care of in this community."

Max chose one of the tea sandwiches and popped it into his mouth.

"Let us know if you hear anything about Joe from the boy's family, will you?" he asked when he'd finished chewing.

"We will," Harriet promised. "Now we'd better be on our way."

✄ --- ✄ --- ✄

"If Joe set the fire at Jade's for someone else, they may have gotten rid of him when he'd completed his task," Harriet said when they were back in her car.

"On the other hand," James said as he pulled out of the parking lot, "he might have been in the wrong place at the wrong time when one of the other murders was taking place."

Luke leaned forward in his seat.

"Have you two considered that Joe could be the one who is killing the people in town *and* set the fire?"

Harriet blew out a breath.

"Somehow, I can't see Joe as the murderer. I mean, why would he?"

"Why not?" Luke countered. "We don't know what he was before he became homeless. Maybe he had dealings with all the victims."

James smiled at Harriet.

"The kid has a point."

Chapter 27

Luke and James were already in the kitchen when Harriet came downstairs, her arms full of packages.

"Are you sure your mom is okay with the dogs coming to their house for Christmas Eve?"

James took the stack of wrapped boxes from her.

"She specifically mentioned them. Since my sister and her family are going to her husband's people this year, I think the dogs are intended to provide the chaos factor usually created by the grandkids."

Luke laughed as he put Cyrano's Christmas sweater on him.

"They can do that, for sure. Fred's going to be a little lonely, though."

Harriet plucked a can of tuna from the kitchen cupboard.

"Fred can have tuna and a new catnip mouse. He will enjoy having the house to himself."

Luke ran his hand over the cat's back. Fred arched and purred.

"If you say so."

James looked at his watch.

"Let's load these two hoodlums up and get going."

"Yes sir," Luke said with a mock salute, and gathered dogs and leashes before heading for the garage.

James pulled Harriet into his arms when Luke was gone.

"It makes me happy to see how relaxed he's becoming in our little family. You're doing a good job as his foster mother."

She kissed him.

"You're doing just as much as his foster father. Let's hope it continues to go this smoothly."

James squeezed her to him.

"Merry Christmas."

She smiled.

"Merry Christmas."

Will Garvin opened the front door while they were still getting out of the car. He was wearing brown corduroy pants, a red plaid shirt, a green pullover sweater, and a jaunty fleece Santa hat on his head.

"Merry Christmas, everyone, Merry Christmas. Here, let me take that," he said and held his arms out to take a large foil-covered pan from James.

Luke carried the presents into the living room and set them under the Christmas tree. He looked around the room. Every surface held decoration of some sort. On the mantle was a ceramic Christmas village, and a narrow table behind the sofa was covered with an eclectic collection of Santas, made from ceramic, carved wood, fabric soft-sculpture, and glazed paper, collected by James's mother over a lifetime of Christmas-market shopping.

"This is amazing."

Will returned from the kitchen and stood beside Luke.

"Kathy does like her decorations."

James's mom Kathy joined them, smiling affectionately at her husband.

"Don't let him fool you. Will bought every one of those houses in the village and more than half of the Santas."

"Only because I know how much you like them."

James brought a platter of Christmas tree-shaped appetizers from the kitchen and set them on the coffee table.

"How did you make these?" he asked his mom.

Kathy smiled at him.

"Don't make fun of me, but the trees are made from crescent roll refrigerator dough cut into small triangles."

He popped on in his mouth.

"Mmm…they're good. Is that guacamole mixed with cream cheese on top?"

"It is," Kathy confirmed. "And before you ask. The secret is, you sprinkle taco seasoning on the dough before you bake it. And as I'm sure you can see, the stars and decorations are cut from red, yellow, and green peppers."

Harriet tried one.

"They *are* good."

Kathy's cheeks turned pink.

"They aren't something James could serve in the restaurant, but they're definitely a hit at dinner parties."

James put his arm around his mother's shoulders.

"Mom, they're great."

Will went to the kitchen and came back with a tray of mugs filled with caramel apple cider, topped with whipped cream. He put the tray on the other end of the coffee table and took a cup from the tray, handing it to Luke.

"I heard you've taken up riding. Tell me about your horse."

Luke launched into a detailed account of his experience with Major. In that moment, Harriet loved Will. He may have been hard on his son when James didn't fulfill Will's dreams of being the father of a Major League baseball player, but he was perfect with Luke. He knew horses and asked good questions without making Luke feel like he didn't know enough. She watched them for a while before retreating to the kitchen to see if Kathy needed any help.

James's mom might not own a restaurant, but her son had clearly learned some of his kitchen skills from her. A golden-brown turkey sat on a platter on the counter while Kathy tucked leaves of curly kale under its edges.

"Can I do anything?" Harriet asked.

Kathy set her kale down and picked up a bunch of grapes, tearing them into clusters of three or four before placing them artfully around the turkey.

"You could put the roasted vegetables James brought onto that blue platter." She gestured toward a stack of serving pieces on the opposite counter.

Harriet took the lid off the pan and began transferring potatoes and carrots to the platter.

"Will is sure good with Luke."

Kathy smiled warmly.

"He's happy to have a young man around the house again. And he loves talking about growing up on his parent's ranch. They were pretty isolated, and his horse was his best friend."

"Luke has really blossomed since he's been going to the stable."

"James told me there was some trouble out there the other night. I know he's worried about Luke going."

Harriet sighed.

"I'm torn. I don't like him being out there, either, if someone is trying to steal a horse, but on the other hand, Luke loves Major, the horse he's been working with, and I hate to take that away from him."

166

Kathy finished with the grapes and got a bag of lady apples from the refrigerator.

"Being a parent is never easy. It has to be especially tough jumping into the teen years. All you want to do is keep them safe, but they think they're invincible."

"Exactly,"

Kathy stood back to look at her creation before placing the apples among the grapes and kale.

"I have to say, with what's going on downtown, I'm afraid to go shopping alone."

"Speaking of that, did you know Valery Melnyk's wife when she was here?"

Kathy thought for a moment.

"I wouldn't say I knew her. I knew *of* her. I attempted to speak to her a few times, but she didn't speak much English. She seemed friendly enough, though."

"Do you know how long she was here?"

"No, but it wasn't very long. I heard from ladies at church that she had elderly parents in the old country, and they needed her. I don't think she wanted to leave the kids here, but she and Valery decided they would have better educational opportunities in the US. I think she thought she was only going to be gone for a year, at least according to the local gossips."

"Instead, her daughter died, and her son got AIDS," Harriet mused.

"Really? I knew about the daughter, but I didn't know about the son."

"I met him at Valery's memorial service. He knew Daniel Muhler because of it."

Kathy raised her eyebrows.

"I didn't know that, either. Although there's no reason I *would* know."

"It's all pretty sad. Especially at Christmas time."

Kathy placed her apples and declared the turkey a masterpiece.

"We'll have to make sure our dinner is extra-festive to make up for all the sadness."

✂ --- ✂ --- ✂

James leaned back in his chair, his cleaned plate in front of him.

"Mom, you've outdone yourself."

Kathy wiped her hands on her napkin and laid it on the table.

"You set the bar high, food-wise," she said, her pride in her son clear.

"You've always been the better cook," James told her.

Will pushed back in his chair.

167

"If you two are done with your love fest, I say it's time to go see what Santa left under the tree while we were eating."

During dinner, he and Kathy in turn had excused themselves to use the restroom or fetch something from the kitchen and had been gone longer than necessary. This must have been how they'd fooled their children into believing Santa had come while they were eating.

James quickly cleared the remaining food from the table as Will led the way to the formal living room, where the tree was set up. Luke stared at the pile of packages that had appeared under the tree.

"Wow, I've never seen so many gifts."

Kathy put her arm around his shoulders.

"We didn't used to go so overboard, but Will enjoys all this. All I ask is for him to buy gifts for the local toy drive and the various giving trees around town. And he's happy to do so."

Will shrugged.

"What can I say, I like holiday shopping."

Luke smiled.

"Works for me."

Harriet figured if Luke ever started to take it all for granted they'd have a family talk about it, but he'd grown up so deprived, she didn't see that happening anytime soon.

"Everyone find a comfortable seat, and Will will distribute packages," Kathy instructed. "When he finishes, everyone can start opening."

✂ --- ✂ --- ✂

"This yarn is perfect," Kathy exclaimed.

James held up a white chef's coat with his name embroidered on the chest pocket.

"Mom, this is perfect. And I desperately needed a new one."

Kathy grinned. "I did my research." She watched as Harriet unwrapped a flat rectangular box. "Let me explain yours," she said as Harriet was about to lift the lid on the box. "I researched yours, too, but my advisors didn't agree so I got you a mix of their recommendations. Okay, now you can open."

Harriet lifted the lid, revealing a smallish quilted bag. She unzipped three sides of the bag and opened it flat. Inside were four pairs of appliqué scissors. She laughed and pulled a pair of Kai scissors from the elastic loops that held them.

"You discovered that my aunt and her friends each swear by a different brand of appliqué scissors."

"So, what could I do?" Kathy responded. "I got you one of each."

Harriet smiled broadly.

"These are fantastic. Karen Kay Buckley and Ginger and Kai are the top scissors for appliqué. I'll put them all to good use."

"Whoa!" Luke yelped and rapidly tore wrapping paper from a large box. He quickly opened the box to reveal a pair of riding boots. He jumped up and threw his arms around Will's neck. "Thank you so much."

Harriet and James looked at each other wide-eyed. They'd never seen such a display of emotion from Luke. Will's face turned red, and he had to clear his throat a couple of times before he could speak.

"Once you figure out what style you're going to ride, you can get some proper riding boots, but I thought you should have something to protect your toes from being stepped on, especially with that big horse you're riding."

Luke pulled on the right boot.

"I did my research, too," Will said proudly. "I asked Vern at the Outdoor Store. I knew you all had gotten hiking boots, and he keeps a record of people's shoe sizes."

"How did Vern seem when you saw him?" Harriet asked.

Will was collecting the tissue paper Luke pulled out of the boots and was wadding it up. He stopped mid-motion.

"Now that you mention it, he was not himself. He was distracted, and he looked like he hadn't slept in a week. I know the holidays are busy, but this was something else. I asked him if everything was okay, but he brushed me off, which is not like him."

"My friend Lauren made the quilt for his store. She's been worried about him. She thinks maybe he's being blackmailed like some of the other vendors in town."

Wills face lost all trace of humor. "Do you think he's in danger?"

Harriet blew out a breath. "That's what's got her worried."

Kathy interrupted by getting to her feet.

"On that happy note, how about we sing a few Christmas carols. If James will play piano, that is."

Harriet turned and looked at James. "Piano?"

He smiled and waggled his eyebrows at her. "I am a man of many talents."

She laughed. "I guess *so*."

"Can I keep my boots on?" Luke asked.

Will put his hands on the boy's shoulders.

"Of course you can. You need to break them in, after all."

"I'll go get the sheet music," Kathy said and left the room.

169

Chapter 28

*H*arriet woke up in the dark, nestled in a bed of straw. Warm, sweet breath filled her nose, and soft whiskers tickled her chin. She opened her eyes to find Becky nuzzling her.

"What's going on?" she asked the horse as she sat up.

Becky looked at her with big brown eyes and pawed the floor with her hoof, being careful not to touch her. She stopped and looked anxiously at Harriet. Harriet stood and patted her on the neck.

"I don't know what you're trying to tell me." She tugged on the bottom edge of her pajama top as Becky rubbed her face against her chest.

"I wish you could talk," she said with a sigh.

"He can't, but I can," James said, and lifted Fred up and off of Harriet.

She opened her eyes.

"Oh, thank goodness. I thought I was in Becky's stall at the barn. She was trying to tell me something, but I couldn't understand what she wanted." She smiled. "It was surprisingly warm, given I was barefoot and in my PJ's."

"Was she actually talking to you?" James asked and pulled her into his arms.

"Of course not," she said with mock indignation. "That would have been ridiculous."

He smiled.

"Because waking up in her stall was so normal by comparison."

She pushed on his chest. "Don't make fun of me."

"I'm not. You just have such interesting dreams. I dream of mundane things like a crowd of people showing up without reservations, and when I go into the walk-in refrigerator, it's either empty or the food is all rotten."

"That's kind of gross."

"See? Not nearly as interesting as your dreams."

"Any indication Luke is up yet?"

"The house is quiet. I'm sure if he was awake, the dogs would have made him go out."

Harriet smiled. The dogs had taken to sleeping in Luke's room since he let them sleep on the bed, something that was strictly forbidden in Harriet and James's room.

"Shall I go downstairs and heat up the cinnamon rolls?" he asked.

"Works for me."

✂ --- ✂ --- ✂

Historically, there was about a ten-percent chance of snow falling on Christmas day in Foggy Point, and this was not one of those rare occasions. The day had dawned crisp and clear and full of promise.

"Be sure you get lots of pictures of Luke as he opens his presents," Harriet reminded James.

He held up his phone. "My battery is fully charged." He reached across the kitchen table, where they sat sipping their coffee and tea, and took her hand. "Don't worry. His first Christmas with us will be perfect. By definition, the fact he's having it with us will make it perfect, no matter what happens."

Luke appeared in the doorway.

"Merry Christmas?" he said tentatively. "Is everything okay?"

James stood up, smiling at him. "Oh, Harriet's just worried about whether Christmas will live up to your expectations."

Luke grinned. "It already has."

"Food first or presents first?" James asked.

Luke looked torn. "Can we do both?"

"Sure," Harriet said. "Grab a cinnamon roll, and I'll fix some hot chocolate real quick. You can take them into the living room."

✂ --- ✂ --- ✂

"Anyone ready for another round of cinnamon rolls?" James asked when all the presents had been opened.

"I am," Luke said without looking up from his new laptop computer.

Harriet closed the cover of her new mystery novel.

171

"I'll help you. I think I need some orange juice to cut through all the sugar."

"Do you think he likes his present?" Harriet asked when they were back in the kitchen.

James put his hands on her shoulders and rubbed the tension from her neck as she poured juice into her glass.

"I think 'like it' is an understatement. He's hardly taken his hands off it since he opened it."

Harriet turned into his arms.

"Did you notice he's wearing his boots? I wouldn't embarrass him by asking, but I wonder if he wore them to bed?"

"I slept with my first baseball glove for about a week, I think."

"I don't think I ever slept with anything, but I did sleep in the manger at boarding school one Christmas. I guess I was researching the whole Mary-and-Joseph thing. I didn't think you really could sleep in a barn."

James laughed. "How did it go?"

"Better than you might imagine. I curled up with our school milk cow. It was nice and warm. It was a little gross when she decided to lick my head, but otherwise, not bad."

"No wonder you dreamed you were sleeping in the horse barn. It wasn't a dream, it was a memory."

✂ --- ✂ --- ✂

Harriet was in the kitchen rinsing her cinnamon roll plate when the phone rang.

"Merry Christmas," she answered it.

"Aren't you just the cheery one," Lauren said.

"It's Christmas, what's not to be cheery about?"

"Oh, you have no idea, but enough about me. I'm calling about Vern."

"Vern, like Outdoor Store Vern?"

"Yes. When I got up this morning, there was a message on my phone from Vern. Unfortunately, it was garbled, like he was getting really poor reception. I have no idea what he might have wanted from me in the middle of the night on Christmas Eve."

"I didn't know you guys were friends."

"That's my point. We're *not* friends. I made him a quilt. I've shopped in his store. That's it."

"That *is* mysterious."

"That's all you have to say? 'It's mysterious?'"

"What were you looking for?"

"I'm hoping you want to go with me to check on him."

172

"I have to be at my aunt's in a couple of hours, and you don't have anything but a garbled message as a starting point."

"Given what's been happening downtown, I would feel better if we at least checked his store."

"By we, are you asking me to go with?"

The phone was silent.

Harriet sighed.

"Let me see if James is okay with this."

"Call me back."

Harriet hung up and went back to the living room. Luke was still putting his computer through its paces while James looked on. She cleared her throat, and James looked up.

"Could you two do without me for a half-hour or so?" She explained her phone call from Lauren. "I'm pretty sure Vern is at home, or with his family, and he probably pocket-dialed Lauren by accident; but she's not going to relax and enjoy her day until we go by his shop and confirm it's closed up tight."

James came over and took both her hands in his.

"Do you promise that if you find anything but a closed-up dark shop you'll drive away and call Detective Morse on your way home?"

"Of course, but that's not going to happen. We're going to meet out front, admire Lauren's quilt in the window, get back in our cars, and return to our holiday celebrations."

"Do you want me to come with you?" Luke asked without looking away from his computer screen.

Harriet smiled. "That's really sweet of you, but there's no need for you guys to spoil your Christmas because of Lauren's paranoia. I'll be back before you know it."

James followed her to the kitchen, where she collected her down jacket and wool scarf. He reached into the closet and got her purse from its hook and handed it to her. He kissed her.

"Promise me you'll be careful."

"Don't worry."

Chapter 29

ow's your Christmas going so far?" Harriet asked as she slid into the passenger seat of Lauren's car.

Lauren put the car in gear and headed down the driveway then toward downtown Foggy Point.

"Any year I can stay out of the line of fire between my parents and my brother, it's good. And before you ask, they have long-term issues which will probably never be solved. I count it as a win that we've finally reached the point we can spend the holidays together. How about you?"

"James's dad is trying hard to win Luke over, and it's working. He gave him cowboy boots for Christmas, and they were a big hit."

"Nice. How does James feel about that?"

"He's good. He wants his dad and Luke to bond. And he understands his dad will probably never get over his rejection of a pro baseball career."

"On the subject at hand. I really do hope I'm taking you on a wild goose chase. It's just weird for him to call me."

"I'm sure you've considered the possibility of a pocket call."

"I have, but I rejected that because of the timing. I could buy a pocket call at three in the afternoon, but not in the middle of the night."

The streets of Foggy Point were empty, and Lauren was able to park in front of The Outdoor Store. She peered in the big front window where her quilt was displayed while Harriet went to the door and pressed the tab on the handle.

"Uh-oh," she said and turned to look at Lauren.

"Uh-oh what?"

"Ummm, the door isn't locked."

174

"So, he's open for business." Lauren started to push past her, but Harriet grabbed her arm.

"I promised James we'd call Morse if the shop was anything but locked up tight."

"Are you kidding?"

"No, I'm not. Three people are dead. Two of them in this very downtown. And I've had my own encounter with whoever is doing all this, and it's an experience I don't want to repeat."

Lauren gave a dramatic sigh and pulled her phone from her pocket. She dialed Morse's private number and had a brief conversation before ending the call.

"She'll be here in a few minutes. She agrees we shouldn't go in."

"Did you expect anything else from her?"

Lauren laughed.

"I guess not."

Morse parked behind Lauren at the curb and got out, zipping her coat as she came to join them at the open door of the Outdoor Store.

"Don't you two ever take a day off?" she grumbled. "I left a perfectly good plate of eggs Benedict on the table."

"I'm sorry," Lauren said. "I wanted to go in and check things out myself, but Harriet had promised James we'd call you if anything was out of place."

Morse shook her head.

"Don't even try to tell me this is James' fault. So, what's going on? Why do you think it's anything but Vern forgetting to lock his door when he went home after what was probably his busiest day of the year."

Harriet shuffled her feet.

"When you say it that way…"

"I'm worried," Lauren said. "Vern called me in the middle of the night, and when I answered, the line went dead. I've been trying to get hold of him ever since with no answer. Maybe it was a pocket dial, like Harriet thinks, but we came here to reassure ourselves and found the door unlocked."

Morse sighed.

"Okay, I'm sorry. You're right. It *is* a coincidence, and I don't like coincidences. Not that it's an excuse, but at the PD we've all been on overtime trying to solve these murders; and so far, we aren't getting anywhere." She took her gun from its holster. "Wait here while I check it out."

She returned a few minutes later.

"You can come in, but don't touch anything." She held the door open for them to enter. "His desk chair is tipped over, and the door to the basement is open, but I don't know if that's normal or not."

Lauren looked toward the back of the store.

"I've never seen it open before."

"Can we go down there?" Harriet asked.

"I checked it out, but go ahead."

Harriet went across the store and down the stairs.

"Vern, are you down here?" she called out, and then stood in the dark basement and listened.

"Did you hear something?" Lauren asked, having followed Harriet down the stairs.

"I'm not sure."

"Vern?" Lauren called in a loud voice.

There was a faint thumping noise.

"Jane?" Harriet called up the stairs. "I think we may have something."

Lauren turned on the flashlight function on her phone and shone the light on the wall at the foot of the stairs.

"Try the ceiling," Harriet suggested.

Lauren did as directed and found a string hanging from a socket on a ceiling beam. Harriet pulled the string and illuminated the cluttered room. Jane came down the stairs, and Harriet held her hand up before she could speak.

"Vern!" Lauren called again.

A faint thumping noise sounded. Shelving covered all the walls, and additional storage cabinets stood back-to-back in the middle of the room next to a large workbench. Dust coated every surface.

"It sounds like its coming from the walls."

Morse scanned the room.

"This can't be all there is to the basement. The shop is huge, and the rest of the shops we've been in have full basements."

"Vern!" Harriet shouted, and then listened intently. Once again, they heard thumping in response.

Harriet stepped toward the noise, facing a shelf full of paint cans. She ran her hands lightly along the two sides of the shelf.

"What are you doing?" Lauren asked as she joined her in front of the shelf.

"Look at the floor."

176

Morse had also come over, and bent down to examine the scrapes in the dust Harriet was pointing to. Harriet continued her examination of the shelf.

"This shelf swings away from the wall. We just need to find the latching mechanism."

Her hand found a curved piece of metal on the back of the middle shelf. It was attached to a spring. She pulled, and at first nothing happened; but then something released, and the shelf moved ever so slightly. Morse grabbed the opposite edge of the unit and pulled it forward. A disheveled-looking Vern Jenkins tumbled out through the opening, nearly knocking her over.

"Oh, thank heaven," he gasped. "I've got to call my wife."

He bolted for the stairs before anyone could stop him. Morse followed him while Harriet and Lauren started through the opening behind the shelving, but then Harriet stepped back out and found a loose two-by-four segment. She wedged it in the opening in case the shelf decided to close on its own.

"Look at this place," Lauren exclaimed when Harriet had returned. She was standing behind a carved mahogany bar. A large mirror covered the wall behind the bar, with the rest of the walls covered in heavy drapes. Seating groups featuring Art-Deco sofas and chairs, and stylized tables were scattered about the room.

"It's a blind pig." Harriet moved to the bar, where a used plate and cup sat beside a half-full glass of amber liquid.

"A blind what?"

"It's a speakeasy. Or it was during Prohibition. Look at the furniture. Classic nineteen-twenties."

"It's like a museum."

"When alcohol became legal again, they didn't need it anymore. This building used to be a pancake house when I was growing up. I'll bet it was a bar before that."

"Someone knew about this room."

Vern came back downstairs and entered the hidden room.

"Sorry about that. I had to call my wife. As I expected, she was by turns worried, relieved, and then angry at my unexplained absence. I called her last night to say I was locking up and heading home and then..." He gestured. "...all this happened."

"So, what *did* happen?" Harriet asked him.

Vern ran a hand over his thinning hair.

"As I told my wife, I was at the register at the back of the store, closing it out for the day, going through my closing-up process. I heard the doorbell chime and came around the counter, where I discovered a tall, thin figure dressed in black. He or she had on a black balaclava with full-face coverage. They held a little electronic contraption in their hand. It turned out to be a voice distortion thing."

He reached for the glass of liquid on the bar and took a sip. He gave them a sheepish grin and held the glass up.

"One of the perks of owning a former speakeasy. Anyway—and I'm saying 'he' only for simplicity, as I truly have no idea of the gender here —he pulled an ugly little gun from a pocket and gestured at me with it, indicating I should go downstairs. We came down, and when he saw a length of rope on one of the shelves, he said, 'Perfect, you'll be another hanging'.

"I said, 'This rope is too old. If I'm going to hang, I don't want it to break halfway through.' I indicated I had a new coil of rope on the back shelf. He gestured for me to go get it, and as you can guess, I opened the speakeasy door and slid inside, locking it behind me. I just barely made it inside in time, and I guess I slammed the door hard, jamming the lock."

Morse was scribbling in her little notebook. She looked up at Vern when he'd finished speaking.

"That must have frustrated your would-be assailant."

Vern smiled.

"I could hear him pounding on the shelves, but that door was built to keep the Untouchables out. A skinny person in a balaclava wasn't going to be able to break it."

Harriet shook her head.

"You were really lucky." She paused, studying the floor. "Did anything about your assailant seem familiar? I know the voice was distorted, but was there anything?"

Vern thought a moment.

"I had a lot of time to think while I was locked in here. There was something familiar about the figure. I can't quite put my finger on it."

Morse ran a hand through her close-cropped hair. She looked like she'd aged years in the last few weeks.

"Do you have anywhere you can go away from Foggy Point? I don't want to scare you, but I think whoever tried to kill you won't give up. Our department doesn't have the means to maintain a safe house to protect you and your wife, so your option is either the Foggy Point Motel or the jail."

Lauren chuckled. "Choose the jail."

Vern thought for a moment.

"Our daughter lives in Portland. They're at her in-laws today, then they were going to come here. We could go there instead. Would that work?"

"Yes. We'll provide transportation. Call your wife and ask her to throw a few things together for both of you. I'll have an unmarked pick her up and bring her to the station. We need to take your statement, then someone will take you to your daughter's. We'll talk to the Portland police and get them to keep an eye on you."

✂ --- ✂ --- ✂

"Will that be safe?" Harriet asked Morse while Vern stood at the top of the stairs calling Mrs. Vern.

Morse shook her head.

"I wish I could do better for them, but I do think our killer is centered on Foggy Point. I don't think he or she is going to go far. And no, I have no reason to think that other than a feeling. I *am* going to ask Portland to have an officer stay outside their house."

"Will they do that?" Harriet asked.

"All I can do is ask."

Harriet stared at Morse, not sure if this was the right time for what she was going to say next.

"What?" Morse finally said.

"This is a little anticlimactic after all this, but in the spirit of full disclosure..."

"For crying out loud, spit it out while there is still some hope of me getting home before dinner."

"There's a gray sedan that seems to be following me around. I haven't said anything because they don't seem to be doing anything else."

"Yet," Morse said, anger in her voice. "They aren't doing anything else *yet*." She shook her head, turned her back on them, and went to her car, driving off a moment later.

"That went well," Lauren said with a grin.

Chapter 30

James met Harriet in the kitchen when she returned.

"Is Vern okay?"

She shrugged out of her coat, and James hung it in the closet with her scarf and purse.

"He is. He had a bit of a rough night, but lucky for him his store came with a speakeasy hidden in the basement. One with a strong lock."

"Really?"

"I'll tell you all about it later. How's Luke doing?"

James pulled her into his arms.

"Judging by how long he's been talking to the charming Miss Emily, I'd say he's doing just fine."

"So, you guys didn't miss me?"

He kissed her.

"We were counting the seconds until your return." He laughed. "Or at least I was."

She smiled. This marriage thing was okay.

He took her hand and led her into the living room.

"Do you have time to sit and have a cup of tea or cocoa before we have to get ready to go to Beth's?"

Harriet glanced at the grandfather clock across the room.

"I would love a cup of cocoa."

"I will be right back."

She sat in a wing-back chair next to the fireplace. Luke was curled up on the end of the leather Chesterfield sofa, two dogs tangled in the afghan at his feet and the cat peering over his shoulder from the back of the sofa. Fred appeared to be reading along with Luke as he studied his new book on horse care. He looked up as Harriet sat down.

"How was Vern? James said you went to check on him."

"It turns out he's fine, if a little worse for the wear. He spent the night locked in an old speakeasy that's hidden in the basement of his shop."

"What's a speakeasy?"

"Back in the days when alcohol was illegal, people created secret bars and sold bootleg liquor. Vern discovered there was one in his basement that's been pretty much untouched since Prohibition."

"Was it the guy that got us?"

"It seems to have been. They intended to hang him, but he was able to get into the secret room before they could do it. Unfortunately, the lock got stuck, and he had no cell reception."

"He was lucky you and Lauren went to check on him."

"Yes, he was." James set two mugs on the table next to Harriet and took the chair next to hers. "Although I suppose Mrs. Vern would have gone looking eventually."

Luke, wide-eyed, had lost interest in his book.

"Why is someone trying to kill all the shopkeepers in Foggy Point?"

Harriet blew gently across the top of her steaming cocoa and took a sip.

"I wish I knew. The only thing the Threads and I could come up with is Valery Melnyk's wife or family coming from Ukraine to avenge his death."

"Didn't Daniel die before Valery?" James asked.

"I didn't say it was a perfect theory. We're missing something. I keep going over everything that's happened since this all started. There's something that's just out of reach. If I could figure out what it is, this would all make sense."

James sipped his cocoa.

"Lucky for you, that is Detective Morse's job and she's very good at it. I'm sure she'll figure this out and put a stop to it."

"I hope so. But enough about that. Are you two sure you're up to facing whatever awaits us at Aunt Beth's house?"

Luke laughed.

"I keep telling you, if no one pulls guns or knives and we don't have to call an ambulance for anyone OD-ing, I'll consider the event a success."

Harriet shook her head, smiling.

"I'm really sorry that is your measure of success."

James took her hand.

"Luke's right. We've all experienced Aiden's poor behavior, and we are not going to let anything he does spoil our evening. Besides, isn't Jorge's son going to be there? I would think that might cause him to act a little more mature than usual."

"I hope so."

✂ --- ✂ --- ✂

Harriet led the way to the front door of her aunt's cottage. Colored lights surrounded the arched opening of the porch, and a large wreath surrounded the door knocker. Beth opened the door as Harriet stepped onto the porch.

"Come on in."

Jorge stood behind her, resplendent in his colorful Christmas sweater. "*Feliz Navidad!*" he said, swinging the door wide.

As Harriet passed her aunt on the way in, she realized Beth's sweater matched Jorge's. James caught her eye as he noticed the same thing. He leaned in and whispered in her ear, "We won't ever do that, will we?"

Harriet suppressed a laugh.

"Not a chance."

Jorge put his arm around Luke's shoulders and guided him into the living room.

"Come meet my son Julio. He's a lawyer in Seattle." He parked Luke beside his son. "Julio, meet James and Harriet's son, Luke."

Luke's cheeks flamed red. Julio smiled.

"You'll get used to my dad. He likes to make sure everyone has a good time."

Jorge brought Luke a cup of steaming spiced apple cider. Luke took the cup, grateful to have something to do with his hands.

"My dad tells me you're learning to ride out at the stable," Julio continued.

Luke looked uncomfortable, and Julio's smile turned into a grin.

"If you haven't learned it already, everyone knows everything about everyone else in Foggy Point. You'll get used to it. And if Aiden and I are any example, it will keep you from getting in trouble. Everything you do will be noticed by someone who knows James's parents or Harriet's aunt or my dad."

"It's kind of nice that they care," Luke finally said.

"Yes, it is. And Foggy Point is a nice place to grow up. Have you lived here long?"

Luke started to answer, but he was silenced, along with everyone else, by Aiden's arrival—with his date.

182

Harriet unconsciously took a step closer to James. He put his arm around her and squeezed.

The girl on Aiden's arm was a show-stopper. She equaled his six-foot, three-inch height and surpassed it with six-inch stiletto heels. Every time she stopped, she tilted her foot just enough to show off the signature red soles of her Christian Louboutin shoes. Her black leather skirt seemed more like a wide belt, and Harriet was pretty sure the white fur stole tossed casually over her silk blouse was real.

Luke was staring, mouth open, at the creature who had just entered. Harriet wasn't sure if it was the short white hair with red and green streaks or the red fishnet stockings—or both—that had him mesmerized.

Aiden grinned, obviously aware of the effect his date would have.

"This is my friend, Calithea."

Jorge recovered first.

"Welcome, Calithea. Can I get you anything to drink?"

"Do you have celery juice?"

"I think I do in the kitchen. I'll be right back." He turned to his son. "Julio, take their coats."

Julio had gotten up and started to do as asked when a dark-haired young woman came out of the kitchen and, with a smile at him, took Aiden's jacket and Calithea's stole. Harriet assumed this was Julio's fiancée.

Calithea laughed at whatever Julio said, resting her hand on his shoulder. Harriet noticed the fiancée visibly tense. Calithea scanned the room, her gaze passing over Luke and coming to rest on James.

Beth emerged from the kitchen and joined Harriet and James.

"Merry Christmas."

James raised his mug in salute. "Merry Christmas to you, too."

"Is it?" Harriet asked dryly.

The smile left Beth's face.

"It was until our latest entry," she murmured. She looked at Harriet. "I shouldn't have insisted you come. You were right. We could have had a lovely dinner tomorrow night and maybe Aiden wouldn't have felt the need to upstage Julio."

"Well, if it's any consolation, I didn't expect him to arrive with an exotic maneater on his arm, either."

Beth smiled a grim smile.

"You notice the way she's been taking the measure of all the males here?"

James sipped his cider.

"As long as she leaves Luke alone, we're good. I can handle her if she takes a run at me, but I feel sorry for Julio's fiancée."

183

"Julie's got a good head on her shoulders," Beth said.

Harriet laughed. "Julie? Really? Julie is going to marry Julio?"

Beth put her hand on Harriet's arm.

"You hush. What do you expect them to do? Change their names?" Harriet was still smiling.

"No, I guess not. The heart wants what the heart wants."

Jorge brought a glass filled with pale-green liquid to Calithea. She smiled and kissed him on the cheek. Beth glared at them. James squeezed Harriet's arm.

"I'm going to see if I can help Jorge in the kitchen. Will you be okay?"

"I'll be just fine. Aiden and his antics won't bother me."

✂ --- ✂ --- ✂

James and Jorge returned a few minutes later, James carrying a tray of canapés, Jorge a tray with glasses of champagne and sparkling cider. They carried both around until all the dinner guests had a snack and a glass of something bubbly.

Jorge set his tray on the coffee table and picked up his glass and held it up.

"If I may have your attention, please."

Conversation stopped and everyone turned toward him, glass in hand.

"I'd like to welcome everyone to this gathering of family and friends as yet another Christmas day is coming to a close. Over the next few days, we shall begin reflecting on the last year, our highs and our lows, and we will begin making plans for the new year. Before all that, I'd like to thank you all for joining Beth and I." He raised his glass in the air. "To friends and family."

Everyone raised their glasses and took a sip. Harriet watched Julio. He was nervously fingering something in his pocket. She smiled. Her aunt had been right. He was about to propose.

Aiden left Calithea's side and stepped into the middle of the room. *Wow*, Harriet thought, *Julio must have an elaborate proposal planned if he's having Aiden give a pre-speech.*

Aiden cleared his throat.

"As Jorge just reminded us, this is a time for reflection and a time to think of the future." He turned to Calithea. "I can't imagine a future without you in it." He dropped to one knee and pulled a black velvet box from his pocket and popped it open. "Calithea, will you marry me?"

Harriet looked at Julio. The color had drained from his face, and his fists were clenched at his sides, the muscle in his jaw twitching. Calithea

184

took the ring from the box and squealed. Aiden stood up, and she threw her arms around his neck.

"Yes, yes, yes." She slid the ring onto her finger. "I love it."

Julio spun on his heel and left the room. His girlfriend, standing next to Aunt Beth, looked confused.

Jorge cleared his throat loudly. The fire in his eyes was at odds with the words coming out of his mouth.

"It seems congratulations are in order."

Chapter 31

Aunt Beth asked Julie to join her in the kitchen, and Harriet took the opportunity to search out Julio. She found him standing on the back patio.

During the day, the patio offered a panoramic view of the Strait of Juan de Fuca. At night, everything was dark. She stood beside him.

"Hey."

"Is Julie okay?" he asked.

"Aunt Beth has her helping in the kitchen."

"How could Aiden be such a total jerk?"

"I've asked myself that on more than one occasion lately."

He turned to face her, the hurt plain on his face.

"He knew I was proposing to Julie while we were here. How could he not see that my dad was introducing my proposal?"

Harriet shrugged.

"Who is this Calithea person, anyway?" she asked.

"I've never met her until tonight." Julio started pacing. "He's so self-centered. He can't accept the fact that you got tired of his antics and moved on with someone who treated you better. And now he does this. He's my best friend...or was my best friend. Now I don't know."

"If I could figure out what to do or say to make him move on in a healthy way, I would," Harriet said. "I won't go back to him. I have a family now. And besides, it's not clear to me his behavior would get better if I did go back to him."

"I'm not blaming you. And don't think I'm suggesting you should go back to him—I'm not." He ran both hands through his hair. "I just can't believe he ruined my proposal. He's known for weeks I was going to do it."

"Not to defend Aiden, but did he know you were going to do it tonight?"

"I didn't tell him specifically the day and time, but come on! I said I was going to propose while we were here for Christmas."

"Did Julie know tonight was going to be the night?"

"Not specifically. I mean, I'm pretty sure she suspected it was coming during the holiday, and she probably guessed it would be tonight, but she didn't know for sure."

"So, what's your plan B?"

"Plan B?"

"Surely you had an alternative in case dinner went sideways."

He chuckled grimly.

"Not really. I would have never guessed my best friend would torpedo my proposal. Now I don't know what I'm going to do."

They stood in silence for a few moments, staring at the black water.

"I think I may have an idea for you," Harriet said. "I need to talk to James first. In the meantime, you may need to rescue Julie—my aunt's idea of a distraction may feel more like kitchen servitude."

✄ --- ✄ --- ✄

James slid his arm around Harriet's waist and pulled her to him when she came back inside.

"How'd it go out there?"

"He's feeling betrayed, as you might imagine. Aiden knew Julio was planning on proposing to Julie over the holidays. He feels like Aiden stole his thunder, which, of course, he did. The sad thing is, Aiden probably wasn't trying to do anything to Julio. He's just being his usual self-centered self."

"Don't you think he was trying to do something to you, and Julio was just collateral damage?"

"He seems willing to go to any lengths to get my attention—"

"You mean to hurt you?" James interrupted.

"I just feel for Julio. Aiden is his best friend, and he betrayed him without even giving it a second thought."

"I wish there was something we could do for him."

"There might be. I have an idea." She explained her plan to him.

He smiled. "I can make that happen."

Julio had followed her inside and gone into the kitchen to find Julie. Aiden sat in the living room with Calithea glued to his side, admiring her

187

new ring. Harriet glanced toward Aunt Beth's guest bedroom. Luke had gone there to check on the dogs and was still with them.

"I'm going to check on things in the kitchen. If I can, I'll tell Julio I need him to help me with something in the garage and explain the plan," she said and stepped behind the sofa, avoiding Aiden and his fiancée. "How soon till dinner?" she asked her aunt.

Aunt Beth looked at her watch and then Jorge. They exchanged a look, and he gave a small nod.

"Thirty minutes," Beth said.

Harriet gave her a long look, and Beth nodded, indicating she understood she needed to go with whatever was said next.

"Can we use that holiday platter I brought you from Sweden?" Harriet asked.

"Sure, it's in the garage in that blue box. Maybe Julio can reach it for you."

"Lead the way," he said.

When they were in the garage and the door was shut, Harriet went to a shelving unit and collected the blue box.

"As you can see, I didn't need help. I wanted to offer an alternative that might salvage your special proposal."

"I'm listening."

"James has given the staff at his restaurant the next two days off, so it will be closed. We would like to offer it to you. James will do up some finger foods for you, and have champagne. If you want to invite your dad, my aunt, or anyone else, it's up to you. Just let us know so the set-up will be right."

"That's incredibly generous of you."

"I can't help but feel partly responsible for your ruined chance tonight. I know Aiden is responsible, but I also know I'm the trigger for his recent bad behavior."

"You're not responsible at all. He's been messed up since his mom died. He needs to talk to someone. I suggested counseling, but he wasn't ready to hear it."

Harriet shifted the box in her hands.

"I better take this inside. If you can get James alone, you can refine the plan and agree on a time. Again, I'm really sorry your proposal was ruined."

Beth and Jorge were alone in the kitchen when they came back in. Julio went on to the living room to find James.

"I don't know what's gotten into that boy," Jorge was saying to Beth.

"I don't know, either," Harriet said, joining their whispered conversation. "James's restaurant is closed tomorrow, so we've offered it to Julio as an alternative proposal location."

Jorge smiled. "Tell James I can prepare food for them. He's my son, after all."

Beth put her hand on Harriet's arm.

"If James wouldn't mind, I could bring all these poinsettias I bought for today over there to decorate."

"I think that would be lovely," Harriet said. "I better go check on Luke. He's been hiding in your spare room with the dogs."

Jorge laughed. "I wish I could hide with the dogs."

✂ --- ✂ --- ✂

To say the dinner was painful would have been an understatement. Jorge tried to keep a conversation going, talking about Christmas traditions and then entertaining everyone with past holiday cooking disasters. Aunt Beth's turkey was perfection, and Jorge's Mexican hot chocolate and cookies were the perfect dessert, but Harriet could hardly taste them.

She and James started carrying empty dishes to the kitchen as soon as they reasonably could. Julio and Julie joined them.

"Could I ask you a favor?" James asked Julio.

Harriet and Julie paused, dishes in hand, curious as to what the favor might be.

"Sure, what's up?" Julio asked.

James looked at Harriet as he spoke.

"Your dad may have told you what's been going on in Foggy Point?"

Julio wiped his hands on a Santa-patterned dish towel and flipped it onto his shoulder.

"He said a couple or three business people had been killed recently."

"Harriet and Luke stumbled into another killing in the basement of the yarn store the other day, so we—or at least I—have been a little paranoid about security. Anyway, there's been a car parked a few houses from Harriet's a few too many times lately. And tonight it followed us here."

Julio drew his brows together.

"Have you told the police?"

Harriet froze and stared at James, wondering what this plan of his was.

"Yeah, Harriet mentioned it to a detective earlier today, but we don't have a plate number," James went on. "and besides, with the murders, we're sort of low on the list, especially since whoever it is doesn't seem to be doing anything but watching."

"How can I help?"

189

"I was hoping you could follow us home, from a distance," James explained. "If he's still out there, he'll pick us up within a block of here. If you leave a few minutes after us, you could follow him and see if you can get a license number for us."

"Don't do anything risky," Harriet cautioned. "If he stops, drive right on by."

"Definitely," James agreed.

Julie looped her arm through Julio's.

"We can say we're going to look at the Christmas lights. Julio's been promising to do that, in any case."

Harriet liked the way this girl thought.

"Let me give you both my cell phone number. If we *are* being followed, text me. We're going to drive into the garage, which is connected to the house, so we'll be fine, but I'd like to know."

Julio typed Harriet's name and number into his phone, followed by James's. James started rinsing dishes and putting them into the dishwasher.

"Hopefully, this will be much ado about nothing, but if someone is spying on us, I'd like to know."

✂ --- ✂ --- ✂

Harriet slipped her coat on and gathered her purse before hugging her aunt and Jorge and promising to call the following day. She ignored Aiden.

"Why would someone be following us?" Luke asked Harriet when she'd explained what was happening on their walk to the car. She told him Julio and Julie would hopefully be behind whoever was following them.

She looked up and down the road in front of her aunt's cottage, but didn't see any cars that didn't belong. James clicked the button that locked all the doors while they waited for the car to warm up.

"Here we go," he said and guided the car onto the road. "And there are lights coming up behind us already."

Harriet pulled her phone from her pocket and tapped in a message.

"I let Julio know we have a potential escort."

"Good. I'm going to take a circuitous route just to see if our follower sticks."

"Should we call Detective Morse?" Luke asked from the back seat.

Harriet turned to him.

"I don't think we need to bother her as long as the car is keeping its distance. I don't like that someone seems to be watching us, but as long as that's all they're doing, we'll let Morse enjoy her Christmas."

When they got closer to town, James guided the car into a neighbor-hood of Victorian homes that had coordinated their Christmas lights in a spectacular display. It allowed them to legitimately slow their speed. The lights followed them. A distance behind the following sedan, Harriet could see Julio's pickup's lights.

James glanced into the mirror.

"Don't be surprised, but I'm pulling over to the curb. Nothing's wrong, and don't worry, I'm not getting out, but our follower will probably drive past us. Maybe we can get a look at him or her."

He drove another block, signaled, and pulled to the curb just beyond the driveway of the corner house, leaving no space for the following sedan to park within sight. It had no choice but to keep going. All three peered out as the vehicle drove past.

Luke leaned back in his seat.

"That was creepy. Who drives around wearing a black mask over their face."

James put the car in gear.

"Let's hope Julio got the plate number."

The mysterious driver knew very well where Harriet and James lived, and as expected after their little maneuver, it didn't follow them the rest of the way home. James drove directly into the garage and used the remote to shut the door before unlocking the car and letting them out.

Julio and Julie drove up a moment later. Harriet called to them from her studio door and ushered them to the kitchen.

"James is making hot chocolate. Would you two care for a cup?"

"That sounds great," Julio replied as he helped Julie out of her jacket.

James took their coats while Harriet set a plate of cookies on the kitchen table.

"Were you able to get the plate number?" Harriet asked when they were finally seated with their drinks.

Julio leaned back in his chair.

"Yes, and no. We got the first three digits."

"There was mud smeared on the license plate," Julie added.

Harriet sipped her cocoa and set her cup down.

I can give what you have to Morse and see what she can do."

Julio bit a leg off his gingerbread man.

"I can tell you the make and model, if that helps."

"It should," Harriet said. She got up, grabbed her shopping list tablet and a pen, and handed them to him. He scribbled notes about the car and handed it back. Harriet set them back on the counter and returned to the table. "I'll drop it by the police station in the morning."

They sipped their cocoa in silence for a few moments. Julie toyed with her cookie.

"Can I ask you guys something?"

Harriet smiled.

"Sure, anything."

"Do any of you know that…woman…Aiden proposed to tonight? I mean, everyone seemed a little shocked."

"I've never seen her before," Harriet said and looked at James.

"Me, either," he agreed.

Harriet twirled her spoon between her fingers.

"Aiden was gone to Uganda for months, so maybe she's someone he met there."

Julio barked a laugh.

"Somehow, I can't see that person living rough in Uganda."

James grinned.

"Well, Aiden's not sharing any secrets with me."

"Me, either," Harriet laughed.

Chapter 32

Harriet and Luke were sitting at the kitchen table eating leftover cinnamon rolls for breakfast when James returned from the restaurant. He took off his coat and hung it on the closet doorknob.

"I waited down the street from the restaurant until they pulled in. Julio has a key, but I left the warming tray on, so I wanted to be sure they actually arrived."

"I'm surprised Julio wanted to do a breakfast proposal. They were here till...what? Eleven o'clock?" Harriet said.

James laughed.

"He's a guy in love, he didn't want to wait any longer than he had to. I can understand that."

"Can we go see Major today?" Luke asked as he finished his second cinnamon roll.

Harriet wiped her mouth on her napkin.

"Fine with me." She looked to James. "Did you have anything else planned?"

"Not really. Just rest and not cook. I did grab a bin of bagels from the freezer. I was going to pick up some cream cheese at the store and take them out to the homeless camp, but I didn't have a specific time in mind to do that."

"What if we take Luke to the stable, then deliver the bagels and cream cheese and then go back to the stable," Harriet suggested.

James picked a cinnamon roll off the plate and took a bite. He chewed thoughtfully then held up the remainder of the roll and examined it.

"Do you think these have too much cinnamon?"

193

Harriet laughed. "They're delicious. Now, what do you think of the plan?"

He took her hand.

"If it works for Luke, it works for me."

Luke jumped up.

"I'll be ready in a flash."

"Don't hurry too fast, we still have to walk the dogs before we go," Harriet called after him as she carried their plates to the sink.

✂ --- ✂ --- ✂

James carried the plastic bin of bagels to the common area of the homeless camp and set it on the table.

"Good morning, Joyce. We brought you a little snack."

"Thank you, James. Can you stay for a cup of coffee?"

James looked at Harriet, and she nodded.

"We could have a quick cup."

Joyce moved the coffee pot toward the center of the fire grate then opened one of the large wooden storage boxes that defined the back of the common area, pulling out three cups before closing it again.

"The Lutheran church sent a bus for us on Christmas Eve," she said as she filled the mugs with coffee. "It was a lovely service. I was hoping to see Joe, but he wasn't there. He has a daughter in Foggy Point. Maybe he's with her."

"If you mean his stepdaughter Arinda, she's looking for him, too," Harriet told her.

Joyce shook her head. "It's just not like him to not tell anyone where he's going."

"We can ask around when we're in town," Harriet offered

Several other camp residents drifted into the common area as the smell of coffee permeated the area. Harriet got up when she and James had finished.

"I hope you find your friend."

"Thank you for that, Harriet. And thank you for the bagels, James."

✂ --- ✂ --- ✂

James turned the car around and headed out of the parking lot.

"Do you think Luke will mind if we watch him ride?"

"I don't think so. He doesn't seem inclined to hide his blossoming friendship with Emily."

"Do you think he's doing okay?" James said in a quiet voice.

"I'm not exactly an expert parent here, but he seems to be doing well enough. I think coming out to the stable has really helped him. He seems really attached to that horse."

James let out a breath.

"I know I'm not a real father, and I haven't been a foster parent very long, but I worry. What if something happens because we didn't do something we should have or say the wrong thing or something."

Harriet reached across the space between the seats and took his hand.

"I find it incredibly sweet that you're so worried, but I think you're doing fine. *We're* doing fine. We may not have much experience, but Aunt Beth does, and she would tell us if we were making any missteps."

"I hope so."

✂ --- ✂ --- ✂

Harriet held up a teal-green laminated card when they turned into the stable driveway. A gate that had previously always been open was closed. A private security guard stood in front of the gate; and when he saw the card, he swung the gate open, closing it again when they were through.

"Now I really do feel like a negligent parent. This seems like a dangerous place to let our only child come to alone." James said.

"They have a locked gate and security guard, and there are security cameras in every barn aisle and both arenas. I think he's safe here."

They parked the car and headed for the barn. Harriet took James's hand and led him to the arena.

"They should be riding by now."

No one was in the main arena. They walked around to the smaller warm-up arena but found it empty, too. Harriet hurried as they headed toward the barn. No one was visible in the aisle.

"Luke?" Harriet called when they entered.

A horse nickered. Harriet jogged inside. James caught up and grabbed her arm. He held his finger to his lips, gesturing for her to be quiet. Muffled voices were coming from a stall.

Harriet could tell the male voice was Luke's, but she couldn't make out what he was saying, so she crept closer.

"I have to tell Harriet," Luke said.

"I promised not to tell anyone. If you tell, I'll get fired."

"Some weirdo is camping out on our street for who knows why, and it didn't start until Jade gave Harriet this horse."

"How will telling Harriet change any of that? Jade gave her the horse. That's done."

"She needs to know," Luke insisted.

Harriet strode to the stall the conversation was coming from and pulled the door open.

"Okay, that cat's out of the bag," she said. "What is it we need to tell Harriet?"

James came in behind her. Luke looked from Emily to James and back to Emily.

"I'm sorry," he said to her quietly.

Tears welled up in her eyes.

"Emily just told me that Jade has been hiding out here at the stable."

"How long?" Harriet asked.

Emily hung her head.

"She never left. She wrote you the note about giving you Becky and moved out here."

"So, the whole 'I'm joining my parents' bit was a ruse?"

Emily nodded.

"Where is she?"

"I don't know."

"Come on," James said. "You expect us to believe that?"

"I *don't* know—for real."

"Emily," Luke interrupted, "are you or are you not hiding Jade?"

Emily wiped her nose on a sleeve as tears dripped down her face. She shook her head.

"But she's here?" Harriet persisted.

Emily nodded.

"Is Marcia hiding her?"

She pulled a tissue from her pocket and handed it to Emily as the girl's tears began falling in earnest.

Chapter 33

A quick search of the barn did not turn up either Jade or Marcia.

"Where has Jade actually been living?" Harriet asked Emily.

Emily dabbed at her nose.

"I don't know, and that's the truth. No one even told me she was staying here. I discovered her by accident. I took my hat off to put my riding helmet on,"

"Wait a minute," Harriet interrupted. "When was this?"

Emily thought a moment.

"Wednesday, I think. A couple of days before Christmas Eve. Anyway, when I was done riding, it was snowing hard, so my mom came to get me and my bike in the car. I didn't remember I'd left my hat in the tack room until the next day. I wasn't scheduled to be here, but I came by to get my hat and I saw Becky's stall door was a little bit open."

"So, you went to see why and found Jade." Harriet finished for her.

"Jade said we needed to talk to Marcia, so we did, and Marcia said someone was stalking Jade so she needed to hide out here for a while. She told me it was important not to tell anyone."

"But you decided to share with Luke anyway?" James asked.

Emily looked exasperated.

"No, I didn't. I mean I did, but he figured it out first. Jade braided red and green ribbons into Becky's mane, for Christmas, I guess. She was going to take them out before anyone came to the stable, but I guess she forgot. Luke noticed and figured out she was the only person who would have done it. He asked me, and I cracked." She looked at Harriet. "I'm not a good liar."

Harriet put her arm around the girl's shoulders.

"It's okay, honey. They shouldn't have asked you to keep their secret." Harriet felt like she was channeling her aunt. "If Jade were going to stay here, where do you think she'd sleep?" she asked.

Emily thought for a moment.

"Probably in the dorm room in the barn attic."

James and Harriet shared a glance. Why hadn't she told them about the attic dorm before they'd searched the whole ground floor?

"Lead the way," James told her.

A door next to the feed room revealed a staircase that led to a second-floor room that contained two rows of wooden bunkbeds divided by a central aisle. Two open doors, one on each side at the end of the bed rows, revealed bathrooms with showers. All but one of the beds had a rolled-up thin mattress enclosed in a clear plastic trash bag. A lone bed had the mattress unrolled and covered by a sleeping bag and pillow.

James picked up the pillow and smelled it.

"It's Jade, all right. This pillow smells like her store."

Harriet came to the bed and took a sniff.

"You're right. But where she is now? For that matter, where's Marcia? I've never been out here day or night without her making an appearance."

"Now that I think about it, I haven't seen her since I've been here," Luke offered.

Harriet pulled her phone from her pocket.

"What's Marcia's house number?"

Emily recited it from memory. Harriet tapped it into her phone and listened, but no one answered. When she heard the voice mail come on, she hung up.

"She didn't answer, but for completeness's sake, we should check the house."

"We could ask the security guard at the gate," Luke suggested.

Harriet smiled at him.

"You're right. If they're doing their job, they should be able to tell us if she's here, and if not, when she left."

✂ --- ✂ --- ✂

Harriet stood behind the guard in the room that housed the stable's security station and stared at the screen.

"So, there's Jade," She pointed. "Going down the aisle and into Becky's stall. She comes back out, walks halfway down the aisle and disappears. How is that possible?"

"Rewind it," James said, and the guard did. "Can you slow it?"

198

The guard pushed another button and played the section again at half-speed.

"See? Right there."

Harriet looked where he pointed.

"Did someone erase a section of the recording?"

James stepped back from the screen.

"Sure looks like it."

"How could that happen?" Harriet asked the guard.

"We don't monitor the screen constantly. We do a walk-around once an hour. It takes about fifteen minutes. Someone could have done it then. It would have to be someone who was on the list to get through the gate."

"Can we look at the list?" James asked.

The guard shook his head.

"You can call my supervisor, but I'm not allowed to give out that kind of information to anyone but the people who hired us. I've already stretched the rules by letting you look at the video."

Emily and Luke had waited just outside the small room.

"We could go to the house and get Marcia. She's probably authorized," Emily said.

"Do it," Harriet said. "We'll wait here."

The guard switched the view on his monitor as the two young people ran for the house.

"They won't find her."

"What?" Harriet and James said at the same time.

"They won't find Marcia. Her car pulled out while we were looking at the other video."

The video system usually showed four small views simultaneously, but any of the four options could be switched to to full-screen.

"Can you replay it for us?" Harriet asked.

He tapped a few keys, and the driveway filled the screen. A gray sedan passed into view, empty except for the driver—Marcia Hamilton.

James leaned closer.

"Can you sharpen the license plate."

The guard laughed.

"That only works on TV. The police may have technicians and equipment to clean up video like that, but we can't do it on a commercial system like this."

Luke and Emily came back.

"She didn't answer, and we looked in the garage window and her car isn't there."

Harriet pressed her lips together.

"You might as well take Major out for some exercise while we're here."

Luke went to Major's stall; he led the big horse out into the aisle and fastened him with the cross ties. Emily watched as he got the grooming kit and started brushing him.

"Will you be okay if I go get Fable?"

"We'll be fine," Luke said, blushing. "Harriet knows about horses if I get stuck, but I think I've got this." Major nudged him as if to affirm his statement.

Harriet watched, but Luke was clearly a quick study. He groomed and saddled the horse without missing a beat. He got a bridle from the tack room and stopped in front of her.

"Could you help me get the bit in his mouth? Emily sticks her finger in his mouth, but I'm not sure exactly how."

Harriet went with him.

"There's a space between his front teeth and his molars where you can tickle his gums to let him know he needs to open his mouth," she explained.

It turned out Luke didn't need much technique. Major opened his mouth as soon as he saw the bridle nearing his head. She waited until Luke headed to the arena.

"There are bleachers in the arena so we can watch him ride," she told James.

"Before we do, don't you think we should call your buddy Morse?"

Harriet slid her arm around his waist as they started after Luke.

"Yeah, I was thinking about that. She needs to know Jade is still in town, and I'm hoping she can check Marcia's license number and see if it matches what Julio got from our stalker." She tapped Morse's number into her phone and listened to the voice message. "Call me when you get a chance," she said after the beep.

She slid her phone into her pocket and put her glove back on. "I'll try again when we're done."

✂ --- ✂ --- ✂

James gestured toward Luke and Emily as they rode in a big circle around the arena.

"Is it just me, or is Luke's horse a giant."

Harriet laughed. "He's a giant."

They continued watching as Emily instructed Luke, having him guide Major through a series of spirals, first turning to the right, then the left. He had been riding for about thirty minutes when James's dad called asking for help setting up the new table saw Santa had brought him.

"Do you mind if Luke and I go help him?" he asked Harriet. "I know I said we were going to spend the day together, but Mom's not home, so it might be boring for you to come with."

"You and Luke *should* go help him. Lauren texted me earlier and wanted to get coffee if I had any time."

"It shouldn't take us more than an hour or two."

"That's fine. I think Lauren wants to decompress after Christmas with her family. It may take at least that long for her to work through it all."

"I'll call Dad back and let him we'll be there in an hour or so. That'll give us time to go back to the house and take the dogs out. Luke and I can take the restaurant van to Dad's so you can have your car."

"Perfect."

She pulled her phone from her pocket and sent Lauren a text, explaining the plan.

Chapter 34

An icy drizzle was falling as Harriet hurried from her car into The Steaming Cup. It had taken less than an hour to deal with the dogs and switch cars, but Lauren had beaten her there. Her Christmas must have been a doozie.

She ordered a London Fog latte and, when it was prepared, carried it to the table where Lauren sat, nursing a large black coffee.

"Yesterday must have been bad if you're drinking the hard stuff."

"It was the usual fun event at the Sawyer household. My parents picking Les apart and me trying to make peace among everyone, all set to the background of my aunt spouting the latest pop psychology on the topic at hand. How was your first Christmas with your baby boy?"

"Christmas Eve at James's parents was great. Christmas Day dinner was bizarre." She described Aiden's girlfriend, the surprise proposal, and the aftermath. "Hopefully, Julio's second attempt this morning at the restaurant went better."

Lauren sipped her coffee.

"That definitely tops Christmas combat at the Sawyer's."

"I felt sorry for Julio."

"Great minds think alike," Aunt Beth said as she came up to their table. "Is this private, or can we join you?"

"We?" Harriet said and looked behind her aunt.

"Connie and Mavis will be along in a minute."

Harriet got up and dragged a couple of additional chairs to the table.

"We got a partial license plate number for the gray sedan that's been hanging around my house," she said when everyone was seated with their drinks.

Mavis set her mug down with a *thunk*.

"And?"

"And...nothing yet. This just happened last night. I left Morse a message, but I haven't heard back. We may not need her help, though. We took Luke to the stable this morning, and he got Emily to confess that Jade did not, in fact, leave the country but instead has been hiding out at the stable.

"Before we could track her down, she disappeared, and then the stable manager drove off in her gray sedan. We're making the assumption Jade was hidden in the car."

"Could you tell if it was the same car?" Lauren asked her.

Harriet smiled.

"It looked like it to me, but you know I'm not good with cars. We're lucky I knew they were both gray sedans."

Connie tapped her spoon on the table.

"So, we're back to thinking Jade is our killer?"

Harriet sipped her latte.

"I wouldn't go that far. She could be hiding from the killer. And I guess I can understand why she would lie to me about her whereabouts."

"But we can't rule her out," Lauren finished for her.

Mavis pulled a piece of wool felt from her bag and began attaching a flower petal to the black background with a blanket stitch.

"So, does that mean we're back to square one?"

Harriet leaned back in her chair.

"You know what I've been wondering? We know, or suspect we know, that a number of the shopkeepers in the downtown area are being blackmailed. Then, that whoever is doing this escalated to killing people—or attempting to kill them, in Jade's case."

"Okay," Lauren said.

"Who is the one merchant among them who didn't make much of a secret about being blackmailed and yet has not had a hint of an attack on her person?"

"Sunny," Mavis and Beth said at the same time.

"And," Harriet continued, "while Jade has had her store burned, and an apparent attempt made to steal her horse, nothing has happened to her personally. What if Sunny has been helping Jade?"

"*Diós mio*, why would Sunny and Jade want to harm the rest of the downtown merchants?"

Lauren made a face as she took another sip of her black coffee.

"Were they both friends of Valery's daughter? Maybe they blamed him for her death."

Harriet stood up. "That doesn't explain all the deaths." She walked to the service counter and came back with a thermos of half-and-half and several packets of organic sugar. She handed both to Lauren.

"I can't stand watching you torture yourself any longer."

Lauren took the seasonings and began stirring them into her coffee.

"What if its plain old greed? Maybe Sunny and Jade are having money problems and decided to prey on their more prosperous competitors?"

"Why did they select the particular shops they did?" Beth asked.

Harriet sipped her latte thoughtfully.

"Their victims have skeletons in their closets they wouldn't want exposed, otherwise, it wouldn't be blackmail. Vern was implicated in Val's daughter's death. He was exonerated eventually, but I'm sure he wouldn't want to be dragged through the mud for a second time. Daniel had AIDS, and Millie had a convicted killer working for her."

Lauren sipped her doctored coffee and smiled. "That's better. Now, what about Valery?"

"We don't know, but judging by the two thugs who were pretending to be family at Val's funeral there could be something there," Harriet said.

Beth dunked the leg of her gingerbread man in her tea and bit it off, chewing slowly as she considered the idea.

"Not that this should be a reason in this day and age, but Val's son also had AIDS. He said he met Daniel at a support group. Maybe Val was Old World enough to pay to keep that quiet."

Harriet sat back in her chair.

"Still, it doesn't seem like multiple people would stop paying the blackmail all at the same time, resulting in them being killed. You'd think after the first murder they'd be scrambling to scrape up the cash to pay the blackmailer."

Lauren took another sip of her coffee. "Or leaving town," she said.

Mavis tied off the thread on the back of her piece and cut it with her little scissors.

"I still think it's Valery's wife, seeking revenge for her daughter being killed and her son getting AIDS."

Lauren pulled her tablet from her bag and typed in a reminder.

"Sorry, I was supposed to follow up on her, but I got distracted with all the Christmas festivities. I'll see what I can find."

Mavis patted her hand.

"It's okay, honey, it's probably nothing anyway. And we shouldn't take your computer skills for granted. You do have a real job, after all."

Lauren blushed. "It's not exactly a burden. I just got distracted."

"What's not a burden?" Jane Morse asked as she sat down with her cup of coffee. "I got your message," she continued to Harriet, "and was on my way back to the office when I saw your car in the parking lot."

Harriet stood up again. "Let me run to the ladies' room, and then I'll tell you all about it."

Jane was catching up with everyone when she returned.

"I'm not sure how significant this is, but we were at the stable this morning so Luke could ride, and he was talking to his friend Emily, and it came out that Jade did not leave the country to join her parents but has been staying in an attic dormitory in the barn there."

Morse pulled out her notebook and made a note. "Did you talk to her?"

Harriet shook her head. "No, we didn't see her. I did attempt to find the barn manager, but she drove off as we were reviewing surveillance video trying to locate Jade."

"Tell her about the car," Lauren prompted.

"I'm getting to that. There's been a gray sedan hanging around my street, and I've seen it several other places I've been. While we were looking at the video, the barn manager drove off in a gray sedan. And before you ask, I'm not good enough with car types to tell what make and model it was. It looked like the generic cars they give you at rental places."

"She did get a partial plate off the one in her neighborhood last night," Lauren added.

Morse wrote another note and looked up.

"I'll go out to the stable and see what I can find out. With the enhanced security they put in after the attempt to steal Jade's horse, there should be plenty of video footage to look at."

Harriet twirled her stir-stick in her fingers.

"It looked to us like someone has edited it. We caught a glimpse of Jade, but she winked out while she was walking down the aisle."

"Define 'winked out'," Morse asked.

"Like someone erased a segment. She was in one frame and gone in the next."

Morse closed her notebook.

"It's never easy, is it?"

She started to get up. Beth reached out and held her arm.

"Sit down and have your coffee. You won't do anyone any good if you get sick from not taking care of yourself. Have you eaten anything?"

Morse sat back down.

"I was going to get a bagel to take back to the station."

Beth stood up.

"You sit. Crime can wait a few minutes. Do you want your bagel toasted?"

Morse nodded, and Beth went to the counter to order her snack.

✂ --- ✂ --- ✂

Harriet drained the last bit of latte from her cup and set it on the table.

"It still bothers me that Sunny was being blackmailed but, as far as we know, had not had any sort of threat to her wellbeing."

Lauren tore a fringe on the edge of her paper napkin.

"Maybe Sunny is the only one who didn't run out of money to pay the blackmailer."

"That's hard to believe," Connie said. "It doesn't seem like a cupcake bakery would be that much more lucrative than an outdoor store or a print shop or any of the other businesses."

Harriet balled up her napkin and put it in her cup.

"How about we go to Sunshine Bakery and have a chat with her? We can see if there's a gray car there, for one thing; and maybe, if we're lucky, we'll find Jade. If nothing else, we can flat-out ask Sunny what's going on with the blackmail business."

Lauren picked up her used dishes.

"I'm in."

Connie slid her arms into her coat and looked at Beth and Mavis. "What do you two think?"

"I could use some cupcakes. My granddaughter is coming over tomorrow," Mavis said.

Beth picked up her purse and her dirty dishes.

"If you guys are going, count me in."

Lauren and Harriet stood by the door while the other three put on coats and bussed their table. Lauren leaned toward Harriet and whispered, "I love their decision-making process. Mavis drove them, so once she said she was going, the others didn't have a choice unless they were going to walk home."

"That's how they've stayed friends so long. They're considerate."

Lauren laughed. "I guess you and I are doomed, then."

Harriet shook her head and joined in laughing.

"What's so funny?" Beth asked.

They just continued chuckling as they went out the door.

Chapter 35

There were two customers ahead of Mavis in line at the bakery. Connie and Beth sat down at a table while Harriet and Lauren examined the offerings in the display case.

"How can I help you?" Sunny asked Harriet when she'd boxed up Mavis's choices.

"I'll have one of the double lemon and a peppermint patty."

"I'll have the same thing," Lauren said and handed Harriet a five-dollar bill.

Sunny began picking cupcakes from the case and putting them on two plates.

"What we'd really like is to talk to you for a few minutes," Harriet said as she handed her the money for their purchases.

Sunny took a step back. "What about?"

"Could you just come over to the table and talk to us?"

Sunny pulled the disposable glove from her right hand and tossed it in her wastebasket before following them to the table where Beth, Mavis and Connie sat. Harriet pulled two chairs from another table so they could all sit.

"Is Jade Meyers staying with you?" she asked without preamble.

Sunny pulled her head back and looked confused.

"I heard she left town to go work with her parents."

"I know that rumor is circulating around town," Harriet pressed, "but what I'm not hearing is you saying no."

"I'm saying it now—no. Why would she be?"

"Weren't you two friends?" Lauren asked.

Sunny blew out a breath and shook her head.

"We ran around together in high school. It wasn't a healthy relationship…for me, anyway."

"Because she sold drugs?" Harriet asked.

"That was a long time ago. It was a phase for her. She's not into that anymore."

"I thought you weren't friends." Lauren said.

"We're *not* friends, but this is a small town. We run into each other once in a while."

Harriet cut her cupcakes into fourths and slid the plate toward her aunt.

"Have you seen Jade in the last few days?" she asked.

"No, I haven't. What's this about?"

Harriet got to the point. "Are you being blackmailed?".

Sunny adjusted her hairnet.

"Why would you think that?"

Beth cleared her throat.

"Our friend saw you holding a letter made up of letters cut from magazines and pasted on a page."

"That was just—"

"Sunny, stop," Harriet said. "Whatever lie you were going to tell us, don't bother. Several business owners in downtown have been blackmailed, and now most of them are dead or have had attempts made on their lives. In Jade's case, her business was burned and an attempt made to steal her horse.

"Our friend saw you holding a blackmail letter in your hands. I have to ask myself, Why is everyone else who got letters being attacked while you remain untouched? Could it be because you were a holding a blackmail letter before sending it to yet another business?"

Sunny's eyes widened, a shocked look on her face.

"No…no! You have it all wrong. I *was* being blackmailed. When I couldn't afford it anymore and was going to lose my business, I called my brother. I didn't want to, but the blackmailer said if we called the police we'd regret it."

Lauren pulled her tablet from her bag. "What's your brother's name?"

Sunny sighed, and her shoulders slumped. "You don't have to look him up. He's Wah Ching."

Lauren tapped.

"The Asian gang Wah Ching?"

"He's an enforcer," Sunny said. "I'm not proud of that. It broke my mother's heart when she found out. After people started being killed here, I didn't know what else to do. He came immediately."

"So, where is he?" Beth asked.

"He's staying with me. He stays in during the day. As you might imagine, he's got tattoos that might draw attention on the streets of Foggy Point. He went out the first couple of nights he was here to the local bars and wherever else his type hangs out, and put the word out that if anyone came near me, they'd regret it." Tears started to fill her eyes. "Are you going to tell the police?"

Harriet considered for a moment.

"If you're honest with us about Jade, I don't see why you or your brother needs to come into this."

Sunny closed her eyes and let out a breath. "I feel like I'm throwing her under the bus."

Connie took Sunny's hand.

"Just tell us the truth. If Jade has been killing people, she needs to be caught before anyone else dies. She needs help."

"She's not the killer," Sunny protested. "She could never do anything like that."

"If you say so," Harriet said. "If not, she is in grave danger. She needs to talk to the police and let them protect her."

"She's afraid. Our letters all said no police or we'd regret it. She's afraid if the killer can't get to her, they'll kill her horse."

Harriet ate a bite of her lemon cupcake.

"They've increased the security at the stable, but I'm sure Jade knows that, because I know she's been staying there."

"So, why don't you talk to her there?" Sunny asked.

"Because she isn't there anymore," Harriet said. "She disappeared."

The color drained from Sunny's face. "Do you think the killer has her?"

Harriet paused and went over to the cooler adjacent to the front counter for a glass of water.

"I don't think the killer got her. I think the stable manager helped her leave without being seen. But she needs real protection."

Sunny pulled a cell phone from her pocket and scrolled through her recent calls, holding the screen up so Harriet could see, as if that made what she was saying more believable.

"She calls me every night so we can be sure we both survived another day, but her number is blocked."

Harriet thought for a moment.

"Would you be willing to talk to our detective friend? We won't tell her about your brother, and will leave it up to you if you even want to tell her you've been a victim of the blackmailer. Maybe she can talk to Jade when she calls you tonight, maybe talk her into coming in."

Sunny looked Harriet in the eye.

"Swear you won't tell her about my brother?"

"If you don't want her to know you're a victim, that's your business. As for your brother, that's none of *our* business."

Sunny rubbed her hands over her face.

"I can't promise she'll call. Can you ask your detective friend to come buy cupcakes like she's a regular customer? Tell her to come just before closing, and that Jade will *possibly* call."

Lauren turned her screen lock on and slid the tablet back into her bag. "We can do that."

Sunny stood up.

"Would you like some coffee to go with your cupcakes?"

Connie smiled. "That would be nice, honey."

✂ --- ✂ --- ✂

Harriet pulled her phone from her pocket and tapped in a text message to Detective Morse. *Have a lead on Jade. Can you be at the bakery just before five?* she typed, and pushed send. Her phone rang before she could put it away.

"What have you got?" Jane asked.

Harriet explained what Sunny had told them.

"Tell her I'll be there," Morse said, and hung up.

Harriet picked up her empty plate and carried it to the counter.

"Detective Morse will be here just before five," she told Sunny.

Sunny took the plate and set it on the pass-through ledge that connected the sales area to the kitchen.

"What do you think she'll say to Jade?"

"I don't know. She'll probably ask if she knows who is doing this and why she's hiding at the stables instead of coming to the police."

"That isn't going to go anywhere. Jade will say the same as I did—the note said 'no police'. And obviously, she's hiding to avoid being killed. I asked my brother if he'd protect her, but he said he's already exposing himself helping me. His people, or whatever they are, understand protecting blood, he says. They're already worried he's too conspicuous to be operating in a such a small town. He says a clever policeman could cause him problems."

"You're right. Hopefully, Morse has a better plan than just asking Jade to fill out a report about her blackmail."

"Could you and Lauren come back when the detective comes? She scares me."

"I can come back, but the Foggy Point Police have made it very clear I'm to stay out of police business."

210

Sunny gave her a weak smile. "Still, I'd feel better if you were here."

Harriet sighed.

She could hear Morse echoing in her head, but she needed to ask Jade about Becky, didn't she? Surely, Morse would be able to see that. Besides, Lauren would be disappointed if they didn't come back, and she couldn't let her friend down, could she?

"Let me check with my family and see if they have any plans for us."

Chapter 36

Harriet met Lauren at Sunshine Bakery at quarter after four.

"I don't know about you, but I can't eat another cupcake this soon," she told Lauren

"I don't think Sunny will mind if we have hot cocoa." Lauren said. "I'm guessing your men had something to keep them busy while you're here."

Harriet laughed.

"You could say that. They barely looked up when I said I was leaving for a while. James's dad got a table saw for Christmas. They went over to help him set it up, and they've moved straight on to Grampa Will teaching them how to make wooden boxes. Luke is working on a carrier for Major's brushes and beauty accessories."

"I didn't realize horses were into beauty."

"You'd be surprised."

"Do you guys want anything?" Sunny asked from behind the counter. She looked like she'd aged ten years since the last time they'd been there.

Harriet smiled and did her best to look encouraging.

"Do you have any of that peppermint hot chocolate?"

"Sure," She turned and went into the kitchen, returning a few minutes with two mugs and a carafe. She set all three on their table and returned to the kitchen without saying anything.

Harriet picked up her mug and took a sip.

"She looks a little the worse for wear since we were last here."

Lauren pulled a plastic bag full of homemade ginger cookies from her messenger bag.

"Here." She handed Harriet a cookie. "Yeah, she does look more worried than I would expect her to be if meeting with Morse was the only problem. Hard to guess what else has happened, though."

Harriet looked toward the kitchen.

"I think someone else is in the kitchen. I just saw someone flash by the little window. I wonder if it's the brother."

"Not sure why that would stress her out any more than she already is."

They sipped their cocoa in silence and munched cookies. Harriet held a cookie up before taking a bite.

"These are really good."

"It's my grandmother's secret recipe."

The front-door chime sounded as Detective Morse came into the shop. She shook her head as she came over to their table.

"I guess I shouldn't be surprised to find you two here."

"Hey," Harriet protested. "Sunny asked us to be here when you came."

"Did she, now?"

Lauren smirked. "She's afraid to be alone with you."

"She said that?" Morse asked.

"Why else would we be here?" Harriet said with a smile.

Sunny appeared and asked Morse if she wanted anything to eat or drink. Morse smiled at her in an obvious attempt to put her at ease.

"Coffee would be great."

Sunny was gone longer than she should have been if all she was doing was pouring coffee. She finally reappeared carrying Morse's mug of coffee...and followed closely by Jade Meyers.

Morse looked Jade up and down.

"A lot of people have been looking for you. They seemed to think you left the country."

Jade's face turned red.

"I'm sorry for that. I didn't want to leave my horse unprotected, but I wanted whoever has been killing people to think I was gone so they wouldn't come after me."

Morse took her notebook from her purse and flipped the cover open.

"I find it a little strange that our murders seem to have happened with no prelude, and now after they've killed several business people in town, you're asking me to believe the same person wants you dead but is fooling around trying to steal your horse and burn your business." She turned to Sunny. "And you were blackmailed, and yet no attempt has been made on your life, either."

Sunny just stared at Harriet and shrugged.

Morse looked around the small room.

"Okay, Ms. Meyers, I'd like to talk to you over there." She pointed to a table diagonally across the room. "Ms. Mason, I'll talk to you when I'm done."

Sunny crossed the floor and collapsed into the chair opposite Harriet.

"She doesn't believe us," she said in a shocked tone.

Lauren sipped her cocoa and set her mug down.

"You'll be lucky if she only thinks you aren't targets of the murderer. She could very well be thinking you two *are* the murderers."

"How could she think that?" Sonny screeched.

Morse looked up from her discussion with Jade. "You okay over there?"

"We're fine," Harriet told her.

Morse turned back to Jade. Sunny's eyes filled with tears.

"Can't you tell her I didn't have anything to do with the murders?"

"What I think doesn't matter. Morse needs evidence," Harriet said.

"Do you know anything that can help her look in another direction?" Lauren asked her.

Sunny pushed her hair off her face with both hands.

"I keep trying to tell everyone—all I know is one day I was minding my own business, becoming a successful bakery owner, and the next I was being blackmailed to within an inch of my life."

Harriet leaned back in her chair and thought a moment.

"Are you positive Jade isn't involved in this in some way?"

Sunny took a deep breath.

"I don't think so," she said slowly. "I mean, why would she? She's like me—trying to build her business up."

Harriet sipped her cocoa.

"Do you think she might have suspected Daniel of being the blackmailer and killed him, only to discover it wasn't him?"

Sunny looked shocked.

"And then she killed Mr. Melnyk?" she said with a note of sarcasm in her voice. "And then the guy that worked for Millie? Killing each, thinking they were the blackmailer and moving on to the next one when she found out it wasn't?"

Lauren smiled. "When you say it like that, it does sound a little crazy."

Morse got up and approached their table, Jade on her heels.

"All right, Ms. Mason, can I talk to you over there?"

Sunny looked panicked, but she got up and followed Morse to the other table.

The color had left Jade's face when she sat down.

"Can I get you a cup of cocoa?" Harriet asked her.

Jade gave her a wan smile and nodded.

Harriet went to the kitchen and found a mug, pouring from the carafe on their table when she returned. She pressed the mug into Jade's hands.

"Here, drink this."

Jade sat and sipped and gathered herself. The color returned to her face.

"What can I do?" she asked. "That detective thinks I killed three people. Because the real killer tried to steal my horse and burned my business, that means I'm guilty? This is a nightmare."

Harriet took a napkin from the dispenser on the table and wiped her mouth.

"Let's think about this again. What do we know so far?"

"The first victim had AIDS," Lauren said. "Or at least he was HIV-positive."

"And he is friends with Ole Melnyk, who also has AIDS," Harriet added.

Lauren got her tablet out and started a list.

"And," she said as she typed, "Valery Melnyk is Ole's father, and we think he was also being blackmailed."

Harriet tore bits of paper from the edge of her napkin, rolling them into little balls.

"Millie's helper William Crowe was a convicted felon," she said, "but as far as we know, he doesn't have any ties to anyone we know. We know Millie was being blackmailed.

"Luke and I did see the mystery figure in Millie's basement after he killed Mark, but that doesn't help much. They could be male or female—we heard them talk but their voice was disguised, and they were covered head-to-toe in black, so we only know they were tall and sort of slender."

Lauren tapped that into her tablet. Harriet waited until she was finished typing.

"Our killer attempted to kill Vern Jenkins, and only because of the hidden room in his store basement did he survive. We know the Melnyk family sued Vern, unsuccessfully, for selling Val's daughter a faulty kayak after she died."

Lauren entered the information.

"So, that covers our murders or attempted murders. All but William Crowe seem to have a connection to Valery Melnyk's family."

"Which brings us to Jade," Harriet said. She glanced at the woman. "We've been told you sold drugs to Valery's daughter."

Jade hung her head.

"That was a long time ago. Not something I'm proud of, but I've turned my life around."

"But it fits with the Melnyk connection. Still, why try to steal the horse?" Lauren asked as she typed.

Jade sipped her cocoa.

"If it's someone who knows me, they would know nothing could hurt me more than harming Becky."

"You're thinking the killer was going to torture you by taking Becky and then would come back and kill you?" Harriet asked her.

Jade blew out a breath. "It's all I could think of."

"What's that?" Morse asked as she and Sunny rejoined the others.

Lauren turned her pad around so Morse could read it.

"We're just grinding on the same few facts we all know."

Morse raised her eyebrows.

"There are a lot of connections with the Melnyk family."

"That's what we thought," Harriet said. "We've wondered if Valery's wife came back to exact revenge. The only problem is Millie's guy, Mark. He doesn't seem to connect to anyone. He *was* convicted of killing a person, although you could argue it was more of an accident than murder."

Morse pulled out a chair and sat down.

"I can't figure out how he fits in with this, either. Of course, it's always possible the killer is choosing random victims, and it just happens they all have a Melnyk connection due to the size of our town."

Harriet put a hand over her mouth and stared thoughtfully out the window for a moment.

"What?" Lauren asked when she turned back to face them.

"If everyone's willing to be a little creative, I think I might have an idea."

Chapter 37

Morse shook her head.

"As you well know, the Foggy Point Police Department isn't known for its creativity, but let me hear it."

Harriet took a deep breath.

"Okay, correct me if I'm wrong, but it seems like you aren't getting anywhere on this case."

"We've eliminated a lot of suspects—the usual friends and family—but it would be fair to say we're getting nowhere," Morse agreed.

Harriet continued.

"It seems to me the killer particularly wants Jade to suffer before he kills her. So, why don't we give her to him?"

Morse began shaking her head. "I thought you had a real idea."

"Hear me out. We don't really give him Jade, but we make him think he can get to her. He wanted to hurt her horse, so what if we make him think he can get to her horse? You could put the word out that a group of horse thieves were caught operating in the Puget Sound area. Then you could remove all the extra security from the stable. Or at least appear to. You could even have a policewoman dress like Jade and be obviously visible at the stable. Just for good measure, you could move Becky somewhere else."

Morse chewed on her bottom lip while she considered.

"I generally don't like elaborate plans, but this has possibilities. And as you pointed out, we aren't getting anywhere." She looked at Jade. "What do you think?"

"As long as Becky and I aren't directly involved, I guess it's okay. But where will we go that's safe?"

"We have a relationship with some of the volunteers in the King County Sheriff's Posse. One of them lives in Gig Harbor. I think she would be willing to put up Becky for a few days," Morse told her.

"That's so far away," Jade protested.

Morse looked at the ceiling.

"It's about an hour-and-a-half-drive. That's not bad. It's far enough to keep her out of harm's way. You could go with her, if you want. I'm sure the woman I'm thinking of would let you stay there."

Jade turned to Sunny.

"If you're asking me, I'd say go for it. Anything to get away from here until it's safe," Sunny told her.

"But how will you get Becky out without anyone knowing?"

Harriet poured more cocoa into her mug.

"If it were me, before I reduced the security at the stable, I'd take Becky out for a ride. I'd take her through the woods to the road, where I'd have her trailer waiting. If you wanted to be really sneaky, you could bring another horse in the trailer and ride that horse back to the stable."

Morse held her cup out to Harriet, and Harriet refilled it.

"I'm not convinced this will be enough to lure the killer in, but I'll run it by my lieutenant. I can call the posse woman and make sure she's on board."

"I wish I could call my parents," Jade fretted.

"If you're not okay with this, it ends here," Morse told her.

"No, no," Jade said. "Something has to happen. I can't go on hiding in the barn attic, hoping some crazy person doesn't find me. But what if it doesn't work?"

"Then you haven't lost anything," Lauren all but shouted. "Geez, what is the question? The rest of us don't enjoy having a killer running around our streets. At least this would be something."

Harriet put a hand on her friend's arm, but Lauren pulled it free.

"You're the one who was captured and narrowly escaped this killer," she snapped, glaring at Harriet. "Don't you want him or her caught?"

Harriet sighed.

"Of course I do, but we can't force Jade to help the police."

"What does she have to do?" Lauren complained. "Keep hiding? She's already doing that."

"You don't need us anymore, do you?" Harriet asked Morse.

The right side of Morse's mouth lifted in a half-smile.

"No, I think you've done enough. I'll let you know if this is a go. I might need to talk to you about the stable set-up."

Harriet stood up.

"Let's go, Lauren."

✂ --- ✂ --- ✂

Harriet led Lauren across the street to the sidewalk in front of Pins and Needles before stopping.

"Before you say anything, yes, I think there's something off about those two. Maybe not the same something, but I don't think either one of them is telling our friend the detective the truth."

"I shouldn't have lost it in there, but come on, she's hiding in the attic of the stable, and she has to think about whether she wants help from the police in catching the guy she's hiding from? There's something not quite right about that."

"Morse didn't say anything about Jade showing up when she was 'possibly calling' tonight, so I didn't think it was my place to mention it, but it makes me think Sunny is a little more involved with whatever is going on with Jade than she wants us to believe."

Harriet looked up and down the street, checking for the gray sedan, but other than a black pickup truck, Morse's sedan, Lauren's car, and her own, Main Street was devoid of vehicles.

"Listen, do you want to come have dinner with us tonight? James and Luke have been at his parent's house all day helping James's dad set up the new saw and then playing with it. Which is all to say, dinner will be something simple."

Lauren smiled.

"I'll take James's something simple any time. Do I have time to go let Carter out? He's been home alone for hours."

"Bring him with you. I'm sure Scooter and Cyrano would love to have company."

✂ --- ✂ --- ✂

Harriet cleared the plates off the table, and James served fruitcake.

"So, let me get this straight," he said as he sliced the cake. "The police are going to put out false information about a horse-theft ring being caught and take away the security at the stable—or at least pretend to. And the killer will come try to steal Becky, only she won't be there, but the police will, and they will arrest whoever it is, and we'll all live happily ever after. What could go wrong?"

219

Harriet set small dessert plates beside the cake dish. James put a slice on one and handed it to Lauren. She took a bite.

"Wow, this is really good. Do you serve it in the restaurant?"

"No, it's my mom's recipe. She won't tell me her secret."

Luke accepted his plate of cake and ate a forkful. He smiled.

"This *is* good." He inhaled the remainder in two bites. "May I be excused? Emily texted and wants me to call her."

"Sure," Harriet said.

James watched Luke until he was up the stairs and out of sight.

"You know he's going to ask if he can go out to the stable and ride tomorrow," he said.

Harriet swallowed her first bite of fruit cake.

"This really is good." She put her fork down. "I know he's going to want to ride, and it's going to be hard to say no when it's his Christmas break."

"Do we think it's dangerous for him to be there while the police are trying to lure the killer?"

"It's not my place to say," Lauren interrupted, "but I don't think the killer is picking people at random. He's blackmailed all the victims first."

Harriet ate another bite of her cake.

"Major seems to be pretty protective, also. I don't think he'd let a stranger approach without raising a ruckus."

James sighed.

"That all sounds reasonable, but you're assuming our killer is a stranger. What if he—or she—isn't?"

Harriet set her fork down.

"If they aren't a stranger, then it could be anyone. If that's the case, we should stay home and never leave the house again."

"Come on, you know what I mean."

Harriet got to take a glass from the cupboard and filled it with water.

"Anyone else?" she asked before sitting down. James declined, and Lauren accepted.

Lauren ate the remainder of her fruitcake.

"It's none of my business, but I'm pretty sure there will be more than one or two plainclothes policemen at the stable once they set the plan in motion."

"And the action will be centered on Becky's stall. I noticed a short row of stalls on the opposite side of the warm-up arena. They're probably for overnight visitors. We can ask if Major can be moved to one of them for the duration," Harriet suggested. "That would keep Luke a good distance away from the action."

Lauren set her fork down. James leaned back in his chair.

"I suppose we can't keep him in a glass bubble," he said.

"It's not obvious the killer will even take the bait. If you ask me, it's pretty weird that someone kills three people they've been blackmailing and then decides to just mess around with the fourth person, who they've also been blackmailing. And I'm not sure what I think of Sunny's whole 'my brother is a feared gang member, so no one will mess with me' thing. I guess it's possible, but how probable is it in Foggy Point?"

James stood and took the remaining fruitcake to the counter to wrap.

"Well, for tomorrow anyway, I can go watch him."

"I'm sorry you're having to do that," Harriet said. "You don't get that many days off."

James smiled. "I don't mind hanging out with Luke. We had fun today."

"Are *you* going to the stable tomorrow?" Lauren asked Harriet.

"No, I got a call from a new customer. She has a Baltimore Album quilt she needs quilted on a fairly short timeline. I haven't seen it, but she says it has a wide border with dense berry vines, leaves, and flowers. It will take a lot of slow, careful quilting. I'd like to receive it and get it on the machine first thing."

"I'll be around tomorrow, if you want to go to coffee when you're ready for a break."

"Okay, thanks. Do you want to stay and watch a British mystery? They have a whole collection of Christmas episodes."

Lauren grinned.

"How can I refuse?"

Chapter 38

The temperature had dropped again the next morning, but at least the rain had stopped. Harriet cut her run to two miles so she could have breakfast with James and Luke before they went to the stable.

Marcia had been fine with moving Major to the stall row away from the main barn and, in fact, decided to move Emily's horse Fable along with another horse to keep Major company and keep Emily out of any possible action.

Luke dug into a fluffy stack of pancakes with maple syrup.

"Where did they take Becky?" he asked when he'd polished off half.

Harriet poured syrup on her two cakes.

"They aren't saying. Since they don't know who's causing the problems in town, anyone could be talking with the perpetrator without knowing it. It might be one of the King County Posse members' places, but that's just a guess. Don't tell anyone my guess. Not even Emily."

"I won't," he promised.

James sat down with his own plate of pancakes.

"When do you think you'll be done with your customer?"

Harriet did a quick calculation in her head.

"Probably a couple of hours. I need to talk with her and receive the quilt, then I'd like to get it on the machine. And I suspect I'll need to go to Pins and Needles and get a couple cones of thread. What are you thinking?"

"I was thinking we could drive over to Port Angeles and ride the ferry to Victoria. Luke's never been."

"That sounds like fun. I'm meeting Lauren for coffee, but I think I can accomplish everything within two hours. Do you want to meet me at Annie's?"

James got up to open the oven and used a spatula to lift three pancakes from the stack being kept warm. He carried them over and slid them onto Luke's plate.

"Do you think we can be done horsing around in two hours?"

Luke drenched his new pancakes in butter and syrup.

"Sure. Emily has to be done by lunchtime anyway."

Harriet stood up and carried her plate to the dishwasher.

"Sounds like a plan. Leave me a message if anything changes." She retreated to her studio to prep her machine and wait for her new customer.

Kimberly Bailey turned out to be a delightful quilter in her mid-fifties. Her appliqué skill level was off the charts. Her quilt was expertly done and, as Harriet had suspected, was going to require a lot of careful stitching in the densely-patterned border.

"Do you think I could get it back by the weekend after New Year's?" Kim asked her when they had finished checking the quilt in.

"That should be no problem. I'll get it on the machine as soon as you leave. I'll have to go pick up thread in town, but from then on, it should be smooth sailing. I should be able to have it done by the Wednesday before that weekend."

Kimberly smiled.

"That's perfect. My friend Jenny said you were the best long-arm quilter in this area."

Harriet laughed. "She might be a little prejudiced, but I will do my best."

With that, Kimberly left, and Harriet got to work setting up the quilt on her machine.

Pins and Needles quilt shop only had two other customers when Harriet arrived to pick up her quilting thread.

"I thought you'd be full of customers," she said to Marjorie.

Marjorie laughed.

"That rush of after-Christmas shopping pretty much passes us by. People usually take a week or two to get over all the stitching they did making Christmas presents. But it's okay with me. I've got a lot of holiday fabric to move to the attic, and I've been collecting some new fabric for winter and early spring that needs to come down."

Harriet raised her eyebrows at the mention of new fabric.

"You want to come up and see what I've got?" Marjorie asked.

"Sure. I'd like to make a new quilt for Luke's bed. I replaced the one in his room with first a Halloween quilt and then a Christmas one. The original I had in that room was floral. It's okay, but not as masculine as I'd like for a boy's room."

"I may have just the thing." Marjorie looked around the shop and spotted her two shoppers. "Are you ladies okay for a few minutes if I go up to the attic?"

The two friends smiled.

"We'll be okay for an hour or two," one of them said, and they both laughed.

Marjorie pulled the stairs down from the hallway ceiling and led the way up to the attic. She stepped over to a large table stacked high with bolts of new fabric wrapped in plastic. Harriet lifted one for a better look.

"Can I remove the plastic?"

"Sure. I'm about to take it off anyway."

Harriet had found the first of a whole line of gray-and-red winter bird fabric.

"That's a new design line I found on the internet," Marjorie explained. "If their winter fabric does well, I may pick up a few more of their groupings. They have some nice neutrals and tonals."

Together, they selected six bolts of fabric and carried them downstairs. Harriet had just listed out how many yards of each fabric she needed when her phone rang. She pulled out her debit card, set it on the counter, and answered.

"Come to my shop, *now!*" Sunny yelled and hung up.

Marjorie had heard, Sunny had spoken so loud.

"Go ahead, I can finish this up."

"Thanks."

Harriet hurried to the corner and crossed the street. The bakery looked closed; the blinds were drawn, and the lights were off. She reached for the door handle, but the door opened before she touched it.

"Sunny?" She leaned in but didn't enter. "Sunny?" she called again.

A hand grabbed her arm and pulled her inside.

"Sit down," an electronically altered voice said and shoved her into a chair.

She looked up and saw a familiar figure dressed in black, including the black ski mask, a small black box held up to their mouth.

"You again," she said. She glanced around the dimly-lit restaurant. Sunny was slumped in another chair to the right of the display case, her hands at an awkward angle behind her back, restrained. Across the room, a muscular Asian man sat by another table in a similar position, his tattooed face covered in blood and one eye swollen shut. His face was too battered to see if there was a family resemblance, but she assumed this was Sunny's brother. The muscles in his chest strained the fabric of his black tee-shirt. He looked tough, but clearly, he'd run into someone tougher.

"I let you go before, but you won't be so lucky this time—unless you tell me where Jade is, and more importantly, where the horse is. I suppose the police thought I would be foolish enough to believe their ruse at the stable. But alas, I'm not that stupid. Now, where is Jade, and where is the horse?"

Harriet shook her head.

"Why on earth would I know where Jade is? I would assume her horse is at the stable."

"You're trying my patience," her captor said. "Everyone in this town knows you're that police detective's favorite pet. And weren't you just here with her yesterday, planning a trap for me?"

Harriet felt the heat rise in her cheeks. She looked at Sunny, but the baker wouldn't make eye contact with her.

The electronic voice made a noise. Harriet realized it was laughter.

"Did you think you could trust that one? Haven't you ever heard a leopard can never change its spots."

"He was going to kill my brother," Sunny blurted.

So much for the feared Asian gang member, Harriet thought. And Sunny's use of "he" must mean that, as she suspected, Sunny knew who the killer was.

Harriet heard a scraping noise to her left—the brother's chair scooting on the floor.

"I still don't know where Jade is, or where her horse is," she said, loudly enough, she hoped, to cover the noise.

"It seems we have a problem, then. What are we going to do?" The intruder grabbed her wrist again.

"Give me your phone," he commanded.

Harriet complied, and he tossed it on the counter with two others. He roughly pulled both her arms around the back of her chair and secured them with a zip-tie.

"Let her go," Sunny said. "She doesn't know anything."

The intruder paced across the room and faced Sunny.

"I think she's made that clear. But she *is* the one who can get that police woman to reveal the information I need."

Harriet gave a harsh laugh. "You overestimate my influence."

"When you tell her what I say, she'll tell you what I want to know."

Harriet never got a chance to find out what that was.

At that moment, the front door of the bakery opened.

"Harriet?" Marjorie called out. She stood outlined in the doorway, purse over her shoulder, Harriet's debit card in her hand.

Before Harriet could say anything, Marjorie flipped the light switch by the front door. She took in the tableau in front of her—Harriet, Sunny, the bloody man across the room and the figure in black.

"You're supposed to be dead," she said in an incredulous tone.

She strode over to Harriet digging in her purse as she came. The man in black turned around.

"Who's supposed to be dead?" Harriet asked as Marjorie pulled the pair of shears she always carried from her purse.

"Put the scissors down," the electronic voice commanded.

Marjorie ignored him and snipped Harriet's zip-tie; she looked up to see the gun in the man's hand.

"Oh, so now you're going to shoot me?" she said. "And then kill all of *them*? Do you think no one is going to notice a gun going off? Valery, we're on Main Street. I know Foggy Point isn't the big city, but there are people out there." She started to gesture toward the outside, then threw the shears at his face instead.

Harriet jumped up as the shears slashed the mask and Valery's cheek. She covered the few steps between them and placed a well-aimed kick at the man's ankles. He fell, knocking over a table and chair. Marjorie jumped forward and pinned his arms to the ground while Harriet shoved the gun out of the way with her foot.

Marjorie was not a small woman and had Valery under control in spite of his struggling, so Harriet grabbed the shears and crossed the room, cutting Sunny's brother loose. He took control of the downed man. Then, he ripped the knitted mask from the intruder's face.

"You're supposed to be dead." Harriet repeated Marjorie's words. "I saw your body."

Marjorie pulled her cell phone from her bag and dialed 911.

"And send Detective Morse," she finished after telling the police operator the particulars.

Chapter 39

The Foggy Point Police arrived in under two minutes. Officer Nguyen came into the bakery with none of his usual comments about Harriet; and for once, Harriet was glad to see him. He went immediately to Valery Melnyk, who was still on the floor. He clamped handcuffs on him; but when he tried to make him stand up, Valery wasn't able to get his feet under him.

"He's wearing some sort shoe lifts," Marjorie told him.

The officer lifted Valery's pant leg, exposing a cut-down version of the sort of stilts worn by construction workers when they're putting drywall on a ceiling. Nguyen started untangling the straps that tied the stilts to his leg. Harriet could see a nasty bruise above the edge of his sock where she'd kicked him.

Detective Morse arrived as Officer Nguyen was walking Valery out the door, hands cuffed behind his back. She looked around the bakery. Sunny had gotten a wet towel and was wiping the blood from her brother's face at one table while Marjory and Harriet sat at a table on the opposite side of the room.

Morse joined her two friends first. She pulled her notebook out and looked around the room.

"How did you know it was Valery?" Harriet asked Marjorie before Morse could say anything.

Marjorie took a small bottle of hand sanitizer from her bag, squirted a generous dollop onto her hand, and then scrubbed her hands together.

"His pants. His wife sends him those black pants he wears from Ukraine. He brings them to me to be hemmed. They're a coarser weave than you can get here, and I guess they're warmer for winter wear. I'd recognize them anywhere. And he'd torn the hems out to cover those lifts he was wearing to disguise his height."

"I should have recognized his head shape," Harriet said. "DeAnn pointed out how the Russian nesting doll images on his quilt looked like him. His head is round like they are."

"He was supposed to be dead, so why would you even think about him? If it weren't for the pants, I wouldn't have."

Morse cleared her throat.

"Would either of you like to tell me what happened here?"

"I came in at the end," Marjorie said.

Harriet started with the call from Sunny and explained the sequence of events.

"What I don't understand, besides why he killed everyone," she said with a wry smile, "is why he's so obsessed with Jade's horse. As far as we know, he killed everyone else more or less methodically, but he toyed with Jade, burning her shop and trying to steal her horse."

Morse finished writing in her notebook.

"Do you have anything to add?" she asked Marjorie.

Marjorie smiled.

"Harriet summed it up pretty well. When I saw the blinds were closed, I peeked through the door glass where one of the slats was bent. I dropped the bag of fabric I was bringing Harriet outside and came in like I didn't know what was going on."

"It worked," Harriet said.

Morse shook her head.

"This could have gone wrong so many different ways. I'll admit, this time it seems like neither of you had a choice. Except maybe calling nine-one-one before either of you came into the bake shop."

"I could—" Harriet started.

"Save it," Morse said, holding her hand up. "I'm going to interview Sunny and her brother and go back to the station to see what Mr. Melnyk has to say for himself. I may need to talk to you both again."

"I'm going home." Harriet said. "Would you like to join me, Marjorie?"

"I wish I could, but I've got to close the shop and go check on my new kitten."

Harriet called James to see where he and Luke were. Luke was still riding, which meant another hour before they'd leave the stable.

"Is everything okay?" James asked.

"Yeah, fine."

Harriet had decided there was no need to worry James or cause Luke to have to stop riding early, since everything had come out okay.

Harriet was sipping a cup of Earl Grey tea when Lauren arrived.

"How was your new customer?" Lauren asked and sat down with her own cup of tea.

"She's a good quilter. Her appliqué is incredible."

Lauren started to ask another question about the customer, but Harriet held up her hand to stop her.

"Something happened."

"I thought you looked a little rough."

"I know who killed everyone, and Morse has him in custody."

Lauren leaned back in her chair.

"Why didn't you say so right away?"

"I'm saying so now. I was at Marjorie's getting thread, and Sunny called saying I had to go to her shop immediately. When I got there, she and her brother were being held hostage by our man in black. He'd just zip-tied my hands behind my back when Marjorie came in. She recognized him and brazened her way into disarming him."

"Who is it, already?"

"You'll never believe it, but it's Valery Melnyk."

"You're talking crazy. He's dead. You went to his funeral. Don't you remember?"

"Of course I remember going to his funeral, but I'm telling you, he's not dead. He's the killer. He held me at gunpoint and asked me where Jade was and where her horse was. If Marjorie hadn't come to give me the fabric I was in the process of purchasing when Sunny called, I'd probably be dead."

"So, if he's not dead, whose funeral did we go to?"

"I've been thinking about that," Harriet said and sipped her tea. "I can't be sure, but I'm thinking it's the homeless man, Smokey Joe, who Joyce Elias at the homeless camp has been asking me to help locate."

"Seems like an elaborate set-up."

"He almost got away with it. If he hadn't decided to become obsessed with Jade's horse, he could have killed her and laid low until Vern came out of hiding then killed *him*, and he'd have his perfect revenge, if that's what he was after."

"Hopefully, under Morse's relentless grilling, Valery will crack and tell her everything, including why the horse."

Harriet smiled.

"You should have seen Marjorie. She was amazing. She threw a pair of big dressmaker shears at Valery's face. Cut him, too!"

"How did she know it was Valery?"

Harriet explained about the pants.

"That was lucky."

"Yes, it was."

✂ --- ✂ --- ✂

James and Luke were in the kitchen when Harriet got home.

"What's wrong?" James asked when she taken off her coat, put her purse in closet and collapsed onto a kitchen chair. Scooter jumped into her lap and licked her face.

She explained what had happened, ending with Morse taking Valery Melnyk to jail.

James crouched next to her chair and pulled her into his arms.

"You could have been killed," he said, squeezing her.

"I'm fine," Harriet choked out, and he released her.

"Sorry, I just don't know what I'd..." He glanced at Luke. "What we'd do if anything happened to you."

The dogs, sensing James's upset, began circling them, barking.

"Nothing happened to me, I'm right here, all in one piece." She nudged him and looked pointedly at Luke.

James took a deep breath, and Harriet was glad he'd gotten the message. The color had drained from Luke's face when she'd recounted her story.

"Marjorie was fantastic," she said in a lighter tone. "It was amazing how she recognized Valery from his pants."

"Tell me what we can do for you," James said.

"I don't want to spoil our trip to Victoria."

"I don't mind," Luke said quickly. "We can just stay home and be together."

James took her hand.

"You've been through quite an ordeal today. Luke is off all week; we can wait until tomorrow or even the next day. I don't really have to be back at work until the thirtieth."

"We could stay home and watch those British mystery shows you like," Luke offered.

She reached out to him, and he came over to her side so she could take his hand, too.

"You guys are the best. I think I *would* like to stay home for the rest of the day. And as much as I'd like to watch mysteries with you two, I know neither of you really likes them."

James started to protest but Harriet stopped him.

"I love you both for offering, but Aunt Beth would kill me if I didn't fill her in, and rather than retell the story a dozen times, I probably need to see the rest of the Loose Threads, too."

"How about this," he said. "You go upstairs and rest for an hour or so, maybe take a bath, a nap or whatever else you need. I'll make some pizza dough while Luke calls Beth, and then we'll both cut up vegetables, shred cheese and assemble pizza."

"Are you sure. It's a lot of trouble. We could order out."

"Bite your tongue," James said in mock horror.

Luke laughed.

Harriet gave James a kiss.

"You're the best."

Chapter 40

Aunt Beth and Jorge arrived, she with an armload of paper plates and cups, he with a large bowl of salad.

"Mavis and Connie will both bring things to drink."

Harriet had come downstairs when she heard them.

"Thank you for bringing this," she said, taking the paper goods. Luke, who had answered the door, took the bowl of salad and carried it to the dining room.

Beth hung her coat in the kitchen closet before pulling Harriet into a fierce hug. Her eyes glistened with unshed tears.

"I just don't know what I'd do if something happened to you."

Harriet patted her aunt's back and leaned back to look her in the eye.

"Nothing's going to happen to me. I'm right here, and I'm fine."

Beth moved far enough to take Harriet's hands in hers.

"How many times can you get into these terrible situations and then escape by a gnat's eyelash. I'm just afraid the next time things won't work out, and the bad person is going to..."

Harriet knew her aunt couldn't bring herself to say *kill you*.

"You of all people know I don't go looking for trouble. And I have been able to get out of it so far. I have no plan to find any future trouble, but if I do, I have no reason to believe I won't get out of whatever it is as well."

"Oh, honey," Beth said, and hugged her again. "If only the world were that simple. I'm so glad you moved back to Foggy Point, but I can't help but think you were safer before you did."

"Don't even say that. I've never been happier than I am right now, here in Foggy Point with you and James and Luke and the Loose Threads and —"

Beth hugged her tighter. Then James came in and wrapped his arms around both of them.

"Can anyone join this love fest?"

Aunt Beth pulled a tissue from her cardigan pocket, dabbed at her eyes, and cleared her throat.

"What can we help you with?"

James opened a drawer and took out two pizza cutters.

"You can take these to Jorge in the dining room, and then we just need to wait for the pizzas to come out of the ovens." He waited until Beth was out of the room to continue. "*Are* you okay? I heard part of what she said. I'm sure she doesn't really think you should leave Foggy Point."

Harriet smiled and put her arm around his waist.

"Don't worry, I'm not going anywhere."

✂ --- ✂ --- ✂

Jenny, Robin, and DeAnn had been unable to come for pizza, but the rest of the Threads sat around the table, the remains of their dinner on their plates in front of them. James had insisted they all eat the pizzas while they were hot, so Harriet had only just finished her story of what had transpired at the cupcake bakery.

"*Diós mio*," Connie said. "Valery fooled everyone."

Mavis shook her head.

"It's hard to imagine the amount of pain he must have been in after the death of his daughter to cause him to snap like that."

Lauren sipped her glass of water and set it back on the table.

"Maybe it was the accumulation of loss that did him in. I mean, his wife left, then his son was diagnosed with AIDS—or maybe those events were reversed—then his beloved daughter died, and when he sued Vern, the court determined her death was an accident.

"From what I've been able to find on the internet, his daughter didn't just drown, she was underwater, fished out, and then lingered in the hospital for months before they finally declared her brain-dead and he had to make the terrible decision to pull the plug. Her care, and his insistence on seeking multiple additional opinions, nearly bankrupted him."

"He probably did feel like he'd lost everything," Harriet agreed.

"That's still no excuse to go around killing people," James said.

Jorge wiped his large hands on his napkin.

"There is nothing more dangerous than a man who feels like he's got nothing left to lose."

"It must be a real relief for Jade and Sunny and Vern and Millie and whoever else he might have been blackmailing," Connie said. "Now they can pull their businesses back together."

A knock sounded on the studio door. James got up to answer it.

"I hope you don't mind," Beth said, "but I invited Detective Morse to join us if she could when Luke called me. I thought she might be able to explain a few things after talking to Melnyk. Besides, she eats too much junk from that machine at the station. She needs some real food."

Lauren looked at Harriet, and they both laughed.

"I guess James's homemade pizza rises above the junk-food designation," Harriet said.

Jorge made a space at the table and set a plate with several pieces of pizza on it down as the detective arrived.

"Water, soda, or beer?" he asked her when she'd settled.

"Cola would be fine." She'd combed her hair and reapplied her lipstick, so she didn't look as haggard as she sometimes did after several hours spent questioning a suspect. Maybe it was the holidays, Harriet mused.

The group let her finish her first piece of pizza in peace; she sipped her cola and set her cup down.

"I know you have a lot of questions, and I also know you all know there is a limit to what I can tell you about an active case. However, I think you've guessed most of what I've learned.

"Mr. Melnyk appears to have perpetrated the recent crimes. We believe his motive was revenge for the death of his daughter. His targets are all people he believed contributed to her death, and to the illness of his son. It's not obvious any of what he believes is true. His daughter *had* dabbled in drugs supplied by Jade, and in the occult with Sunny; but at the time of her death, she was clean and sober, and there's nothing to suggest her death was anything but what it appeared to be. She rolled her kayak and became tangled in the underwater roots close to shore, hitting her head in the process. It was nothing but a tragic accident, pure and simple."

Harriet processed that information.

"What about Will Crowe, Millie's employee?"

"That was really unfortunate." Morse paused for a moment. "Of course, it's *all* unfortunate, but Crowe is what might be called collateral damage. He had the misfortune of going to pick up a print order for Millie while Valery was stringing Daniel up.

"He apparently called out and poked around, finally finding his printing and leaving. He looked through the small window in the door to the press room but didn't see anything. At least, he never told Millie he saw anything. But Valery saw *him* and decided to eliminate the possibility of a witness."

"That *is* sad," Mavis said.

Harriet sliced a skinny piece of pepperoni pizza for herself. She chewed thoughtfully while Mavis and Connie asked additional questions about Mark.

"What I want to know," she said when she'd finished, "is why was he so obsessed with Jade's horse."

Morse smiled.

"Now, that's interesting. It made no sense to me, either, until my partner Jason Martinez did some digging. It turns out Jade's horse used to belong to Valery's daughter. By all accounts, she was never very interested, but nonetheless, he was very invested in the idea of her learning to ride. Then, after her accident, when he needed cash to bring in international medical specialists, he sold the horse to Jade."

"It appears his attempt to buy the horse back, and Jade's refusal to sell, is what caused him to hatch the blackmail plan. I guess once he got it going, and Jade still refused to sell, he decided to exact revenge on everyone he felt contributed to the situation."

"So, was he the one who had people following me?" Harriet asked.

Morse picked up another piece of pizza.

"This is really good," she said with a nod to James. "Yes, that was Valery's people. They were following you to get to Jade and the horse."

Mavis blew out a breath.

"Grief does terrible things to people."

"I have a question," Lauren said as she picked little bits of leftover crust from the remains of her third piece of pizza. "Why were the hard drives stolen from the murder victims, and why burn Jade's shop?"

"That's two questions," Morse said with a smile. "You can thank Martinez for that one, too. That little jerk Chris Baker at the computer store had been installing spyware on the hard drives of all the computers he was repairing so he could steal customer information. We haven't figured out if he was selling customer lists or if he was actually stealing identities. That will remain to be seen. He was afraid, with the murders, someone would take a deep dive into the computers looking for clues and discover his handiwork."

"Wow, that little jerk," Harriet said.

"Uh-oh," Mavis said. "He just did some work on my computer."

Lauren, who was sitting beside her, patted her back.

"Not to worry. I can fix it for you. I've got time while most of my clients are on holiday breaks."

Mavis started to protest.

"Don't argue. You can bake Carter some of those dog bones you make."

Harriet could tell Mavis wanted to argue some more about not taking up Lauren's valuable time, but she didn't say anything.

"As for the arson at Jade's shop, he was afraid she'd left incriminating evidence behind when she 'disappeared'. He was searching for emails and letters they'd exchanged about him demanding 'his' horse back."

"What will happen to Jade and Sunny?" Harriet asked.

Morse sat back and rubbed her stomach.

"Oh, I think they'll be okay. I wish Jade hadn't hidden from us, but that's not a crime. And I suspect Sunny's brother may have an outstanding warrant or two, but I also suspect he's already left town. There's no reason for us to pursue him. He didn't do anything here we know of."

Jorge started stacking empty plates and napkins.

"So, Foggy Point can go back to being a sleepy little town?"

Morse laughed. "Foggy Point hasn't been that for quite a while."

Harriet passed her plate to Jorge.

"I have one more question. What about the body Valery used to fool everyone?"

"Right now, we don't have any idea. He doesn't match any of our open missing-persons files. We'll do DNA, of course."

"I might be able to help," Harriet said. "Joyce at the homeless camp has been looking for a guy they call Smokey Joe. He doesn't usually leave without telling anyone, but he went missing right before this all started."

Morse pulled her notebook from her pocket and made a note.

"I'll go out tomorrow and get a description and see if they can tell us anything concrete that will help verify his identity. As you know, the body was cremated, so it will be hard. It makes sense, though."

Harriet stood and picked up the plates Jorge had stacked.

"Thanks for coming and telling us what you did."

"Thank *you* for the great pizza."

Luke brought the teakettle full of hot water to the table and set it on a hot pad before returning with the basket of tea Harriet kept in the cupboard. Harriet smiled at him.

"What?" he asked. "Isn't this what you guys do when you get together?"

"Yes, sweetie, it is. I'm just amazed you noticed. Not a lot of guys your age would."

Luke's face turned red, and he retreated to the kitchen.

236

"He's such a good boy," Beth said. "It's amazing, really, given his early life."

"He *is* a good boy," Harriet agreed.

Chapter 41

Harriet woke early the next morning; the sky was clear, and the air was cold. James and Luke were still sound asleep when she took thez dogs out, so she decided to go for a long run. She had a lot to think about.

She didn't agree with her aunt about it being safer for her to live somewhere else, but if she was being honest she had to admit she'd faced more than a normal amount of dangerous situations since she'd come to Foggy Point. She was going to have to reflect on what about her own behavior was drawing these situations to her.

She had pounded out six miles by the time she arrived back home, but she still didn't have any answers. James and Luke were in Foggy Point; and as long as that was true, that's where she was staying, so she was going to have to figure something out.

That could wait, though, she told herself. Today, she and James had decided they'd go watch Luke ride in the morning, and then take the ferry ride to Victoria they'd missed the day before.

James was up and in the kitchen cooking when she came into the house.

"I made steel-cut oats for breakfast. I hope that's okay."

"Sounds good to me," Luke said as he appeared. He took a bowl of oatmeal from James and sat down at the table.

"Are you sure you don't mind watching me ride again?"

Harriet sat down opposite him, and James set a bowl in front of her.

"I love hanging out at the barn. Riding was one of the best parts of going to boarding school."

"I told Emily we'd probably be there around nine-thirty." Luke said between bites.

Harriet sprinkled brown sugar on her oatmeal.

"I need a quick shower, but I think that will work."

"Sounds like a plan," James agreed as he joined them.

✂ --- ✂ --- ✂

Harriet and James sat on the first level of the bleachers watching Luke guide Major through a series of spirals at a walk as Emily circled the perimeter at a canter on Fable.

"Fable looks like a pony compared to Major," James commented as the two horses passed each other going in opposite directions.

"Too bad we can't keep him," Marcia said, sitting down beside Harriet.

Harriet tensed. "What do you mean?"

"The people who own the stable are very conservative. Even though Major broke out of his stall to protect Becky, they think it's too risky to include him in the therapy-horse program.

"So, what's going to happen to him?" James asked.

"He'll be returned to the mounted police unit, and they will undoubtedly attempt to sell him. Failing that, he will, sadly, probably become dog food."

Harriet and James looked at each other.

"We can't let that happen," he said.

"Agreed," she said.

Marcia smiled.

"I was hoping you'd say that." She handed Harriet a folded piece of paper. "Here's the person you need to call if you're interested in buying Major."

Harriet slipped it into her purse.

"Assuming you're successful, I took the liberty of drawing up a boarding contract—to hold his stall space. You just need to sign it and bring it back to the office."

Harriet pulled a pen from her purse and handed it and the contract it to James. He laid the contract on the bleacher and signed it.

"You can go ahead and file that. We *will* acquire Major, whatever it takes."

Marcia didn't take the contract from him She looked away.

"What's wrong?" Harriet asked.

She sighed.

239

"I can't file anything here anymore. The owners decided my decision to let Jade stay in the dorm when she was hiding from the killer was not the sort of behavior they expected from their now former stable manager."

"They fired you for helping Jade stay alive?" Harriet said, incredulous.

"They said I should have taken her to the police. In any case, it's done. The new manager will be here this afternoon, and I will be gone tomorrow."

Harriet put a hand on Marcia's arm. "I'm so sorry."

Marcia gave her a half-smile. "I should have known better. I knew what sort of people they were when I went to work for them."

"Well, we'll be sorry to see you go. Will you be okay?"

Marcia grinned. "I've had a former client from here who opened their own stable in Ridgefield. They've asked me several times to come work for them. I called them this morning, and they said their offer is still good." She stood up. "I better go, I've got a lot to do. Good luck with Major."

James gestured for Harriet to give him the piece of paper she had put in her purse. He left the arena pulling his phone from his pocket. Harriet was watching Luke working to master his trotting when he came back in.

"What would you think about putting off that trip to Victoria and instead going to Seattle to pay for our horse?"

"Our horse?" she said with delight, and wrapped her arms around him as he sat down beside her. "Do you want to tell him, or shall I?"

"Tell me what?" Luke said as he pulled to a stop in front of them.

James and Harriet both grinned broadly at him

END

Acknowledgements

I'd like to thank my family and friends who support my writing efforts and understand my crazy schedule. And thanks to all the Susans who make my life easier by all sharing the same name. Thank you to the real Aunt Beth who puts up with me and supports my efforts.

I would also like to acknowledge the people who make it possible for you to hear about and buy my books—Deon and Rich Stonehouse at Sunriver Books and Music, who have the best bookstore ever. Linne and Jack Lindquist of The Craftsman's Touch Books, who tirelessly drive all over the US to quilt shows and allow myself and other authors to sign in their booth, are fantastic.

Many thanks to my fellow road warriors and roommates, Marie Bostwick and Patience Griffin.

I'd also like to acknowledge my granddaughter Amelia, who has already declared that she's going to be a writer when she grows up just like Grammy. I must also mention her sister Claire, who will be unhappy if I don't. She is a very good reader.

As always, none of this would happen without my publisher Liz. Many thanks.

About The Author

After working nearly 30 years in the high-tech industry, where her writing consisted of performance reviews, process specs, and a scintillating proprietary tome on electronics assembly, **ARLENE SACHITANO** wrote her first mystery novel, *Chip and Die*.

Quilt As Desired, the first Harriet Truman/Loose Threads Mystery, was published in the fall of 2003 and has been followed by eleven more adventures; *The 12 Quilts of Christmas* brings the popular series to an even dozen.

Arlene is aided in her writing endeavors by her canine companion Navarre. When not writing, she is on the board of directors of the Harriet Vane Chapter of Sisters In Crime as well as Latimer Quilt and Textile Center in Tillamook, Oregon. She teaches knitting at Latimer and, of course, is a quilter.

She's been married to Jack for forty years; they split their time between Tillamook and Multnomah Village in Portland. Arlene and Jack have three lovely children and three brilliant grandchildren. She also has two wonderful friends, one named Susan and the other named Margi.

About The Artist

APRIL MARTINEZ was born in the Philippines and raised in San Diego, CA, daughter of a US Navy chef and a US postal worker. Dissatisfied that she couldn't make use of her creative tendencies, she started working as an imaging specialist for a big book and magazine publishing house in Irvine and learned the trade of graphic design. From that point on, she worked as a graphic designer and webmaster while doing freelance art and illustration at night. April lives with her cat in Orange County, California.

Made in the USA
Monee, IL
20 November 2024

70672269R00152